The Shadow of War

BOOK ONE IN THE DANNY SHAW / MANFRED BREHME TRILOGY

THE SHADOW OF WAR

JACK MURRAY

LUME BOOKS

LUME BOOKS

Published in 2022 by Lume Books

Copyright © Jack Murray 2022

ISBN 978-1-83901-442-0

Typeset using Atomik ePublisher from Easypress Technologies

www.lumebooks.co.uk

Prologue

North Africa: November, 1942

God it was hot.

Rivers of sweat flowed from his forehead, or was it blood? He couldn't see. All around him was a blur. The smoke, the sweat, the watery images caused by the heat stopped his eyes from focusing. His arm seemed to be stuck. He wanted to wipe his eyes. He tried to free his hand. No joy. The air seemed to be draining from the cabin. Each breath he took fried his lungs. His legs also seemed to be locked into a position. Something was holding them down. He needed to wipe his eyes.

The coughing started. Breathe, cough, breathe again. The pain seared his throat like acid. The heat was no longer murmuring now; it was crackling. All around him the metal of the cabin seemed to be melting. The sound of the fire was intoxicating, like immersive percussion. He was drowning in its indiscriminate beat. His eyes closed. The temperature was overwhelming him now.

He heard music. His father floated into view and then he saw her. He looked into her green eyes. They smiled invitingly. So much he

1

wanted to say, but how could he? And then they disappeared. He tried to reach out to hold her. Only darkness now. There was a loud rumbling. Like thunder in the distance.

His eyes opened again. The sound of crackling was louder. Getting nearer. Still, he felt weighed down. With a struggle he freed one arm and wiped his eyes. He wished he hadn't. A body was lying over him. He levered it away, freeing up his other arm. The skin on his hand was curdling.

Lifeless eyes gazed at him mockingly. It would be his turn next. Death was all around him. It would soon slowly enfold him in its arms and caress him away from the pain, the heat, and the hate. He closed his eyes.

A series of explosions outside. He woke with a start. Another explosion, more distant. He roused himself once more. Every breath was a struggle now.

Another body lay over his feet. He tried to kick free. Pain knifed his chest as he tried to rise; he flopped back. It was useless. And the crackling fire grew louder and edged closer. He felt like crying. This is how it would be then. The immensity of the moment was too much. The indignity of it. Absurd almost. He was in despair. Panic rose in him, drowning his spirit, his will to live. The cabin seemed airless now. He cried out a name. Her name.

The shapes in the cabin grew indistinct again and the crackling grew dimmer, like a murmur. And then he woke again. And he began to scream over and over again. Not like this. It couldn't be like this. He screamed again. He screamed until the pain in his throat threatened to overcome him and then he kept screaming.

2

Part 1: Britain 1933

Part I: Britain 1935

Chapter One

Little Gloston: February, 1933

The air was cold and green with shadow under the trees hinting at the first bloom of spring. The brightening sky had lifted Danny's mood of despondency as he pounded up the road. Blood pulsed through his veins. Ribs vaulted with every stride. Muscles drew and flexed and pumped through the morning ground mist and his head jerked from side to side until he finally darted clear. His adversary gave up the chase with the shake of a fist accompanied by a few words unlikely to be repeated in front of the congregation at St Bartholomew's on Sunday.

Danny grinned, gave a mock military salute and slowed to a trot. He made sure to maintain some momentum lest his pursuer find a second wind. The sound of the lad's voice receded into the distance. The lad in question was Bert Gissing. Eighteen and at least as many hands in height: over six feet anyway. Large, too. He liked his food. Perhaps too much. Quick enough over thirty yards but if you could evade his massive paws, then you could outlast him even when weighed down by a couple of dozen apples.

Safe at last, Danny turned around and saw Bert trooping dejectedly back to the farm where he worked. For a moment, Danny felt a stab of guilt. Would Bert find himself in trouble, he wondered? He wasn't a bad sort really. He had his job to do. It wasn't made easier by Danny or his chums who periodically raided the orchard for apples. The farmer could afford it. Still, he'd tell Bob and Alec to lay off old man McIver's farm for a bit.

Reaching into his canvas bag, he extracted a red apple. Moisture glistened like tiny jewels on the skin. He admired the product of his criminal efforts for a moment. Filched fruit seemed to have a fragrance and a sweet taste all its own. The first crunch released watery juices that overran his mouth and oozed down his chin. He wiped it away with his sleeve and continued back to his house, dodging puddles of water on the muddy path as he went.

Eleven years of age, Danny should really have been in school but, of late, his interest in academic life had petered out. He and his friends regularly mitched off for a day if the weather was clement. By early summer they would have abandoned school altogether. Most of the boys left at fourteen, anyway, bound for field or factory. Danny saw no reason why he should not plough the same furrow.

Danny's attendance had decreased with each passing year following his move to 'the big 'uns' side of the partition. He could read well, he thought. There wasn't much more to learn there. He could write, although the neatness was not quite at the same level as the girls in the class. And he could count. Geography seemed pointless, if the folk around him were anything to go by. Everyone tended to stay in the village. Well, except those who had gone to France.

Like his dad.

He had no yen to travel after seeing what it had done to those who had left. Many had not come back. Most never spoke of their time during the war. His dad for one. No, travel was not for him. He ambled along the road enjoying the freedom. The run had warmed him up and he was in fine fettle. He stopped at a clearing in the forest to look down over the valley at the twenty or thirty houses scattered around the slope. Behind them, on the flatter areas, lay the farms. In the distance he could see Cavendish Hall.

The rising sun had cast a shadow over a portion of the valley. He looked up. The sky was cloudless. A few birds fluttered around. He finished his apple and threw the core onto the ground in front of him. Getting up, he made his way towards the brook where he had agreed to meet his pals to share the booty. His feet pushed through the fallen leaves.

As he picked his way through the forest, he thought about the future. He would soon be expected to start earning his keep. There was work out there on the farms. It wasn't well paid, but Danny didn't care if it meant he was out of school. Then, of course, there was the forge with his dad and brother. Neither had mentioned about joining them yet. Anyway, there were choices. But the choice would come soon. He would suggest leaving school this summer. Once you left school you were a man. This was Danny's somewhat limited view of the world.

Physically he was getting there. He'd grown at least two inches in the last year. In two or three years he'd be as tall as Bert, although his body had not filled out so much. He was lean but not gangly. If Bert had caught him, it would have been a one-sided affair even with Danny's special 'throw'. Thoughts of his earlier adventure prompted the desire for another of the apples. He grabbed one from his bag and took a bite. It had been a near escape. This made the apple taste all the better.

As he munched the apple, he passed a youth sitting against a tree. The youth was a little bit older than Danny. His clothing was like Danny's; worn, patched up and a little too small. He looked at Danny and then the apple. It was difficult to say if there was hunger in those eyes.

'Morning, Ted,' said Danny with a smile.

Ted Truscott was a bit daft; all agreed. Harmless, but not all there. He rarely said much. Education had been attempted and abandoned with little regret on either side. His life was spent wandering in the forest. Danny went over to him and offered him an apple. Ted looked at Danny and then the apple. He took it and began to eat. Perhaps there was gratitude in the boy's eyes; it was hard to say. Their hooded emptiness was its own story. Conversation over, Danny left him and continued his way to the brook.

Bird song echoed around the trees providing Danny with a musical chorus as he tramped towards the arranged meeting place. He couldn't see any birds, though. Just squirrels scuttling up trees. Some stopped for a moment to return his gaze before boredom set in. The only other sound in the forest was the crunch of twigs under Danny's boots.

This was the life. He knew it would not last forever. The prospect of joining his dad and older brother at the forge was something he neither welcomed nor wanted to avoid. It didn't occur to him there was anything else. That was it. Life in a village was like this. The future was written in the seasons.

The family were the village smiths. They always had been as far as Danny could tell. Always would be, probably. There was no reason to change this way of life. There was no reason, ever, to leave. His father had left. Not his choice, mind. Much good it had done him, thought Danny. Still, he'd survived. He thought of his friend Bob. His dad had survived the war. In a manner. Injured at Cambrai. One leg went that day. Gassed, too. Danny's dad had seen what had happened. Bob's dad lived just long enough to see his boy walk.

Up ahead he saw a gap in the wood. Through the branches, light danced on the flowing brook. No sign of his pals. Maybe they'd run into trouble. The milk raid was the most difficult of their plundering activities. They took it in turns. Two would do the milk: one as lookout, one to break in. Danny was on apple patrol. They rotated the farms they stole from so as not to raise any suspicions. They didn't take much. Just enough to feed them through the day.

A few minutes later, he broke through some foliage and arrived at their meeting place. Looking around he found a flat spot to sit on and waited. The brook ran fast a few feet away. He listened to it gurgling nearby where it hit the rocks. Further upstream it was deeper. They would probably go for a swim. A few months ago, Alec had fastened a rope from one of the overhanging branches. They could swing from it for hours on end.

Finally, he heard two voices. They sounded full of vim. A successful mission guessed Danny. He hoped Bob had brought some of his mother's bread. She worked in the bakery and the boys loved the fresh bread she dispensed every day from her iron oven in the cottage Bob shared with her and his sister.

'Oy,' shouted Danny, as the boys neared.

'Oy,' shouted Alec by way of response.

Danny looked up as the two boys appeared. Alec was carrying an old bucket full of milk. It would have been quite heavy so they would have taken turns to carry it. As Danny had hoped, Bob was carrying the bread. Two hours out of the oven. His mouth began to water in anticipation as the warm smell enveloped him and caressed his senses.

They sat down and Danny poured the contents of his bag out onto the grass. Neither boy said much but the grin on their faces was pure and grateful as they gazed upon their ill-gotten bounty.

'Any trouble at McIver's?' asked Alec.

Danny nodded.

'Bert?' asked Bob.

'Bert,' confirmed Danny.

Alec looked serious for a moment, and he voiced what was on everyone's mind. 'We should avoid McIver's maybe for a while.'

For the next half hour, the conversation, such as it was, took second place to the grub. Bob had brought a veritable feast and feast they did. He liked his food and food liked him. When the last drop of milk was drunk and the last apple demolished, the boys lay on their backs and stared up at the cerulean sky, broken only by a solitary puffy white cloud floating, almost in embarrassment, looking for some companions.

'What shall we do next?' asked Danny.

'Swim?' suggested Bob.

This was greeted with a biff over the head with Danny's empty canvas bag.

'I meant who will we do tomorrow?'

'Why didn't you say?' complained Bob, but not angrily.

They discussed potential targets for the morrow. Each farm had advantages and disadvantages. Dogs were a no go. Farm boys less of an issue. The three boys had developed a set of ruses that could distract anyone likely to interfere with the commission of their crimes. The discussion lasted around an hour before the boys felt ready to amble down to the pond for a swim.

Predictably, Bob charged forward first, stripping off as he ran and taking a running leap onto the rope swing before completing his splash into the water with a poorly executed somersault. His ample frame caused a deluge of water and the two other boys laughed hysterically.

'Belly flop,' shouted his friends in unison.

'Let's see how you do it, then,' replied Bob, brightly, as he surfaced in the pool.

As they splashed around in the water, they heard an aeroplane overhead. They stopped for a few moments. It was flying low, in the direction of the Hall. For a few seconds it coughed and spluttered before the engine kicked in again.

'He's mad,' said Danny.

'His lordship?' asked Bob.

'Who do you think?' laughed Danny. 'Wouldn't catch me up there in one of those things.'

'I don't know,' said Alec. 'I'd love to try.'

'Maybe you will one day,' said Bob, not meaning it.

A little later, when they had dried off, they began wrestling each other. Despite Bob's weight, Danny always had the better of him and Alec, courtesy of a special throw he learned from his father. He deployed it just as his opponent seemed to be gaining an advantage. One moment they would have Danny at their mercy and then, seconds later, they would be lying on the ground. He claimed his father had learned it during the war. Generously, he had shown his friends what to do, but they had not racked up the years of practice Danny had enjoyed with his brother. They were grateful, however, and never begrudged his ability.

Such was the life of a country boy between school and work. They thought days like these would last forever.

But day eventually gives way to the darkness of night.

The days were longer now. It seemed only a few weeks ago that the village was in darkness by five, save for the lights in the windows. Danny trooped home with the sun on his back. It was a bit cooler now. His shadow seemed to stretch from his feet all the way to the front door of his cottage. To the right of the cottage was the shed which doubled as the forge. He could see his brother, Tom, bathed in the orange of the fire. There were blue shadows around his eyes and torso. His face was stained with dirt and tears of sweat. He turned to Danny, nodded and then went back to the forge.

Tom was older than Danny by four years. He had been working as a smithy for a year now. He was much taller than Danny and the few years wielding a hammer had seen his frame fill out. Danny looked at his brother's shoulder muscles with something approaching awe. If he was not as strong as their father, he was getting closer. His muscles flexed as he lifted a piece of heavy iron out of the fire. After pausing a few moments, Danny continued his way into the cottage.

He walked through the door and shouted, 'I'm home.'

The atmosphere in the cottage was distinctly chillier. He sensed it without having to look at the face of his mother. His father stared at him. He knew that look. His father had never been one to shout or to inflict corporal punishment. But the look of angry disappointment was all too plain.

'What's wrong? Somebody died?'

The words were barely out before Danny was overcome by a wave of regret. His father flinched a little at the word 'died'. Sometimes his charm and sense of humour worked to defuse potentially explosive moments. Not always. He was in trouble, and he knew why.

'You missed school again, Danny,' said his mother. Her tone was sad rather than angry. 'Mrs Grout came by. She told us. Why Danny? You of all people, son.'

What was there to say? It was true. There was no denying it. He could have said he was bored or that it was not going to be of any use to him. The raging silence swirling around his father screamed a warning to him: this was not the time to argue. Yet the sadness in his mother's eyes, and his father's, was less about his cockiness, or laziness, than the feeling he was wasting an opportunity. Yes, school was a bore. But this was not because what he was being taught was uninteresting. Learning things was not the problem. He grasped the teaching quickly. Perhaps too quickly. The others did not. It made the time in the classroom drag. The boredom was stultifying. He felt caged.

'You'll be there tomorrow, boy,' said Stan. There was a tremble in his voice, but it was not fear. Danny could see the distressed rage in the eyes of his father. A tormented man's disappointment in his son. Danny felt wretched. This was the first time Mrs Grout had complained. Too many days had been missed. It was naïve to think that this would continue without comment. They had been too cocky. Worse, their actions had put her and his father in an acutely uncomfortable position. Each had to acknowledge a kind of failure.

Danny nodded and wanted to apologise when he saw his father turn away. His father had returned to a place inside himself. Remote yet caring. He would be unreachable now, a silence that could last hours. It would only be relieved by the pounding of his hammer on metal.

The wireless was on in the background. Danny could hear Al Bowlly singing. None of his friends had heard of him but Danny loved his voice. It caressed the words of a song and brought them gently to life whether it was playful, sentimental, or melancholic.

He found himself falling under the spell of music and the warm balm of the singer's voice. His mother seemed hypnotised too. They looked at one another and smiled conspiratorially. The music seemed to cleanse the atmosphere of its cold rage, replacing it with love and even redemption.

Chapter Two

'Nice to have Mr Shaw, Mr Owen and Mr Leddings back with us today,' announced Mrs Grout to the classroom.

Danny, Bob and Alec looked around sheepishly as the class turned as one towards them. Alec scowled at one boy immediately ahead, but nothing could be done. Their humiliation was complete. Retribution would come to those who mocked them. This was for later; for now they could only sit and accept their fate. Thankfully, the class seemed to be mostly disinterested. Mostly. Danny didn't need to look to the other side of the room to see three smiling faces.

The village school, if a converted barn can be so described, consisted of two classes separated by a canvas partition. On one side were the 'little 'uns' taught by Miss Jarvis. On the other side sat Danny and his pals. They were the 'big 'uns'. The bigger children were taught by the fearsome Mrs Grout.

Mrs Grout occupied an indeterminate age territory between forty and eighty. Although child years seem longer, it was as if she had been around forever. She was just over five feet tall. What she lacked in height she more than compensated for in meanness of spirit, violence of temper and a left jab that would have had Jack 'Kid' Berg's corner reaching for the towel.

She was kinder towards the girls in the class, humane even. Perhaps it was out of sympathy for the fact that many would marry the boys sitting, bovine-bored, with them. This was their misfortune, she concluded. Consequently, Mrs Grout viewed her job as to knock, quite literally, sense and respect into the rebellious young males that ended up in her classroom year after year with the depressing regularity of winter rain.

The three boys sat at the back of the classroom. Another two years and their school career would be over. None of them could wait. They had long since lost interest in anything Mrs Grout had to communicate. This process began with the realisation that what they learned at school barely impacted what they would be required to do on the farms.

They each sat at long wooden desks with inkwells. Pens scratched messily on paper. Surrounding them were walls covered in artwork and even a map of the world. The artwork could, kindly, have been described as modern, although Mrs Grout, in the twenty-five years she had taught in this classroom, had yet to uncover anyone with a modicum of talent. Often the only noise in the classroom, for hours on end, was the sound of pens crunching through cheap paper, suppressed mirth and regular yelps from a casualty in the ongoing war between Mrs Grout and the boys.

The terror rained down by the fiendish lady was extraordinary. Slightly built, she could easily have been picked up and thrown through the classroom window by any of the bigger boys. All of them towered over her. Such was her boiling intensity, however, no boy in living memory had ever challenged her authority. In fact, it was inconceivable. Rebellion took the form of internecine warfare when her back was turned and, of course, truancy.

15

In between bursts of truancy and clips round the ear, the three boys had, somehow, learned how to read and write. Mrs Grout had treated their teaching rather in the manner of a dog handler training a puppy. Reward came in the form of food, or denial thereof. Punishment was delivered quickly, painfully and with a frequency that suggested Mrs Grout had a natural proclivity towards sadism.

Only one boy was excused from this guerrilla warfare. Harold Goodnight was the son of a farmer, although something of the runt of the litter. He had two older brothers, both working on the farm. Strapping lads they were.

Harold was puny but smart. Very smart. Oddly, Danny quite liked him and defended the poor boy on occasion. In return, Harold offered to help Danny and his friends with the occasional homework. Part of this sympathy was because Harold was often picked on by the rival gang to Danny's. It was comprised of three boys. All were thirteen; all were bound for farms within a year. One of them was the biggest boy in the year, Bert Gissing's brother, Hugh.

Like his brother Bert, Hugh was big, probably smarter than his brother, but sorely lacked a sense of humour, at least in Danny's view. The three boys had an ongoing war with Danny and his friends that had lasted as long as they could remember. The cause of the conflict was lost somewhere in the mists of time. No armistice had ever been offered. The war of attrition would go on.

There they sat, impervious to authority, six elder boys, occupying territory at either side of the class. In front were the pupils who were either younger or had some desire to learn. And of course, there were the village girls. The boys had ignored them over the years but now things were changing. It added a fresh dimension to the war with Hugh, Fred and Greg. Soon the males would be fighting over the females. It was the way of the world, wasn't it? The only thing worth fighting for, Bob would say.

The class went on interminably. Outside the clouds were funeral dark. Maybe it was as well they'd gone to school. The sky finally released its weight and rain rattled against the window like a machine gun. Danny shivered involuntarily. It felt like an omen.

After school, Danny ambled back home during a break from the rain. His mum was manning the kitchen like a sentry facing German trenches. She barely noticed Danny's arrival or, indeed, his exit again clutching a handful of bread. The wireless was on in the background. She was listening to the news. Her face seemed grave. Danny, as a rule, ignored the radio unless it was playing music. He walked a few yards to the forge to see if anything was needed. Although he would not admit as much, he was desperate to help.

'Anything I can do?' offered Danny to his eldest brother.

'Disappear?' suggested Tom before his face erupted into a massive grin.

'Funny,' responded Danny. He walked forward and watched Tom take a hammer and beat the hell out of a luckless piece of iron.

'What did it do to you?' asked Danny turning and walking out again. He saw his father arriving through the gate. His face looked troubled, but then, it always did. He looked down at Danny.

'Were you at school, boy? Don't lie.'

'Yes.'

His father nodded and strode forward into the forge. He took off his hat, mopped his brow and looked over Tom's shoulder.

Danny glanced at the two of them and then headed out the garden gate. He didn't begrudge Tom not wanting him around. He knew he wasn't ready yet. They'd bring him in when he was needed. The sky seemed to have cleared but it was getting dark. He wondered about heading down to the brook but decided against it. He turned and saw his mother walk out to the forge and motion for his father to join her. The two of them walked into the house.

Something was up.

Never mind, he thought. I'll hear about it soon enough. He walked towards the village. There was a high street of sorts comprising a shop, a bakery and a post office. Further ahead was St Bartholomew's. Little Gloston was not, and never would be, a metropolis.

Along the way he passed a couple of younger girls from his class. They glanced at him and giggled to one another. Danny ignored them and pushed on. As he did so, he ran into Bert Gissing. His nemesis from yesterday seemed as surprised as he. He was also somewhat laden down with two bags of feed.

They looked at one another for a moment and then Bert grinned.

'Lucky beggar.'

Danny grinned also and said, 'That I am.'

'Don't let me catch you near the farm again.'

'You won't,' replied Danny with a wink, and continued.

Yes, Bert wasn't a bad sort, all in all. His younger brother, Hugh, was a different story. He and Danny were unofficial leaders of their respective groups. They led where others wanted to follow. Neither was academic but both, much to the frustration of Mrs Grout, were clearly smart. This resulted in frequent, unexplained and painful reminders from the diminutive teacher that she was really in charge.

Bob was up ahead talking to a girl from their class. It looked like Beth Locke. She was a redhead but seemed to have been in the wrong queue when volatility was handed out, for there was no more tranquil girl in the village. Even the girls teased her about this apparent misalignment of hair and nature. She took it in good part. This made her universally popular with boys, girls and parents alike. Even Mrs Grout had a soft spot for Beth, despite her apparent lack of interest in classwork.

It was similar for girls, supposed Danny. Their destiny was decided in the womb. The direction of travel plotted. A life that would revolve around kitchen and cradle. Bob already had one eye to his future. Rather than cramp his style, Danny made his way in the direction of Cavendish Hall but then broke off near St Bartholomew's. As he did so, a familiar figure greeted him from the garden.

'Hello, young Shaw,' said Reverend Simmons. 'Where you off to then?'

'Forest,' replied Danny with a smile. He liked the reverend. The stories he told the kids over the years never failed to entertain. He'd fought in the Boer War and boxed against some folk Danny had never heard of but were, apparently, pretty useful if the reverend's cauliflower ears were anything to go by.

'You be good, young man, and let me see you at the church more. I didn't see you Sunday. By the brook as usual, were you?'

'Sorry, Rev. I'll be there. Promise.'

Simmons laughed and called him a cheeky imp. Danny continued his way with a smile on his face. He wasn't heading anywhere in particular but thought to head up the hill and sit overlooking the valley. It would be another half hour before tea. They clearly didn't want him under their feet. That was fine with Danny. There was plenty of time for work.

A few minutes of climbing brought him to his destination. He sat down and looked across the valley once more. The early evening had brought the sun out after the rain. A long shadow lay across the valley; only the Hall remained in the sunlight. Before him lay fields and hedgerows planted hundreds of years earlier. Hundreds? A thousand years probably. It took his breath away. The silent majesty of history and its changing changelessness.

The only noise he could hear was the sound of birds and the gentle rustle of trees in the light breeze. And then, from behind, he heard some twigs break. He turned around and found himself looking up at the grinning figures of Hugh Gissing, Fred Dobbins and Greg Lunn. They looked in the mood for fun.

This wasn't good news.

Chapter Three

'Where was that boy going?' asked Stan Shaw, entering the kitchen. His tall frame filled the doorway. There was no one in the village as strong as Stan Shaw. But strength is not just physical. Stan Shaw knew this. Inside he felt weak. Every day was a battle just to rise from his bed and face the day. His eyes haunted the depths of his sockets; unspoken torment came and went.

The family understood. They understood the silences. They understood the anger. They also felt the brief, rare moments of tenderness from a soul trying to escape the prison of depression.

He strode forward into the kitchen. It was the first room a visitor to the house would see. But it was more than that to the Shaw family. It was the centre of their universe. An all-day glow and the all-night heat came from the Aga cooker, lovingly restored by Stan. The warmth wasn't just physical: it was emotional and spiritual, too.

Stan looked at his wife. They'd married just before the war when she was nineteen and in the bright bloom of youth. Not yet forty, she looked older but the beauty remained. Tom had arrived as Stan had received Kitchener's call. He went over in 1916. He'd survived. Barely. There were scars, though, unseen but vivid, painful and untreatable.

Kate looked up and smiled radiantly at Stan.

'Danny? I didn't see him.'

'He was here a few minutes ago. I saw him walking out the gate.'

'Nothing for him to do in the shed?' asked Kate.

'Tom chased him off. I'd have given him something all right. Lazy little beggar.'

Kate grinned at this. Stan could be very hard on Danny, but the truth was the little 'beggar' was idolised and probably spoiled a little. He'd always been the bright one. The mischievous one. Tom was stolid and true. Big, strong as an ox but soft as well. Danny fibbed, cajoled and charmed his way through life with a ready wit and a smile that could melt granite at thirty paces. Even Tom, a heart as big as his frame and not a jealous bone in his body, let the boy get away with murder.

The result for Danny was a mixed blessing. The boy wielded his magnetism like a sword to cut through any problems he faced. Stan worried he lacked the work ethic that was core to the Shaw family and had been so for many generations.

'What's in the pot?' asked Stan glancing at the cooker.

'Vegetable broth,' replied Kate, 'and I made some bread also.'

'Smells good,' said Stan giving his wife a peck on the back of the head. 'I'm hungry as hell.'

'Watch your language, sir, in front of the children,' admonished Kate.

'They're not babies anymore,' smiled Stan. It was a conversation that was like the well-worn groove in the floor at the entrance of the house.

'That imp better not be late.'

Stan was as guilty as the others in allowing Danny his head, but he was a natural disciplinarian. On things that truly mattered, Danny knew there was only so far he could push things. For some reason, unfathomable to Danny, his family pushed him harder on education

22

than they ever had Tom. In fact, the ease with which he avoided work was matched only by the relative ease with which he managed his schoolwork. When he bothered.

Both Stan and Kate had attended the same school as the boys. They'd both left at fourteen, Stan to work with his dad at the forge and learn the trade of blacksmith and Kate to work as a seamstress. They had been sweethearts at school, and they married as war clouds thickened in the dark sky.

As a smithy, Stan had originally been exempted from service in a reserved occupation. The nature of war had changed, though. It was no longer the clash of armies but of industrial economies. Stan joined the newly formed tank battalions that were part of the Heavy Section of the Machine Gun Corps. It was felt that his skills might be of use in a part of the armed forces where heavy armour was a critical element. Bob Owen's dad had joined with Stan on the same day in the same battalion. He was nearly blown to bits in the tank next to Stan's.

Stan survived the war, but the experience had marked him forever. Even with Kate, the topic was never discussed. His response to the war was silence. In the first few years after his return, these silences would last for hours. And the silences were frequent. The boys and Kate knew to stay away at those times.

They had become fewer over the last few years but recently they had returned. The news from Germany had reawakened something in Stan's damaged mind. Kate could see this but felt powerless to stop the creeping dread afflicting her husband. Tom could see it also but Danny, as ever, was blithely unaware. He was fighting his own wars, his own battles of growing up.

The forge was Stan's escape, his confidant, his redemption. The horse ruled the country. And horses needed shoes. Farmers from around the county came to Stan to have shoes made for their horses. Between one and two hundred horses were on the books and they needed to be shod three times a year.

He also made crucifixes, iron coats of arms, light holders, plough-cutters, nails made of iron, smelted with charcoal that would last centuries. The demand was endless; the orders came like a river flowing unstoppably during the rains. The business grew and grew. He would need Danny soon. Maybe someone else. They'd have to make the barn larger.

Thankfully, Tom had taken to work at the forge quickly and with Danny of age in a year or two, he would soon be helping the business to fulfil the order book. The three of them together, working at the forge; this was Stan's dream.

He unrolled his shirtsleeves, rolled from the inside to avoid sparks catching in the folds, and began to wash his hands and arms.

'Tom shouldn't have sent him away. I'd have found him something to do. He needs to start learning.'

'You know Danny, any excuse,' laughed his wife.

'Yes, I know our son all too well,' said Stan grimly but suppressing a smile.

'Dossing about somewhere, no doubt.'

Chapter Four

In fact, Danny was a long way from loafing about. Hugh, Fred and Greg looked down at him with malicious intent in their eyes. The boys traditionally confined their rivalry to barbed words and occasional playground pranks. As they grew older and began to work off their excess energy in the forest shinning up trees, playing foxes and hounds, and making the first tentative steps to courting, the rivalries deepened, and the dislike spilled out into more physical demonstrations like goats butting heads in the meadow.

Danny looked at the three boys and said, 'Three against one. Not very fair. Are you sure you don't want to run down to the village and get some help?'

The words hid his distinct nervousness. One on one he was more than a match for any of the boys but if they rushed him all at once, they would easily overpower him. Oddly, he did not expect this. Whatever he may have thought of them, there were unspoken rules in combat. Rules that were etched into their bones and blood.

'Very funny, Shaw,' said Hugh, stepping forward. As unofficial leader, he would make the first rush.

'We'll see who's laughing in a minute.'

Danny managed the unusual feat of both relaxing and tensing at the same moment. The fact that Hugh had stepped forward meant they would not all jump him, and this made him feel more relaxed. They would attack one after another. He could handle this, at least until fatigue crept in. However, his muscles tensed as he stood feet shoulder width apart. He moved one foot slightly behind the other in anticipation of a rush.

He didn't have to wait long. Hugh surged forward and they met in a clash of bodies. Another feature of the fighting of the boys in the village was the absence of fists. The two boys wrestled for a moment. Hugh was slightly taller than Danny but, like his brother, heavier of build. At this stage, Danny recognised that Hugh was the stronger. This only mattered when each boy was equal in technique. But Danny had the ultimate card up his sleeve and he deployed it as soon as the opportunity arose. Relaxing his upper body, he bent back as Hugh tried to make his greater weight and strength tell, then quick as a squirrel avoiding an owl, he whipped his body round, throwing Hugh over his trailing leg. Hugh hit the ground with an enormous bump.

Seconds later, Fred Dobbins was on him. Fred had neither height, weight nor technique. He met a similar end in record time. Just as Greg Lunn stepped forward a voice from behind called out.

'What's going on here?'

The boys all turned around. Four people on horseback were on the ridgeway above where the boys were wrestling. A man and a woman on large chestnut horses looked down. Beside them was a young girl. She was around seven years old and astride a grey pony. With her was a boy who was probably Danny's age.

The man jumped off the horse and marched down to the boys. He wore a tweed jacket, breeches and leather boots. Tall, with clear blue eyes and a Roman nose, he looked like the lord of the manor which, in fact, he was. Lord Henry Cavendish stared down at the boys.

'Three on one? A little unsporting, don't you think?' He didn't seem angry, but his face was serious.

Hugh looked shamefaced and was about to speak, when Danny piped up. 'It's nothing, sir, just messing around.'

Henry looked at the four boys for a moment, clearly sceptical. Finally, he said, 'Really? It certainly didn't look like it from up there.'

Nobody said anything for a moment, Danny's intervention having averted a potential crisis for all the boys. Danny glanced up at where Lord Cavendish had just come from.

The woman on the chestnut was Lady Jane Cavendish. Danny saw her from time to time when he bothered to go to the Sunday service. She was the most beautiful woman he had ever seen. Her wild red hair was messily stuffed into the riding hat. From under the brim, he could see her green eyes crinkle in amusement.

Beside her was Sarah, their daughter. Unlike her mother, her hair was ash blonde. The curls were clearly visible underneath the hard riding hat. However, the green eyes were those of her mother. The little girl coolly ignored the activities below and stared stonily ahead. The boy beside her ignored them also. Hateful-looking boy, thought Danny, unkindly. He'd give a sixpence for the opportunity to throw him.

After a few moments, where the only sound in the forest was the gentle rustle of branches in the light breeze, Henry nodded. Scepticism remained; however, he turned back and walked towards his family.

'I see. Well, be sure it is only messing around.'

He used a branch to help pull himself back up onto the ridgeway to re-join his family. One last glance down and then he climbed up onto his horse in one swift movement.

'What's your name, boy?'

'Shaw, sir. Danny Shaw.'

'Stan Shaw's son?'

'Yes, sir,' replied Danny. His eyes never left Lord Henry Cavendish.

Henry nodded, seemingly in approval. With the slightest movement of his reins, Henry's horse moved forward and a few moments later they were all gone. The four boys watched them as they trotted off into the distance. Hugh looked up at the sky. It was clouding over again.

'We should head back.'

They marched back to the village together in a guilty silence. However, after a minute or two they began to chat.

'Who was the boy?' asked Hugh. 'Looked too old to be the son.'

'No idea,' replied Danny. 'Definitely not Robert Cavendish, that's for sure. Probably some other lord they want to marry his daughter to.'

'What a life,' said Fred.

'You'd take it,' said Hugh, giving his friend a friendly clip on the back of the head.

'She'll be all right when she's older,' said Greg. This was more awestruck than coarse. There was no disagreement from the other boys. One by one they peeled off as they passed each house until only Hugh and Danny were left. Finally, they reached Hugh's house. They parted with a nod.

A minute later Danny announced his arrival in the kitchen with a cheery, 'Something smells good.' He tapped his mother on one shoulder and then, as she turned to look, Danny dodged the other side and sampled what she was cooking.

'Actually, it is really good,' he confirmed. Then he glanced at his father, sitting by the wireless, grim-faced. There was something about Germany on the wireless. Danny was relieved it wasn't anything he had done. He went to the sink and washed his hands. This was

28

something his mother insisted on before they ate. Tom was already at the table. At least he had a smile for him.

'Lazin' around as usual?' asked his brother.

'You know me,' laughed Danny, reaching to break some bread off the loaf in the middle of the table. 'Anyways, I offered to help. You didn't want me.'

'Didn't want you under my feet, you little sod. Worse than useless, you are.'

Mother gave Tom a look. His brother mumbled a sheepish apology. Bad or coarse language was not permitted in the household, she reminded him. This rule was applied with rigour by their mother. Nobody, Stan included, was permitted to break the rules. Danny grinned at his brother who merely rolled his eyes.

Stan was still sitting with his ear close to the wireless. The wireless announcer was still giving the news headlines. Danny heard him mention a name several times. He was going to ask his father but one look at the lines tightly etched over his cheeks and around his eyes told him the subject was not for discussion. His mother also stopped what she was doing to listen more closely. Something about a fire in the German Parliament. She glanced at her husband. Stan shook his head and switched off the wireless. Outside they heard the rain begin to slap against the roof and the ground.

Part 2: Germany 1933

Chapter Five

The leaden grey sky was heavy with cloud. Rain and who knows what else was coming. The prospect did little to improve Manfred Brehme's mood as he stared out of the window. Rage coursed through him. Rage and a desire to inflict violence. He kept his attention on the window. Just in front of him a man was on his feet. He paced to and fro, footsteps echoed in the sullen silence of the classroom. He was speaking a heavily accented English, although Manfred was not to know this. The man tapped the blackboard crisply and read to a class that was as bored as he was.

Manfred continued looking away from the teacher, the blackboard and, critically, the person beside him. Normally he liked English class, and why not? He was probably the most accomplished speaker in the class. Second most accomplished. Diana Landau was better but then again, she had the advantage of being half-English so that didn't count.

No, the problem was the boy beside him: Erich Sammer. What had started out as a few playful punches before the class, had escalated steadily during the class. Now they carried real venom and neither boy was prepared to give way until they had struck the last blow. A glance at the clock on the wall confirmed there was another fifteen minutes of this war of attrition left to run. A few classmates were aware of the undeclared conflict and would no doubt press for a more explicit resolution to the hostilities at the next break.

This was now a problem. He and Erich were normally friends. However, these episodes happened from time to time. Rarely did they reach a point where a fight would end the quarrel. If they stopped now, the issue could be resolved, if not amicably, then at least without bloodshed.

Manfred felt a stab of pain in his shin. He turned around quickly. The two boys looked at one another. Erich was clearly angry. The look in his eyes suggested he wanted to get another blow in. Manfred widened his eyes slightly and then shifted them behind to indicate others were looking. Erich paused for a minute while he tried to assimilate the communication. A voice from the front of the class interrupted them both and caused the rest of the class to giggle.

'Silence,' shouted the English teacher. 'Herr Brehme, I asked you a question. Will you answer it please?'

Manfred reddened; he had absolutely no idea what had been asked, such was his intense focus on ending the fighting with Erich. He had to think quickly now. Risking all, he plumped for the least embarrassing response he could think of.

'I'm sorry, sir,' he replied in English. 'I didn't hear the question.'

'Was that because Herr Sammer was hitting you?'

'No, sir,' lied Manfred. His face reddened as he said this. Burning shame and anger rarely stay hidden long.

An angry glint appeared in the eye of Franz Fassbender. He was a man renowned for a very un-Teutonic lack of self-control. His nickname was Franco due to this Latin-like volatility. His skin even

34

seemed to take on a darker sheen when he lost it. That, and a rather unattractive eye-popping anger, gave a diabolic quality to his outburst that was, by turns, frightening, violent and comical, depending on your proximity to its original cause.

'Stand up,' ordered Fassbender. The voice was quiet. A sure sign that violence was imminent. Manfred shot to attention like a soldier. 'Both of you,' snarled the teacher in a voice that resembled an animal growling.

The situation was now deteriorating, realised Manfred, and he wasn't sure if he should blame himself or Erich. The post-mortem would identify the causes. For now, they were in trouble. Serious trouble. It was a mess that would extend beyond the classroom.

Any hope that his obvious linguistic capability and a previously unblemished record would stand him in good stead was swiftly put to rest by the malevolent look in Fassbender's eyes. The teacher stalked forward like a hunter about to seize its prey. His arm lashed out so fast that Manfred could not avoid it. Moments later, an index finger and thumb hooked around Manfred's left ear and proceeded to drag him to the front of the class. Nervous giggles were stifled. Fassbender deposited Manfred in front of the blackboard and then spun around. A worried-looking partner in crime joined Manfred at the front of the class.

Rage mixed with humiliation for Manfred as he stood at the front of the class. He and Erich were to be made examples of. This happened very rarely for Manfred, more often for the less-academic Erich. Fassbender was notorious as a disciplinarian. The ordeal the boys were about to face was an almost daily ritual for some poor soul. The eyes of the class all looked up at the two boys. The same thought hung in the air over their heads: thank God it's not me.

Manfred risked a glance at Diana Landau. She looked horrified.

Manfred reddened a little as their eyes met and he looked away in shame. She stood out from the other girls and not just for her intelligence. Her hair was shorter, with no attempt to tie it into pigtails or plait it in the manner of the other girls. He'd never spoken to her in the two years she had been in his class. This was odd as he liked what he saw of her. Such thoughts ran through his mind as he held out his hand.

A swish in the air and a stabbing pain. Manfred grimaced but uttered no sound. He kept his hand out. Experience had taught him that, if you removed it, this merely served to invite a second helping. Fassbender was moralising as he inflicted violence on the children, but Manfred had stopped listening. He moved outside himself and observed the situation as if from a seat in a Roman amphitheatre. This crowd bayed in silence. Blood lust in the eyes of the boys. Horror in the eyes of the girls.

Erich stayed silent, too, as the cane lashed his hand. The pain was almost unbearable. The hatred kept him silent. Like Manfred, his hand remained outstretched. One question was now front and centre in both their minds. Would Fassbender make it two lashes? There was more than enough precedent to suggest he would. However, perhaps conscious of time, or maybe Manfred's previous good behaviour, Fassbender ordered the boys back to their seats.

The class ended soon after and the two boys trooped out. Rather than renew hostilities, they called a truce and compared their injuries. Both had a vicious red pulsing streak across their palms. Their classmates crowded around to see the damage. Whether due to the humiliation or guilt, both boys decided not to mention the event again.

When the school day ended, Manfred walked back along the village street towards his family house. He followed the same route to and from the school every day. The market Platz in the centre of town was full of children and a few older boys in brown uniforms. Many were dotted around the war memorial in the middle of the square.

A few minutes later, he arrived at his house. It was large by the standards of the village. White plaster and wooden beams, painted a vivid red, greeted the visitor and left them in no doubt as to what country they were in. Inside, his feet clumped noisily on the wooden floorboards. The furniture was also wooden and seemed pre-war in its antiquity: the Franco-Prussian War. The house had a forest of such furniture but felt empty, in Manfred's view. The high ceilings seemed to create a sense of vastness in the smallest, most cluttered of rooms.

His mother greeted him with hardly a smile. He walked up to her and kissed her proffered cheek. He said nothing about the events of the day because he was not asked. The housemaid smiled at him, but she tended to speak only when addressed.

'How was your day?' asked his mother after a few minutes of silence, more out of duty than actual interest.

'Fine,' said Manfred, glancing out the window, or was it an escape route? The rat, tat, tat of rain suggested any request to go outside would be denied. He looked up at his mother for inspiration. Her face was drawn. She rarely smiled these days. It had not always been so. But now her eyes looked empty, like a dry well. The chill and the grey seemed to have seeped into the house, inhabiting the foundations, the walls and the people.

Manfred left her and went to the drawing room. It was full of books with characteristic bindings. He thought about reading but realised he was in no mood. The events of earlier had left an impression and not just on his hand. It still throbbed. He went to the sink in the kitchen and bathed it. As he did so, his mind wandered again. He thought of Diana Landau.

She was twelve and generally considered the prettiest girl in the class. Dark haired and dark-eyed, she was exotic not just because she was half-Jewish but also because her mother was English. Lots of the boys had cast eyes in her direction once but, of late, this had ceased. Manfred knew why this was so; it was impossible to ignore and yet still a surprise. He found it difficult to imagine why politics should matter when it came to boys and girls and love.

The tap must have been running for an age when his reverie was broken by the echoing clump of footsteps outside the kitchen. In the doorway stood his father, Peter.

His father was tall and forbidding. He was a serious man doing very serious work as head of the town police force. Whether by way of conversation or, more likely, interrogation, he asked, 'What are you doing, Manfred?' The muted tone was the most unsettling part. His father rarely raised his voice. Instead, it was like a liquid whisper. The sound of it wrapped around your ear and invaded your mind, enfolding, compressing and then suffocating it until you screamed your confession.

'I hurt my hand, Father.'

His father stepped forward and looked at his son's hand. He could see the red welt across the palm.

'How did this happen?' asked Peter Brehme in a low voice. Why do adults do this? Why the low voice. Don't they know we're frightened enough as it is? Fear was now strangling Manfred. His father's glare was hot enough to melt snow. He had a choice now: full disclosure or an outright lie. Neither alternative held much appeal, so Manfred told him the truth. And then held his breath. He didn't have to hold it long. His father's eyes hardened.

'Come with me.'

They passed Manfred's mother on their way out from the kitchen. She sensed immediately the anger in the eyes of her husband. She

38

did not ask any questions, however. Instead, she watched them go into her husband's study without comment. The door closed behind them. She stood in the corridor unsure of what to do.

Then she heard the whistling sound of a cane followed by an almost inaudible groan. Another two followed. She continued to stand in the corridor, almost frozen. Following the three lashes of the cane she heard her husband's voice, barely audible through the thick oak door. Manfred's voice was stronger. It was an apology, but the resentment and the hatred were clear.

Chapter Six

Manfred walked through the market Platz of Ladenburg the next morning. It felt like he could have been in the Middle Ages. All around was the bustle and noise and smells of farm and baking. The market was alive and had been for over an hour. Wagons pulled by carthorses mingled with stalls of vegetables and fruit. Women wearing coifed headdresses of starch and black ribbon, men stamping in buckle boots trying to keep fire and warmth in their part of the square. Preposterous outfits, outlandish claims by the stall holders and young children playing hide and seek.

As Manfred walked up to the school gates, he immediately sensed an atmosphere. The warmth and the exuberance of the square had been replaced by a chill and the pinched, pained faces of the pupils and teachers.

It was the silence, or rather the murmur, that alerted him to the possibility that something was wrong. Huddled groups of children whispered. One teacher was sitting on a bench outside the main building. He seemed to be weeping.

Herr Kahn, the physics teacher, brushed past Manfred, barely acknowledging him, a haunted look on his face. Spotting Erich, he wandered over to his oftentimes friend, sometime enemy, and asked, 'Is something wrong?'

Erich looked at Manfred in surprise and said, 'You mean you haven't heard, Manny?' Manfred shook his head.

'The Reichstag was burned down last night.'

'So?' asked Manfred, mystified at the reaction to the news around him.

To be fair, Erich was no wiser as to what a fire in a government building signified, but it was clear something was awry. The two boys looked around for a few minutes for someone who could enlighten them. A few fellow pupils shrugged in bemusement.

'Herr Kahn is over there with Diana Landau. He'll know,' said Manfred pointing to the teacher.

Erich laughed grimly. 'Of course, the Jews, they stick together.'

Manfred glanced at Erich but said nothing. They walked over to Herr Kahn. Manfred said, 'I apologise, Herr Kahn, if we are interrupting, but we were wondering why everyone is in despair this morning. What has this got to do with the fire?'

Diana looked at Manfred and then up at the teacher. 'Thank you, Herr Kahn. Excuse me.'

Manfred was disappointed she'd left, a fact noticed by Herr Kahn.

'Don't worry, I had finished talking to Fraulein Landau anyway,' replied Kahn although Manfred did not entirely believe him.

'So, you want to know why there is, shall we say, an atmosphere?' Both boys nodded. Kahn looked at them thoughtfully and continued. 'Well, you know about the fire obviously. It seems our leader is blaming the communists for starting it. This may or may not be the case. There are certainly other possible causes.'

'Such as?' pressed Manfred.

Kahn smiled again, and said, 'Well, there we come to the other thought. The government, and by that I mean the National Socialists, may use this fire to implement some of the policies that they have been wanting to do for a while now. This may result in a curtailment of some civil liberties. I'm only speculating, you understand, but it is a possibility.'

Manfred thought for a moment. The implication of Herr Kahn's statement was abundantly clear. He looked at the teacher and asked, 'Do you think the National Socialists were responsible?'

The smile slowly faded from Kahn, and he became very solemn. 'I think it best, Herr Brehme, that such thoughts are left unsaid, even among friends. I think classes are starting soon. Go to your class, boys.'

Manfred and Erich watched him go and then looked at one another.

'Pretty clear what the Jew thinks anyway,' said Erich dismissively. Manfred laughed.

'Yes, but we should do as he says, though. C'mon, let's go.'

The two boys hurried off to class and no more mention was made of the fire from that day forward in the school.

No mention was made, either, when one of the teachers, Herr Fischer, a teacher known to have sympathies with the communist party, did not return to the school. A veil of silence descended on any discussion about politics. No mention was made of the disappearance that evening in the house as Manfred and his family ate in silence.

Around nine in the evening, Manfred went up to his bedroom. He sat on the bed and read for a while. Suddenly he heard a noise at his window. He looked towards it and then back down to his book. It came again. He rose from the bed and went over to the window. Pulling back the curtain, he saw Erich down below, with some other boys. He opened the window.

'What are you doing?' he whispered loudly.

'Come on,' said Erich, motioning with his arm.

'Where?' replied Manfred, mystified. 'It's late.'

'Come on, we're having fun.'

'I can't. My father will kill me if I sneak outside,' pointed out Manfred in a loud whisper.

'Grow up,' sneered Erich, about to turn away.

The gauntlet had been thrown down. Grow up. He'd just turned twelve. Such challenges could not go unanswered. Yet, he also feared his father. Obedience was everything in his family.

'Give me a minute,' said Manfred reluctantly. A few moments later, Manfred climbed out of the window and down to the front garden.

'What's going on?' he demanded. This was the first time he'd ever done something so reckless. At the very least he wanted to know why he was putting himself at such great risk.

'Let's go. You'll see,' replied Erich. Manfred followed Erich and three other boys. All were from his school.

Ahead, Manfred could hear noise levels rising as they neared the centre of town. It seemed like a celebration. There was much shouting and laughter. He glanced at Erich, who merely smiled back without saying anything. At last, they reached the source of the shouting. There were two dozen boys. Most were older than Manfred. They were all wearing brown shirts. All were chanting slogans in support of the Nazi government. Manfred, Erich and the other boys attached themselves to the main group. As they did so, Erich joined in with the chants.

Manfred was unsure of how to react. The atmosphere was celebratory. Everyone looked happy. All the faces around him were young and their eyes were lit with a fire that Manfred found strange and oddly compelling. His own life felt so repressed. He envied the joy and lack of restraint in the other boys. It felt like a release.

These boys seemed to be having a life that he was excluded from. They were able to follow their passions. The mood was triumphant, and Manfred felt he wanted to be part of this. He didn't want to be a spectator. Erich looked at his friend and saw the slow change come over him and then, with a nod of encouragement, Manfred joined in the chant.

Nearby, another boy was wearing a khaki shirt and black shorts with a black tie which looked like a stain across his heart. He produced a tin of white paint and a brush. Then, brandishing it over his head, he shouted to the rest of the crowd. The others quietened but Manfred still struggled to hear what he was saying. It seemed he was urging them to follow him. The crowd was now no longer dozens of individuals. It was a single organism. It followed the boy to the tobacconist's shop. The self-appointed leader dipped the brush into the paint and then brushed the door to the shop with a Star of David and the word 'Jude'.

The crowd cheered and they followed him as he repeated the same message on the doors of shops that were known to be owned by Jewish people. The chants returned, only this time they were directed at the Jewish people: 'Deutschland erwache; Kommen die Juden' (Germany awake; the Jews are coming!). Unlike before, they were no longer random shouts among groups of boys. Now the chant beat a steady pulse. The screaming darkness was lit up by the torches the boys were holding. Demonic shadows danced on the walls of the shops in the square echoing to the abominable noise. Manfred, drunk with excitement, joined in.

They passed some houses and the leader of the mob went to one door and painted the same message. Manfred stopped chanting for a moment. Something was wrong. He looked at the house. It seemed familiar. He looked around to get his bearings. In the night and with the crowd of boys and the torches, he had lost track of where he was. Then he saw a face at the upstairs window. It was a man and he was scanning the crowd. Recognition dawned on him. This was the house of Herr Kahn. Manfred turned away lest he be recognised. Now uncertainty gripped him.

Slipping away quietly, he picked his way back towards his house making sure to stay in the shadows. He saw the police coming towards the mob. He saw his dad. For the first time in his young life, Manfred saw something in his father's eyes he'd never seen before.

Uncertainty.

Manfred's upbringing had been no different from most of his friends'. He didn't know if his father was strict or not. Discipline rarely took verbal form alone. All the teachers, no less than the fathers, seemed to think and act as one in this regard. His father's approach was governed by a certitude, emboldened by his position as head of police, that few of the fathers among his circle could match.

The fearlessness and the youth of the mob were unsettling. His father was looking around. There were only a couple of other policemen with him. They could not possibly halt what the Hitler Youth had set in motion. Unsure of what to do, Manfred watched in fascination. At last his father made a decision. He marched forward alone and sought out the ring leaders.

Peter Brehme did not feel afraid for himself. But a cold feeling gripped him that had nothing to do with the night chill. He'd never seen anything like this before, even during the worst of the country's economic woes. Law and order, Christian values, the idea of father-land had all remained firm and kept the country under control. This was new. A calculated disregard for social restraint but enacted in the name of some distorted idea of patriotism. It felt to Peter that to oppose this was to oppose the fatherland itself. Yet he knew this was not so. What he was witnessing was the antithesis of what he had spent his life upholding as a policeman and as a father.

He could not stand by and allow mob rule even if this was tacitly approved by the government. Scanning the crowd in front of him, he picked out a few men, barely schoolboys, as ring leaders who were responsible for the growing sense of anarchy. He strode forward and picked the tallest of the group, a young man in his early twenties.

'Who is responsible for this?' demanded Brehme.

The young man looked Brehme up and down; he smiled lazily and replied, 'The people, sir. The people.' He looked away in a manner that suggested Brehme had been dismissed.

Brehme felt the rage within him grow. What was happening to this country? Where was the respect? Once upon a time a young person would no more have thought of speaking back to an elder, never mind a police officer, than throw a brick through a stained glass window in a church. Brehme pushed his face right up to the young man.

'Look at me when I'm speaking to you,' shouted Brehme. A few other young men saw what was happening and came over towards them. Brehme ignored them. He jabbed his finger into the breastbone of the young man. 'Stop this rioting immediately.'

The young man glanced down at the finger that had just inflicted a mild amount of pain. His face twisted into a half smile, half snarl. 'What are you going to do? Arrest all of us?' He gestured to the mob.

It was Brehme's turn to smile. He looked at the new arrivals steadily. 'No, I can't arrest a mob on my own,' he admitted. Then he took his gun out of the holster and pointed it at the young man. 'But I can arrest you. Now, you little bastard, tell these friends of yours to go round and disperse the mob.'

The young men looked at his friends and then back to Brehme. There was uncertainty in his eyes now.

'Now,' screamed Brehme, causing the young man to flinch.

* * *

Standing in a shop doorway, hidden by the shadow, Manfred watched the group surround his father. Unsure of what to do, he stayed rooted to the spot. A dilemma was presenting itself. If they attacked him, he would have to help his father. But that would, itself, reveal that he'd been part of the original mob.

He heard a loud voice shouting in anger. He couldn't see who it was but he didn't need to. He knew his father's voice. He tried to get a better view to see his father shouting at the group. Some things never change, he thought. The group dispersed giving Manfred a clear view of his father holding a gun pointed at the young man.

This was unexpected but Manfred was relieved that he would not have to help his father. Or was he relieved that he would not have to oppose the people in the mob? He had been one of them, after all. With his father's attention now completely fixed on the young man, Manfred realised this was his chance to escape. He broke out from the shadows and darted past his father. He did not stop sprinting until he'd reached his home. His heart was pounding as he reached the door, driven by fear, driven by excitement and something else.

Elation.

Chapter Seven

His father's mood, always serious, was now more volatile. The uncertainty had been replaced by fear. There had been no repeat of the mob-like behaviour of the other night, but Manfred could see the change that was transforming both the town and his father. Each day, as Manfred returned home, the warm familiarity of the market Platz was replaced by a coldly threatening atmosphere. Young men dressed in brown shirts paraded around town.

Manfred longed to join them.

A few days later at school, Erich opened his bag and showed Manfred the contents. 'Look,' he said, 'look what father has bought me.'

Manfred reached inside the bag and pulled out a brown shirt. A black scarf fell out of the bag, too. Manfred bent down and picked it up. He held it in his hands. The texture was rough. There was a tightness in his chest. Envy.

'Your father gave you this?' said Manfred breathlessly.

'Yes,' said Erich delightedly.

'He doesn't mind?'

'No, he's really happy that I want to join. He supports Hitler. Doesn't everyone?'

Manfred was unsure how to answer this. His father certainly appeared to have little respect for Nazis but said nothing on the subject. Who knew what his mother's views on the subject would be these days?

'You seem surprised,' pointed out Erich. Thankfully he did not push for an answer to his original question.

'My father,' said Manfred by way of answer, accompanying it with a shrug. As he said this, Herr Kahn came into the classroom for their science lesson. Erich smiled and rolled his eyes. He understood. Manfred's father was unlikely to be supportive of the Hitler Youth. Were they not competition? Manfred replaced the shirt in the bag. He was burning inside. Looking around the classroom he knew a few of the other boys had joined. It felt like he was an outsider. He didn't want this. He wanted to be with his friends.

Herr Kahn began the lesson, but Manfred barely listened. His mind lay elsewhere. He wondered, at one point, if Kahn was aware that some of the boys he was teaching had daubed the front of his house with paint. He suspected that Kahn knew this was very likely. Manfred was uncomfortable about this but also recalled the excitement he'd felt. The sense of release. The sense of power.

There was no doubt Herr Kahn was the best teacher in the school. This was Manfred's view, and it was one shared by many others. He was certainly the most lenient. In the two years he had been in Herr Kahn's class, Manfred could not recall a single incident where violence had been deployed to control the classroom. In fact, Manfred realised this made him almost unique within the school.

Yet things had changed. He could see this on Kahn's face: the doubt, the loss of authority. There was a carefulness about him now. Where once he taught with a freedom and sense of joy about the wonders of science, his classes were now conducted with a muted restraint as if he sensed in the classroom the presence of an enemy.

And the enemy was there all right. It was almost palpable, brushing against his face, reaching inside the heads of the children. A reckless energy crackled in the air that was moments away from igniting. The least flammable substance in the classroom seemed to be the chemicals themselves.

It was clear both pupils and teacher were waiting for something. A moment when the changing balance of power could be made explicit. Kahn seemed to understand this. Each day the pressure built, unspoken but recognised, unhurried but all too fast.

At home, too, tension was mounting. Manfred's mother was openly dismissive of the Hitler Youth, but this was based on a contempt she felt for all young people. How could he not have known what she would think?

'Well, they seem to have fired up the young people. It's very distasteful,' commented Renata Brehme. Each passing day seemed to make her more distant and mean-spirited. His father, however, became more circumspect. He would never be openly supportive of any political party but there was something about the Nazis that clearly made him uncomfortable.

'Fires run their course,' replied Peter Brehme sourly. He tried mockery, aware Manfred was listening. Manfred understood it was a message to him.

'They think they're little soldiers with their uniforms. They don't know what war is.'

Nor do you for that matter, thought Manfred. He knew his father had remained in the police during the war and avoided service. Just briefly Manfred's anger flared up, but he quickly supressed it. How long before Erich brought up the subject of his father's contribution to the Great War? Manfred knew he would never be able to live down the shame if that happened. One thought raced through his mind, burning everything in its path: my father was a coward.

Peter Brehme walked through the town towards the large grocery store in the centre, Geschafft Ladenburg. He picked up his usual order of cigarettes from Arnold Weber and wandered through the square. He was acutely aware of the number of Hitler Youth now. They were everywhere. No wonder Manfred was so keen to join. Yet surely, he could see why this was impossible. How could he, the head of police, countenance a quasi-military organisation parading through town with impunity?

The Hitler Youth was not part of the state. As far as Brehme was concerned, they were the youth wing of a political party. Nothing more. It was untenable for his son to be seen to be favouring this party when he was a state official and, by definition, neutral from politics. His role was to uphold the law made by the government. It was inconceivable to him that his family should align itself implicitly through membership of a party, even its youth wing. Manfred should have understood this. Yet he hadn't. With a stab of pain Brehme realised that he'd done little to foster that understanding. He'd demanded obedience instead. But matters were coming to a head.

Manfred was a member of the church scouts. This was something that Peter Brehme had been in favour of. Manfred had embraced the scouts eagerly if only to be away from the house. That his father approved, was a relief. It made a change for him to be interested in anything outside of education. His mother was, as ever, ambivalent. Manfred was less worried about his mother. Instead he threw himself into the activities and the opportunity to be with his friends during the evening.

As he arrived at the church hall, later than usual, he sensed something was different. It was quiet. When he opened the door, he could see why. Marius, the group leader, was standing to one side, fear and shame etched deeply on his face. He was looking at three young men, all dressed in Hitler Youth uniform. Marius turned and walked away from the group towards the door Manfred had entered through.

He saw Manfred and said bitterly, 'You can stay if you want to; that's it for me. I'm having nothing to do with the Nazis.'

Manfred looked from Marius to the rest of the group. There were about twenty boys, all young teenagers. Some, like Erich, also wore Hitler Youth uniforms. They were all looking at him. Manfred looked at Marius and then back to the group. His heart was beating so loudly he wondered why it was not echoing in the hall.

He walked forward without looking back at Marius. All at once the group broke into a celebratory song 'Vorwärts! Vorwärts!' Manfred didn't know the song. He felt as if his feet were being carried on air. He bathed in the acclaim of his rejection of Marius, a young man in his early twenties who had run this group for the last three years. They all liked Marius.

Later that evening, Manfred returned home. The exhilaration of the last few hours was dissipating quickly as he wondered how he would tell his parents that he wanted to join the Hitler Youth. Each step closer to the house clipped away at his courage. His previous mood of elation was replaced by anxiety, then fear and a desire to keep it a secret. But how could he? It was a small town. Soon everyone would know of what had happened to Marius. The poor fool.

The thought of Marius brought a stab of guilt. He had not led the coup d'état, but his final denial of the young man had sealed his fate as surely as Nero turning his thumb downward or Peter denying

Jesus. What two hours ago had been a moment of triumph becan. his shame. Manfred knew Marius deserved better.

As he thought this, he grew angry. Angry at Marius. Why hadn't the fool joined them? Couldn't he see what was happening? The Hitler Youth offered so much more than the scouts. The scouts was for children. How could they be prepared for the responsibilities of manhood, of rebuilding their shattered nation by talking about God and how to help your parents in the house? What use was that? Now his mood had changed. His exasperation towards Marius had changed his sloping walk into a stride and his back straightened as he thought about how Marius had slunk out of the church hall. This would not be his fate. He arrived at the door of his house.

He walked into the house. His mother ignored him, and his father was in the study. Leni, the housemaid, smiled at him but he ignored her and thought about going straight up to his room without saying goodnight. For a moment he was undecided; then he decided to go to his mother.

'Yes?' asked his mother looking up from her book.

He gave her a kiss on the cheek and said, 'Goodnight.' Then he walked along the corridor to his father's study. His heart was beating fast, and he felt his throat constrict.

Two quick knocks on the door were greeted with a curt 'Enter.' Manfred did so and found himself in front of his father who was sitting behind his desk.

'Yes?' asked his father.

'I've come to say goodnight.'

His father glanced at his pocket watch and looked back to his son and said, 'A little early, isn't it?' Manfred remained impassive. His father had not reached a position as head of police without some

ng of when someone was holding something back. 'Is

rong, my child?' he asked, sympathetically.

r Youth have taken over the scouts.'

This seemed to trouble his father and he sat back in his chair. After a few moments he said, 'Marius is now with the Hitler Youth? I'm surprised.'

'Not Marius. He left tonight.'

'Really?' exclaimed his father. Now he sat forward and looked at his son. 'Are the rest of the boys happy about this?'

'Yes, Father.'

His father nodded slowly. It was immediately apparent what had happened. What was happening. He looked his son in the eye and asked in a dangerously soft voice, 'Are you happy about this, my child?'

Manfred bristled at the tone. He knew his father. He knew when he was angry. But something new, important and unstoppable, was happening to Manfred, to Germany. His fear evaporated and was replaced by the only thing that can help defeat the inner voices of denial, of shame and inertia.

Anger.

'Yes, Father. I want to join the Hitler Youth.'

His father slammed the palm of his hand down on the desk and roared, 'Never.'

Chapter Eight

The next week was governed by silences and looks of recrimination between Manfred and his father. This would have been uncomfortable for Manfred had it not, in his opinion, represented the usual situation. It was almost funny. Each night at the dinner table had been characterised by staged conversations between Peter and Renata on the ridiculousness of the Hitler Youth. Manfred grew bored very quickly but remained silent.

He had a plan.

The toppling of Marius would have been the major topic of conversation in the classroom had not one other even more shocking event taken place. It happened midway through the week during a chemistry lesson.

From the beginning of the class, it was apparent to Manfred and his friends, when they chatted afterwards, that there had been an atmosphere in the room. Professor Kahn was particularly ill at ease. Of late, though, he always seemed so. Erich claimed that he saw the looks between Diana Landau and the professor. He said he thought the two of them were 'having it off' which was a cue for much ribaldry that made Manfred burn inside, but he smiled along anyway.

Midway through the class, there was a knock at the door. Professor Kahn went to answer it. Manfred looked on as he seemed to be having a conversation with someone outside. Although he couldn't see, he was told afterwards it was Diana Landau's mother. When Kahn returned, he asked Diana to collect her books. Moments later Diana Landau floated out of the classroom.

Manfred never saw her again.

The incident provoked a lot more comment the next day when it was clear that Diana was not going to return. Klaus Steicher, Manfred's classmate, provided the confirmation.

'She's gone; the whole family has flown. The house is empty,' said Klaus. He added to this, 'Pity.' The smile on his face required little interpretation.

At the weekend, the silences had been replaced by lectures from his father on duty and obedience to family. They came randomly. Anything that Manfred did was used as an opportunity for Peter Brehme to extract a meaning that Manfred found scarcely credible, and even pathetic. In the space of a week, his view of his father had transformed from one of fear mixed with love to one of contempt mixed with pity. In a moment of shock, he realised he felt more derision for his father than love.

Even his mother seemed to weary of the lectures and there was also a tension between her and Peter. But then there always had been. Manfred often wondered if his parents had ever loved one another or was the match borne and preserved out of a sense of duty. Her interest in either him or the man she married seemed to vary by the day. Some days she would be communicative, others less and, more frequently now, not at all.

The pressure was building to the point when it required release. But Manfred only realised this afterwards. His mood raged between unhappy, angry and impotent. In his home there was no outlet for him to express this openly. This was just how it was. Not only in his home. Every home. So every look, every word, every silence was pregnant with implication, at least in Manfred's view. But Peter Brehme was no fool. Years of dealing with offenders meant he was aware of what Manfred was feeling.

'Peter, you're overreacting,' said Renata in a rare moment of engagement with her husband and with a household matter. 'It seems harmless to me. Just boys dressing up in uniforms and singing ridiculous songs.'

Manfred's father looked at his wife, the rage building up in him. But rage with his wife was pointless. She was as indifferent towards him as she was towards her son. This was her power and his impotence. In the end he shook his head and stalked off to his study saying, 'He will not be going to the meeting tonight.'

Manfred made sure to stay around the house that day. He knew what was coming and he didn't want to be accused of instigation, but then how could he not be?

The knock on the door came just before seven in the evening. The family were at dinner. Leni came into the room. She looked very uncomfortable.

'Yes?' demanded Peter. 'Out with it. Who is it?'

'Some people for Manfred, Herr Brehme.'

Peter glared at his son and said slowly, 'Really? Well, we'll see about that.' He rose sharply from the table and strode out of the dining room into the corridor. There were muffled voices in the corridor at the front door.

Sometimes the world seems to stop. Time ceases to exist. There is only you. Your breathing. Your heart beating. The air screaming in your ears.

The conversation seemed to last an eternity. Even Renata Brehme was, for once, curious about what was going on. She stood up and went to the door to listen. Manfred did not look at her, although he felt her eyes on him. He wondered what she was thinking. This was unusual. Normally he spent little time thinking about her. He suspected this was reciprocated. And still the talking went on.

At long last, Peter's father returned to the room. There was no hiding the anger behind his eyes but the slump in the shoulders told a different story. He looked at his son. The anger seemed to leave him at that moment. His eyes were almost pleading. This time, Manfred felt a stab of pity. It was beginning to dawn on him that something important had happened, but he was too young to understand what. The lines on his father's face became more apparent to him. They seemed deeper almost. The downward curve of his eyes, which previously had an almost self-righteous piety, now seemed to whisper one word: defeat.

And then he said, 'You can go.'

Manfred leapt from the table and left the room without saying goodbye. Peter sat down at the table silently and picked up his knife and fork. He put something in his mouth. After a few moments of chewing, he dabbed the side of his mouth with a napkin, stood up and left the room without a word of explanation.

Renata heard the door of the study slam shut. Leni looked from the table to Renata.

'Do you want me to clear up?'

Renata nodded absently, 'Yes. Perhaps you should.'

Part 3: Britain 1938–39

Chapter Nine

Little Gloston: Christmas Eve, 1938

Snow fell softly at first, fluttering in the wind like white butterflies. Soon it became heavier, falling steadily, covering the ground outside the forge in a white blanket. It began to cling to the leafless trees and the houses. The cold had teeth now. There was a bite to the air. It felt almost like a physical presence everywhere except the forge. The forge was its own world. A heated haven.

Inside the shed, Danny was stripped to the waist, sweating madly only a few feet away from the furnace. He was hammering together two pieces of metal on the anvil. Stan walked in smoking a pipe. He looked at his youngest son. Danny was now as tall as Tom at six feet two. His wide shoulders were heavily muscled yet there was not a spare ounce of flesh on his frame.

'What do you think you're doing, you young fool?' were Stan's first words as he came into the forge.

Danny looked down at his shirt which he'd removed. His father had told him before about hammering iron in this manner. The sparks could burn naked skin. He grinned at his father and said, 'Don't worry. Nearly finished. I didn't want to dirty the shirt. I don't have anything else to wear for the carol concert.'

His father shook his head and turned away but then a thought occurred to him, and he walked back to the forge.

'By the way, Charles Desmond spoke to me yesterday. He said you'd put the price of horseshoes up.'

'I have.'

'When were you thinking of telling me?' asked Stan.

'You asked me to handle the business affairs. I am. What did you tell Mr Desmond?'

'That you're handling the business affairs now,' replied Stan, looking at his sixteen-year-old son, not without a degree of wonder. The boy had been working at the forge for nigh on three years now. He'd grown into a man so quickly. When was it apparent he'd also taken over the business? Stan knew that neither he nor Tom had a head for commerce. Danny had taken to the business side like a bee to flowers. Desmond wasn't the first farmer to complain to Stan about the change in prices but, oddly, none complained about Danny. They liked him. But they didn't want to pay more, which was hardly a surprise.

'I've put the price up on the shoes. It hasn't changed since 1929.'

'That long?' exclaimed Stan in shock. Danny nodded and continued beating the hell out of the iron on the anvil. 'We should put the prices up then,' agreed Stan.

'Aye, we should,' said Danny, grinning.

'You can tell 'im yourself, then. I can see him coming now.'

Danny looked up and, sure enough, in the distance he could see the old farmer walking along the road towards their house. Stan nodded to Danny and left him to deal with the farmer. Putting down his hammer, Danny walked over to the outside sink and pulled the handle for water. He quickly cleaned himself off and then used a towel to remove the excess water. By the time the farmer had arrived, Danny had his shirt on and was sitting waiting for Desmond.

'Hello there, Danny,' said Desmond. The farmer was a stout man of fifty, with a florid country complexion and grey whiskers impressively resplendent on his cheeks. 'Did I just see your father there?'

'You did,' said Danny, grinning widely. 'He was asking when we'd increased the prices of the shoes.'

'Ah yes, that's why I've come to see you,' said Desmond. 'I had a feeling your father knew little about it. He said to speak to you.'

'Is there a problem?'

'Yes. This letter you sent says you're nearly doubling the price. Look Danny, wheat prices are less than they were ten years ago. I can't afford this increase, really I can't.'

Danny looked sympathetically at the farmer. It was true, the price of wheat had been stagnant for a long time due to imports from abroad and over-capacity in the industry.

'I'll tell you what, Mr Desmond. We do need to increase the price otherwise we're losing on every shoe we make. Why don't we leave the price as it is, but you give us three dozen eggs each week?'

'I see you still want to steal eggs from me, you young scamp. Two dozen.'

'Three dozen, Mr Desmond. You're not just here to talk to me about the horseshoes, are you?'

Desmond looked at Danny in surprise and then smiled slowly. Finally, he said, 'No, I'm not just here to talk about the price of shoes.'

'Your boy Ben wants to work at the forge.' It wasn't a question.

'He does. I can't interest him in the farm work and as he's the youngest, the other two lads and the other workers are all I need. Can you use him?'

'Yes,' responded Danny.

'I'll send him along.'

'Along with three dozen eggs,' said Danny with a grin. He held out his hand and the two men shook on the deal.

After the farmer had left, Danny returned to the house. His father looked up from the table.

'So?' asked Stan.

Danny took him through the conversation with Desmond. His father nodded. He was impressed. The solution was fair and took account of Desmond's situation on the farm. The forge was doing well, and an extra pair of hands was needed.

'What age is the boy?'

'Fifteen.'

'More children,' said his father grumpily, but he was quite pleased with how things had worked out. Danny shot his father a look and laughed.

'I knew you'd be pleased.'

Tom came down the stairs, dressed in his Sunday suit. He'd caught the end of the conversation.

'More children?' he asked, looking at his father in surprise.

His father looked shocked also and removed the pipe from his mouth. Danny, always on the lookout for a prank said, 'Yes, didn't Dad and Mum tell you?'

Tom looked from Danny to his father in shock and even a little disgust. Stan said nothing, half amused at the exchange. Finally, Tom asked, 'Dad? We're going to have a baby?'

By now Stan was in on what Danny was thinking. 'You look surprised.'

'You're both a bit old,' pointed out Tom.

'And you, son, are a bit of a ninny,' replied Stan more sternly than he felt.

Tom turned from his sombre-faced father to his brother, who was now laughing so much he had to sit down.

'Very funny.' Tom turned towards his dad who was also smiling now.

'Danny has organised for the Desmond boy to join us. We need it.'

'We do,' agreed Tom, sitting down, and giving Danny a gentle clip around the head to stop him laughing. Then he continued. 'How did he take the price rise?'

Stan told Tom about the new arrangement.

'Good idea, Dan, we'll be able to feed him n' all.'

'That's what I was thinking, too,' said Stan. 'Desmond was one of my first customers; we're doing right by him and us.'

This was as close to praise as either Stan or Tom was ever going to get. Not that Danny was worried. As long as they left him to run things, he was happy. Both men also seemed happy that Danny had taken the lead in business matters. So far it seemed to be working well.

Stan glanced at the two boys together. His boys. Boys? They'd grown up and he couldn't have felt prouder. Both good, hard-working young men. His eyes blurred with the images of events long ago. Stan knew how much the future is connected to a past they had no part in shaping. And the skies were darkening for reasons that had nothing to do with snow.

Chapter Ten

Around two o'clock, the Shaw family left the house and walked towards St Bartholomew's church. The church was tiny with light grey brick speckled by dark spots. Alongside the church was a small grave-yard. A few odd headstones peaked out from underneath the snow.

Outside the church, a small crowd had gathered consisting of almost every inhabitant of the village. Young and old alike stood waiting for Reverend Simmons. He would lead them from the church, after his usual prayer, towards Cavendish Hall where they would sing carols, drink punch and mulled wine. The children would be given presents by the lord of the manor, Lord Cavendish.

Kate Shaw walked out from the cottage. She was arm in arm with Stan. Their sons followed, nodding to their friends as they arrived in the square. Everyone was dressed in their Sunday best. This was one of the major celebrations in the village calendar, alongside Easter and Harvest.

The Shaw family joined the throng. Kate Shaw spotted Bob Owen with Beth Locke and walked over to say hello.

'When are you two going to get hitched?' asked Kate. Beth gave Bob a playful dig in the ribs.

'You hear that?' she said. Bob rolled his eyes at Danny, who was enjoying Bob's discomfort immensely. This turned into a frown as Tom joined his mother. 'Yes, Bob, how long have you two been together? If you're not careful she may look to another better-looking man.'

'Time enough,' responded Bob eventually, but with a smile.

At this point Reverend Simmons made an appearance. The village cheered the reverend who made a mock bow. He glanced up at the sky. It was a metal grey with speckles of yellow threatening to break through. The snow had stopped for the moment.

Reverend Simmons held his arm up and a hush descended on his outdoor congregation. He was wrapped up well against the cold. Looking around the crowd he nodded and smiled.

'Let us pray for Christians around the world as we celebrate the birth of Christ. Bless all those who are entrusted with Christian ministry that your Word might be proclaimed with truth and courage across our world. Bestow your wisdom on all who govern, that in honouring the earth and its people, we may celebrate the light of God. Grant reconciliation to those beset with conflict and violence, that they may live in the peace of this holy night.'

Not a sound could be heard aside from the reverend's rich baritone voice. When he finished there was silence and a moment of reflection. Then Simmons looked up and said, 'Musicians, make ready.'

To his right stood three musicians. Danny recognised Hugh Gissing on the tuba. The other musicians were older: Gerald McIver, the farmer, on trombone, and Ronald Annersley, the postmaster, on trumpet. They traditionally started with 'God Rest Ye Merry Gentlemen' as they walked towards the hall.

Reverend Simmons made a start towards the driveway leading to the Hall, his feet crunching through the dusting of snow. Meanwhile

Ronald Annersley led the carols and played the introduction for half a minute as they walked towards the Hall. Then the village began to sing in unison:

God rest ye merry gentlemen
Let nothing you dismay
Remember Christ our Saviour
Was born on Christmas Day

They sang as they walked, and arrived at the front entrance within a few minutes. Standing on the steps of Cavendish Hall were the Cavendish family and staff. There were also a few guests that Danny did not recognise and one, with some dismay, that he did.

The singers completed their first carol and then Henry Cavendish stepped forward to greet Simmons.

'Tom, how many times have we done this?' he said shaking hands.

Simmons laughed. 'Too many! I'm not sure how long I'll be around to do this in the future. These old bones are creaking.'

'Nonsense, Tom. You're indestructible. Do come inside. I think you and the children deserve warmer surroundings and something for your efforts.'

The carol singers marched in first, followed by the villagers and about twenty children and toddlers. Once they were all in the main hall, Cavendish stood before them to give his traditional Christmas speech to the village.

'My grandfather used to say, "I feel there are a few of you who could probably give this speech now, you've heard it so often." I know how he feels.'

There was some laughter at this from the older villagers and carol singers. Henry continued. 'But no matter, tradition must be followed.

As many of you will remember, as a young man it was a tradition I didn't much care for. I do now. I care for it very much and I hope that it is as welcome to you as it is for those of us who live and have lived at Cavendish Hall.'

This was greeted by many saying, 'Hear, hear.'

'As my grandfather would say, I hope this tradition of ours will go on for many generations to come.' This was greeted with applause by all. Danny noticed Lord Cavendish glance when he said this to his mother, a rather formidable woman, who remained impassive throughout until that moment. She smiled when he said this and the two of them seemed to share a moment of genuine warmth.

Henry continued. 'As you know, we shall serve mulled wine, lemonade and mince pies to you all. Doing so, as usual, will be my children whom you know very well, Lady Sarah and Lord Robert. Joining us are our guests this Christmas.' Henry mentioned a few names. Danny did not know or care who they were, but he guessed the mention of Lord Augustus was a reference to the young man standing near Lady Sarah. He hadn't changed much from his last sighting of him, nearly five years previously: taller, not bad looking but with an air of boredom, or was it contempt? His face did not make any attempt to hide his displeasure at what he was being asked to do.

He looked at Sarah. She, also, seemed unhappy. He wondered whether she found the festivity a chore or if it was because of his lordship. Was there anything between them? With the upper classes, who knew? In Danny's opinion she was still too young to be courting, if she were his daughter, anyway. He glanced again at Lord Augustus. What a poncey name, he thought.

By now the carol singers were all assembled in the large entrance hall where tables had been laid out with all manner of food. Dominating the hall was a large Christmas tree, which brought squeals of delight from the children who were itching to run towards it to find their presents. Danny followed his father towards the table where Henry Cavendish was serving drinks with his son, Robert. The boy was around eleven years old with fine features, very slim and clearly destined to be as tall if not taller than his father.

'Mr Shaw,' said Henry, filling a cup of wine and handing it to Stan. 'A pleasure to see you again. And this is young Tom and Danny, if I remember correctly.'

Young Robert filled the cups with wine and handed them out to the young men. Stan grinned. 'Not so young now. Tom will be married next year.'

'Really? My word, how the time goes. Congratulations, Tom. And what of you, Danny?'

'Too soon, sir,' laughed Danny. 'Plenty of time yet.'

Stan rolled his eyes and shook his head. It was clear he had given up on this son.

'Actually,' continued Henry, 'I'm glad I've met you again. Would you be willing to come up to the Hall some day and show my son that throw you did all those years ago?'

This caused Danny to laugh and his father and brother to turn to him, both confused. Danny shrugged and said, 'I'd love to. When would you like me to come?'

'Perhaps the day after Boxing Day,' replied Henry. He could see that the other two men were baffled by the conversation.

'You may be wondering what this is about. Clearly Danny never mentioned anything. Your son, Mr Shaw, was alone in the forest a few years ago when my wife and I came across him being attacked by several other boys from the village. To say he dealt with them very handily would be an understatement. Apparently, he learned a particular throw from you, Mr Shaw, that you were taught in the army.'

At this point recognition dawned on Stan and he looked archly at his son. Tom smiled also. It sounded like Danny all right.

Danny looked down at young Robert and said, 'So how about it, Lord Robert? Do you fancy learning a few wrestling moves?'

'Yes, please,' said the boy, beaming. He had a likeable, open face. So different from his sister.

'I can tell you he is very much like his grandfather and not a bit like me at this age,' said Henry with a smile. But behind the smile there was sadness also. The remembrance of a man whom he'd lost because of the war.

'I remember your father, sir,' said Stan. 'A fine man. He had a word for everyone, didn't matter who you were.'

Henry nodded and said nothing. The memory of his loss would never leave him. Stan, recognising the look on Henry's face, turned to his sons, and said, 'Right, boys, we've taken enough of his lordship's time. There's others want a sup.'

This seemed to break the spell and Henry smiled at the big blacksmith as he moved aside. The three Shaw men moved into the centre of the hall and looked around. As big as it was, it was still thronged by the villagers who looked forward to this day and spoke of nothing else for many weeks in advance.

Danny spotted his mother over by the table where Lady Jane and her daughter Sarah were serving mince pies. Sarah was almost as tall as her mother now but very gangly. Unlike her mother, who seemed very relaxed with the visitors, Sarah looked ill at ease. Augustus was whispering to her. He seemed amused.

Danny found he couldn't take his eyes away from her. The green eyes compelled his attention. Then, just for a moment, their eyes

71

met. She turned away immediately. Danny looked away also and went over to join Hugh Gissing who was now minus his tuba and was guzzling every cake he could lay his mitts on.

'You ready for the concert then?' asked Danny with a grin.

'Aye, been practising for weeks,' replied Hugh between mouthfuls.

'I know, the whole village has been listening,' joked Danny. Hugh laughed at this. The animosity that had marked their time at school had long since disappeared. Danny realised it probably dated from the moment he had not given them up to Lord Cavendish. Since then, the two rival gangs had gradually merged as other things captured their interest.

Alec was now courting Fred's sister. Tom was to marry Greg's cousin. This was village life. A cycle of renewal that had begun centuries before them and would go on long after they were dust in the ground. Or so Danny had once thought. But even he accepted that things change. Sometimes for the good, though often not.

He drifted through the crowd trying to avoid the small children who were running underneath his feet. It was the same every year. Once upon a time he had been one of those children. There seemed to be more of them now. The crowd was as big as he could remember.

Up ahead he saw Reverend Simmons clap his hands to gain everyone's attention. The crowd became silent and gave him some space so that all could see. Danny looked at Simmons, his back a little more crooked, his cauliflower ears partially covered by a felt hat. He'd lived a life. Danny wondered about his own future. Would it draw out lazily year after year in the village or would events in Europe force his life along a different course? The serious look on the face of Simmons suggested he was thinking along similar lines as he began to speak.

'My friends, it is time to work for our food and' – he held his glass up – 'wine.' The audience laughed at this. Simmons continued,

'Normally such a day as this should be one of joy as we anticipate the coming of our Lord. Alas, the world is facing a great evil once again. I wonder how long we will be able to enjoy such gatherings before the young men of our country must, once again, be asked to make the ultimate sacrifice. I hope and pray that day never comes. I fear that it will.'

There was silence in the hall as Simmons spoke. The Cavendish family looked on solemnly. Everyone recognised that to ignore the looming war would be a disservice to those who had lost family in the previous conflict. A few of the villagers, including Lady Jane, already had eyes brimming with tears as Simmons spoke movingly of that time.

Finally, Simmons finished by saying, 'With our hearts in the present, our memories for those we have lost in the past and our prayers for the future, can I ask you, the carol singers, to begin.'

There was a round of applause and then the singers grouped together. Following the short introduction by Simmons, the choir rapidly changed the order of the songs they had decided to sing. On the trumpet, postmaster Ronald Annersley began to play the opening bars of 'Silent Night'. The whole hall echoed to as emotional a rendering of this carol as anyone could remember. Danny sang along also. He looked at his father. Tears ran down his father's cheeks. So used to the silence, the void that sometimes seemed to be his father, Danny was shocked by what he saw. And, for the first time, he felt something that he had never felt before.

Fear.

Chapter Eleven

December 28th, 1938

Danny rose just after seven and dressed quickly. He walked outside. The cold stung his face. It was still dagger-dark but there was a glow of light from the snow blanketing the ground. His feet crunched through the snow towards the forge. There was always a fire lit. Danny added more charcoal causing the forge to burst into life. Flames snapped up and outwards. He turned to the wall and reached for a pair of ancient bellows his grandfather had probably used. Grabbing the two handles and pumping vigorously, he forced air through the bag into the forge causing the fire to roar with approval. Job done; Danny returned to the cottage following an aromatic trail of bacon. A light was on and he could see his mother through the window preparing a cooked breakfast for the three men.

'Smells good,' said Danny giving his mother a hug. 'Tea ready?'

Kate frowned at her son. 'I've only two hands. Why don't you boil the water?' Danny ignored her and sat at the table with his arms folded and a grin on his face. His mother smiled also.

'I'm not a servant y'know,' said Kate but the effect was ruined by her laughter.

Tom joined them a few moments later and then Stan. Soon they were tucking into bacon and eggs.

'What time are you going up to the Hall?' asked Tom between mouthfuls.

'The note said eleven,' replied Danny, looking at Tom with a smile.

'How long will you be?' asked Stan. Business as usual, semi-impatient with the interruption but the pride was unmistakable.

'As long as it takes,' interjected Kate. 'What if his lordship invites him for lunch?' This brought guffaws from Tom. 'Well, why wouldn't he?' continued Kate. 'My boy's as good as any that go there.'

'Maybe he'll eat with the servants,' laughed Tom.

'You're just jealous,' replied Kate, any attempt at rebuke let down by her laughter.

Danny was enjoying all of this immensely and chipped in after his mum. 'Always has been jealous, Mum. Can't blame him, living in my shadow all these years.'

Kate pointed her finger at Danny and warned, 'Don't you start.' But her youngest was already laughing loudly, and so was Tom.

At his mother's insistence, Danny scrubbed up and changed his clothes, which resulted in a volley of friendly abuse from his brother as he set off for Cavendish Hall. Danny responded in kind, which left his mother scolding her two sons and Stan looking on with a pipe in his mouth and a broad grin.

As he approached the Hall, Danny realised he was unsure whether he should go to the front or make a left and head to the back of the Hall where the trade entrance was located. He opted for the latter and had made about twenty yards when he heard a voice calling him.

'Mr Shaw, would you care to come this way?'

Danny turned around and saw Mr Curtis, the venerable butler of Cavendish Hall. Curtis was a dignified man doing a dignified job. The grey hairs suggested, truthfully, that he was on the wrong side of seventy. He had been butler at the Hall since the Bronze Age, according to Danny's classmates. Looking at him, Danny thought that was being generous.

'Hello, Mr Curtis, are you sure?' replied Danny. 'I'm happy to go this way.'

'No, if you please, Lord Cavendish insisted you come through the front entrance.'

Danny shrugged and followed Curtis through the front doors as requested, into the large entrance hallway where he had stood a few days previously. The Christmas tree was still there but the absence of tables and people emphasised the hall's size. Directly ahead, Danny had an unobstructed view of the great staircase leading up to the open second floor corridor with a series of imposing portraits of the descendants of Lord Cavendish. A fairly motley crew thought Danny.

'If you'll come this way,' intoned Curtis as if he was reading from a pulpit. 'Lord Cavendish suggested that I take you to the games room.'

Danny had never been beyond the confines of the entrance hall so was fascinated to continue through to previously unseen parts of the manor house. The two men made their way down a corridor before arriving outside a door. Curtis gave a brief knock and then walked in.

The room was large, containing a billiard table, a leather chesterfield sofa and matching armchairs. There was a table with a green baize top for playing card games. To the other side of the room was a table with a chess set laid out and two chairs either side. The middle of the room was clear.

76

'If you'll take a seat, I'll let Lord Cavendish and Lord Robert know that you have arrived.'

Rather than sit down, Danny had a look around the room. He went to the window and saw that it overlooked the back garden. There wasn't much to see. The snow had done a good job in covering anything of interest.

A noise from behind. The door opened and into the room walked Henry Cavendish and Robert. The youngster looked very excited.

'Hello, Mr Shaw,' said the young noble. He walked directly to Danny and shook his hand.

Danny laughed and replied, 'If I'm going to be showing you how to throw someone to the ground, perhaps you should call me Danny, young sir.'

Robert glanced at his dad, who smiled and nodded.

Henry looked at Danny and said, 'I shall take it that I can call you Danny also.'

'Yes, Lord Cavendish,' said Danny with a grin.

'Well, then,' continued Henry, 'we are quite literally in your hands. Perhaps if you demonstrate to Robert using me as your mortal enemy or some such, he'll have an idea of what we're doing. In fact, perhaps before that you could tell us more about how you learned it. You said your father taught you?'

Danny looked at Henry and understood immediately that this was an opportunity to talk about the war.

'Yes, sir, my father taught me,' replied Danny. He looked at the young lord and said, 'You will know all about the last war, Lord Robert.'

'Yes, Danny, my grandfather fought in it. He died.'

'Yes, sir, he was a very brave man. When you're in the army, like my father was, they give you basic instruction in hand-to-hand combat.

77

It's part of the training. Comes in useful I'm told. Apparently, there was quite a lot of it in the trenches.'

'I know. I read all about it, Danny.' The young lord was more excited than horrified by what he'd read.

Danny glanced at Henry. The look on his face was amusement but Danny sensed there was a tinge of sadness for his late father. A nod from Henry and Danny continued.

'My father showed my brother and me some of the things they'd taught him. My brother and me, well we practised a lot. I became pretty good at it in the end. It's fairly easy to do as you'll see.'

Henry stepped forward and Danny showed him where to stand. A few moments later, Lord Henry was thrown, quite gently, onto the floor.

Henry burst out laughing. 'My word, Danny, you made that seem very easy.'

Robert clapped excitedly. For the next half hour, Danny instructed both on a few wrestling techniques Stan had taught him. It was clear in the conversation between throws that Henry was keen that his son be prepared for life at a boy's public school. It sounded as if boys were the same whatever their station in life.

'Well, Robert, I think perhaps we should allow Danny to return to his work. You look like you have the idea now.'

Robert looked very unhappy at this. He was having such fun he couldn't imagine why anyone would want to end it.

'One last throw, young sir,' suggested Danny. This brightened the youngster's mood. Danny and Robert stood face to face and then gripped one another's arms. 'Remember what I told you, sir.'

A moment later, Robert stretched his leg out and threw Danny over it. Danny cushioned his fall by expertly rolling as his back was about to hit the ground. When he looked up, he saw the bemused faces of Lady Jane and Sarah looking down at him.

'Hello, darling,' laughed Henry. 'I asked Danny Shaw if he would come up and show Robert that throw, do you remember?'

Jane's green eyes crinkled in amusement.

'I certainly remember the throw. I don't remember you mentioning that Mr Shaw would be coming up to show Robert.'

'Ah yes, I may have forgotten that bit,' said Henry shamefacedly.

'A little too conveniently if you ask me,' said Jane, with one eyebrow arched. Danny rose to his feet and dusted himself down a little.

'Thank you, Mr Shaw, for giving us your time. I must admit, the ways of men are often a mystery to me, but it seems like my son has had an enjoyable morning.'

'Oh yes,' exclaimed Robert. 'We've had a wonderful time.'

Sarah rolled her eyes at this and turned to walk away. Up close Danny was conscious of two things about her. Firstly, she was still every bit as snooty as the first time he had seen her in the forest clearing. Secondly, she was probably going to be a stunner.

The two women left the boys to their play. Henry laughed at the intrusion and suggested that they have a lemonade. Danny was intrigued. He had never been to this part of Cavendish Hall and agreed to this immediately. He was led down to the kitchen where he met Elsie, the aged cook, and the housekeeper, Polly.

'What've you three gentlemen been up to?

'Fighting,' said Henry truthfully.

Ethel looked at him sceptically before Robert provided a more detailed explanation of the morning's activities. All of which amused and appalled Ethel in equal measure. Three glasses of lemonade were put on the table and the three men gulped down the contents in record time. Three refills followed and were despatched with equal rapidity.

'I think it's time to let Danny go now,' said Henry after they had well and truly quenched their thirst.

Danny rose from the table and was about to head towards the back door when Henry added, 'No come with us. We'll go up via the entrance hall again.'

Danny felt a surge of pride. This was something of an honour and he felt they were treating him as an equal. Changed times, he thought. They climbed the back stairs and arrived back in the hall.

Robert chattered away happily, asking questions about the forge. He seemed fascinated by the work of blacksmiths. Danny glanced at Henry, unsure if he should suggest the young lord should visit. The raised eyebrows and the smile on Henry's face emboldened Danny.

'If you'd like to come along some day, I'm sure we could use an extra pair of hands down at the forge. We've just taken on another young lad, just a bit older than you,' said Danny, grinning down at Robert.

Robert's eyes widened in excitement, and he turned to his father. Henry nodded. This was greeted with a squeal of delight by Robert. Henry looked on in pride. He was delighted by the interest shown by his son in the work that took place on the estate and the village. It was something he was keen to encourage. His own life had been more closeted. His mother had discouraged such interests. He was going to ensure his son had the widest possible exposure to life outside the narrow world of nobility.

They stopped at the main doors and Henry grew serious for a moment. He looked at Danny with some sadness.

'What did you think of Reverend Simmons' speech before the carols the other day?'

Danny nodded grimly and said, 'We may be at war soon. My dad has been following this chap Hitler for years now. He's been saying as much for a long time.'

'I think you're both right, sadly. Everything I hear about this beastly man leads me to believe he won't stop at Austria and Czechoslovakia.

80

From what I understand, there's a growing disillusionment with the chances of maintaining peace. We lost a lot of men last time. I wonder if there'll be so many stepping forward this time.'

'I will,' said Danny quietly.

'I know your father was in the other lot. He may be against you doing this, and your mother,' replied Henry.

'They'll understand. I think you'll find the men of the village will still be prepared to do their bit.'

'For he today that sheds his blood with me shall be my brother,' said Henry, almost to himself.

'Henry V,' said Danny.

Henry looked at Danny in surprise. Then he smiled. 'Yes, forgive my surprise.'

'I remember we read it at school. I quite liked it. Full of blood and thunder. I wish I'd read a bit more back then. I wasn't very keen on school.'

'I remember,' laughed Henry. 'If you have a moment, come this way. I want to show you something.'

The two men and Robert walked into a nearby room, which turned out to be the library. The room was full, from wall to ceiling, with books. Henry led Danny over to a photograph on the wall. It was very wide and showed an army battalion. The date read June 1914.

'That's my father there,' said Henry pointing to an officer, sat in the middle.

Danny looked at Henry and nodded. Henry then led Danny over to the books. He picked a book from off the shelf. The title read, *The History Plays*. It was Shakespeare. He handed it to Danny.

'A lot of blood and thunder in there. If you're interested, you can keep it. We have a lot of Shakespeare as you can see.'

Danny looked at the book and laughed. 'Thank you, sir. I'll definitely have a read.'

As he said this, the door opened. Sarah and an older lady walked into the room. Sarah looked in surprise at Danny before her face returned to its usual cold mien.

'Hello, my darling. I was just showing Danny our library. It transpires he likes Shakespeare.'

Sarah looked entirely dubious about this but said nothing.

'Danny, this is Governess Curtis. She taught both myself and my wife, funnily enough.'

Danny shook hands with the lady.

'Pleased to meet you, Danny. It always gladdens my heart when I see someone likes Shakespeare. I'm sure you'll enjoy reading it.'

'I will, Mrs Curtis,' replied Danny.

Henry gently touched Danny's arm and said, 'Well, I think, Robert, you have a lesson now. Danny, let me walk you to the door.'

A few minutes later Danny was walking through the snow back to the forge clutching his book. His senses were filled by the memory of the warm hospitality of the Cavendish family, the enthusiasm of their son and the coldly beautiful green eyes of their daughter.

Chapter Twelve

January, 1939

'Now, pick up the shoe and place it in the forge,' said Stan to Robert Cavendish. 'Yes, just there.' The boy did as he was instructed. 'Now release the shoe.' The two of them stood back and looked at the shoe beginning to glow. Stan clapped a big hand on the shoulder of the young lord and said, 'Your first shoe, well done, sir.'

'Thank you, Mr Shaw,' said Robert enthusiastically.

Danny walked in and looked at the boy's handiwork. He gave the boy a nod and said, 'Now, you have to do the tidying up bit.'

Robert did as he was told. By the end of the day, his enthusiasm and friendly nature had won over the family. Around five in the evening, Jane Cavendish stopped by the Shaw house to pick up the boy. Like Kate, she was in her mid-thirties, but she looked much younger.

Tall and willowy, she moved with a grace that would have had a prima ballerina crying in her beer. She was popular among the villagers for the principal reason that she was one of them. Far from being born with a silver spoon, she was the daughter of Bill Edmunds who was the former groundskeeper at Cavendish Hall. She had been the stable girl for the family but, unbeknown to them, had also been the sweetheart of the future Lord Cavendish, Henry. Against his mother's wishes, Henry had married her as soon as both were of age.

'Hello, Mrs Shaw,' said Jane, knocking lightly on the open door.

'Lady Cavendish,' said Kate Shaw, turning around from the Aga.

'Mummy,' exclaimed Robert, leaping up from the table where he had been gorging himself on freshly made, toasted bread. He ran into his mother's arms and began to tell her everything that had happened that day.

'Slow down,' laughed Jane, rolling her eyes at Kate. 'How was he?'

Danny appeared at the door and answered the question. 'We'd happily take him on, Lady Cavendish. Not sure we could afford his wages though.'

'Can I come back, Mummy?' asked Robert.

'Well, that's for Mr Shaw to decide, not me.' Danny nodded and Robert looked pleadingly at his mother. Jane shrugged. 'As long as it doesn't interfere with your studies then, yes. I can see no problem.'

Robert let out a cheer and immediately ran over to hug Danny.

'Are you sure, Danny?' asked Jane, smiling.

'He's a good lad and a great help. He worked hard today, didn't you?' asked Danny looking down at the future Lord Cavendish.

Robert's response was to begin a list of everything he had done, which, to be fair, was not insubstantial. He'd clearly had a ball.

'Well, I hope you put as much effort into your studies,' commented Jane sternly. She knew she had few worries on this score but felt the need to say something her parents might have said. Such is the way of things. She caught a look on Kate's face and the two women smiled conspiratorially.

They walked out of the kitchen and Danny accompanied them up the garden path.

'Thank you,' said Jane, and she meant it.

Over the next few months, Robert became a frequent, and welcome, visitor to the forge. Henry looked on in approval as he saw his son grow in stature. The time spent with the Shaw family had done wonders for the boy's physical strength and confidence. From his own upbringing, Henry knew he would need reserves of both for when he was sent away from the Hall to boarding school. This was something he wasn't looking forward to, but it was expected and probably necessary.

And so, summer gave way to autumn. The lambs grew bigger; the harvest was made ready and blossoms that had floated through the air became copper leaves, deserting the trees to be carried hither and thither in the wind; the days became shorter and darker and colder.

Chapter Thirteen

3rd September, 1939

The Shaw family gathered around the wireless. The air was thick with fear and sadness. Kate's eyes were milk wet as she waited to hear the inevitable news. An icy chill gripped her as she looked at her two boys. Both strong young men, but boys. One seventeen, the other twenty-one. Their life was meant for other things, not this. What had happened to the world? The natural order of life was working in the village, falling in love, marriage. The family was being ripped apart by forces that Kate did not understand. Life was not meant to be this.

Neville Chamberlain's reedy voice halted all thoughts. She listened to the words that she'd dreaded hearing for days, if not years. Stan stood up from the kitchen table and walked to his armchair, puffing on his pipe. Danny and Tom stared at the wireless, in a mixture of excitement and dread.

'This morning,' announced Chamberlain, 'the British Ambassador in Berlin handed the German government a final note stating that, unless we heard from them by eleven o'clock that they were prepared at once to withdraw their troops from Poland, a state of war would exist between us. I have to tell you now that no such undertaking has been received, and that consequently this country is at war with Germany.'

Danny sat back from his hunched position. His senses tingled as he listened to the Prime Minister continue relaying the sombre news.

'You may be engaged in work essential to the prosecution of war for the maintenance of the life of the people – in factories, in transport, in public utility concerns, or in the supply of other necessaries of life. If so, it is of vital importance that you should carry on with your jobs. Now may God bless you all. May He defend the right. It is the evil things that we shall be fighting against – brute force, bad faith, injustice, oppression and persecution – and against them I am certain that the right will prevail.'

The family looked at one another when Chamberlain had finished. They waited for Stan to say something. Instead, Stan remained silent, staring ahead with a stony countenance. Unreadable.

'What does it mean for the boys, Stan?' asked Kate, unable to hide the fear in her voice.

Stan thought for a moment and then said, 'For the moment, nothing.'

'For the moment,' replied Kate fearfully. The answer hung in the air, like mustard gas. But Stan remained silent, lost in his own thoughts. He looked at his wife. His eyes were like sunken pits, and she felt like crying. As young as he was, Danny could read his father's mind.

'It means we're all on alert,' said Danny. 'If this Polish thing finishes well and Germany leaves, then we're back to where we were. If they don't leave and we commit troops then it's a mess and it will not end quickly. I think we'll have to deal with Hitler once and for all.'

He looked at his father as he said this and could see the sadness in a man who recognised, with all due sense of fear and dread, what the next few years would bring. At last Stan rose from his seat and trooped out of the kitchen and headed back towards the forge. The family watched him go. They looked at one another. Tom put a comforting arm around his mother but could find nothing to say.

Later that evening, Danny sat with a group of his friends in the centre of the village. All the young men of the village were there. Normally such get-togethers were marked by robust banter. However, the mood was solemn. Instead, there was discussion about what they would do. A few of them had lost family during the Great War and there was an unspoken agreement that, amongst them, there would be no bellicose behaviour. The conversation centred on one topic.

'They'll start calling us up in the new year, wait'll you see,' said Hugh Gissing with absolutely no evidence to back up this claim. But they knew he was right. It was just a question of when.

Danny was unusually quiet. His thoughts were scattered like the leaves on the ground. He felt an emptiness that he couldn't be sure wasn't fear. The certainties he'd felt as a child had slowly begun to erode over the last few years. War was a hastening rather than an end to a process that had been developing in the library at Cavendish Hall.

Over the last few months, he'd begun to make frequent trips, at Henry Cavendish's invitation, to the Hall. Much of his spare time had been spent in the library. His reading had been focused on history initially but slowly expanded out as Henry introduced him to science.

His reading of history suggested that the war would take time to progress. Listening to Henry made him comprehend just how unprepared the country was. Any call up might take much longer to occur than they realised. As the nation made provision for the coming struggle, it would need to develop strategies that encompassed military and civil life: the building of armaments and ensuring the security and continuity of food production was more important now than battle planning.

Without dismissing Hugh's comment, Danny explained this to the group, who listened in silence. Afterwards it was clear that, to a man and boy, they would all volunteer to serve. Some of the farm hands wanted to volunteer immediately but Danny counselled against this.

'I'm telling you, right at this moment the best way we can help is to do what we're doing. The country needs food,' said Danny, looking at Bert Gissing and his friends, who had been most in favour of immediate enlisting. 'We'll hear soon enough what's needed of us.'

There was a quiet authority in Danny now that seemed at odds with the lad they had grown up with. The person they remembered was someone always on the lookout for a bit of mischief. Now he'd changed. They had all changed of course, but the change in Danny went beyond the merely physical.

They all knew of the friendship with the Cavendish family. All knew how much time he spent up at the Hall. No one begrudged him this. He was still one of them.

Of course, boys will always be boys. The gravity of the day gradually gave way to the enthusiasm and irreverence of youth. War was on everyone's mind now but no more or less than the other overriding interest of these boys.

A few girls began to appear in the village street in groups. The boys soon forgot about their fears and joined them in the dance that has existed since the beginning of time. Some of the girls came over and joined Danny's group sitting in the middle of the village. Soon the steps of the Great War memorial, listing all those who had died in the previous conflict, were covered with young people. The memorial had been erected at Henry Cavendish's wish and expense.

'What will you do now?' asked Margaret Desmond, the sister of Ben who was now working at the forge.

Hugh and Tom turned to Danny, now the unofficial spokesman for the group. He told them what he had told the rest earlier. Another asked when they would be leaving for the fight.

'After I marry you, gorgeous,' came the reply from Hugh. This brought a host of jeers from the girls. But the mood had been lightened and the comments took on a more risqué nature as the young people of the village chased away the dark thoughts of war.

In its place came a more intense focus on the things that mattered to them. Driven by the fear for the future, friendships deepened between the girls and the boys. Thoughts and feelings, once undeclared, became common currency that night. The air became sweeter, and colours more vivid as all developed an appreciation for a life that once had been taken for granted.

Sitting apart from this was Danny. His thoughts were elsewhere. A few of the girls tried to engage him in conversation but gave up and sought solace and company with other more willing boys. As the evening light was replaced by darkness the centre of the village became quiet again.

For all his comments about the time it would take before the call-ups began, Danny returned to the certainty that it was when and not if. Like his father, he would answer the call, fearfully but willingly. It was no more or less than what his country would expect. It was what other young men would do. What his father had done. This made things explicit. The consequences of the wireless broadcast were all too apparent, the cost incalculable, the outcome unknowable.

Danny trudged back to the house knowing his world was going to change. He had no power to direct its course. He could only respond to its prompt. This, more than any sense of fear, was what he hated: the inscrutable uncertainty of war.

Part 4: Germany 1938–39

Chapter Fourteen

Ladenburg (nr. Heidelberg): Christmas Eve, 1938

The church hall was full of song and a lifeforce so strong it seemed the place would explode with the energy within. The rafters of the wooden hall were certainly being put to the test by those present. Manfred and Erich were now the group leaders of the village Hitler Youth group. They sat in front of the boys leading the singing 'Es Zittern die Morschen Knochen' (The Rotten Bones are Trembling).

> *Trembling are the rotten bones*
> *Of the world before the Red War.*
> *We smashed the terror,*
> *For us it was a great victory.*
>
> *We will march on*
> *Even when everything falls in shards,*
> *For today Germany is listening to us*
> *And tomorrow the whole world.*

Manfred could see tears in the eyes of some of the children. They sang with passion, with volume and with their hearts. There was little beauty in the noise they made. Instead, the music was more primeval. It seemed to emanate not just from the souls of the young people but also from the core of the building.

All the boys were dressed in a similar uniform: khaki shirts and black scarf. This group now included children as young as ten, members of a separate group Deutsches Jungvolk in der Hitler Jugend (German Youngsters in the Hitler Youth). But age does not matter when you are sharing a common dream. Like when you go to a football match, men, young men, and boys become one. Free from responsibility, free from the need to impress others, free to be themselves: unconstrained and happy. Manfred looked around at the faces of the boys under his and Erich's command. Euphoric faces beamed back at him. He felt his heart surge with pride.

Erich motioned with his head towards the door. He was right, of course, how could they hope to contain such emotion within the small confines of the hall. They needed to share their joy with the world outside. Make them see that the future was with them, in their hands. The hands of the young.

The group of boys marched out into the street singing, led by Manfred and Erich. The eldest boy was given the responsibility of holding a large flag emblazoned with a swastika. Tears stung his eyes, and he accepted his duty in muted adoration as if he was holding the Holy Grail itself. Manfred felt almost embarrassed by the intensity of the boy's reaction. Was it the flag itself or the coming-of-age symbolism of leading the young army out to the world?

People in the street stopped and looked at the line of boys emerging before them. There was a surprise for Manfred outside. He could see his father watching the procession. He had reluctantly ordered the policemen to stop the traffic to let the group of boys pass. Father and son looked at one another. Manfred felt almost drunk with power. He gave his father a brief nod as he passed him. His father's face was unreadable.

Snow fluttered lazily onto their faces as they marched. The pavements were blanketed by snow. Manfred sensed the ludicrousness of trying to keep in formation as they risked slipping and falling on the crushed snow. The chill cut the faces of the boys as they marched through the town singing Nazi marching songs; their hearts, as much as the drums, beat the pace of their march.

A few women made attempts at saluting, but Manfred could see their hearts weren't in it. This made him angry. He stopped the boys in the middle of the street, holding up the traffic behind. For a minute they marched on the spot and then he moved them forward again towards the market Platz.

All around them, the shops were decorated for Christmas. In the market Platz, alongside the war memorial, stood a very tall Christmas tree. The marchers stopped by the Christmas tree and sang the 'Horst Wessel Lied' (The song of Horst Weisel), a song dedicated to the memory of a Nazi murdered by a communist. When the song finished, they applauded their own efforts. Erich stood up and addressed his audience.

'I think maybe it is time that we …' He paused for effect. Then with a wide grin he said, '… have a snowball fight.' In a flash, he bent down, scooped up a handful of snow, compressed it with his other hand and threw it at Manfred.

This was greeted with loud cheers. Moments later, Manfred was hit on the side of the head by another snowball. Ice flowed down the side of his face like an open wound. He roared with laughter and set about avenging himself on the culprit. Snowballs whistled past him, and he felt the melted snow trickle down the back of his neck. He compressed the snow together in his hand, the cold stinging his hands, and he let fly. Another snowball hit him and then another. He was a natural target for the small boys, and they were now liberally pelting him, emboldened by a fire within. Snow crunched under Manfred's boots as he sought cover, realising he was hopelessly outgunned.

Passers-by joined in the snowball fight and soon battle lines were drawn between young and old. Erich stayed with the young boys, but Manfred led counter attacks by the adults. The effort was telling on Manfred. His breath came out in white puffs; his heart was beating fast, and the cold of the snow chilled his fingers so much they could hardly bend.

Manfred's adrenalin was now surging through him. He led a bunch of his army in an attack on the enemy. They pinned Erich's rather ramshackle militia into a corner and proceeded to bombard them mercilessly, laughing all the time.

The fight ended when Erich sued for peace and re-assembled the boys around the Christmas tree for another rousing rendition of 'Heil Hitler Dir'. A few of the adults joined in saluting as they did so. Many of the other townsfolk returned to finish the last-minute shopping, tired of the songs, tired of children screaming 'Heil Hitler', tired of the cold.

The air was full of snow and the vapour from the mouths of the combatants. There was much laughter. The simple joys of a snowball fight never leave you. Manfred grinned at Erich and they both giggled at the madness of it all. There was a poem he remembered from an Englishman; he couldn't remember it exactly, but it reminded him of this moment with Erich. To be young and in Germany at that moment was a type of heaven.

'This is the best fun,' said Erich shaking his head in wonder. His hair was wet, melted snow dripped down his face like sweat in summer. Both were breathing plumes of vapour from the cold and their exertions. Manfred's fingertips were beginning to hurt, such was the cold. He looked at their throbbing redness and felt relieved that Erich had surrendered. The last thing he needed was a war of attrition.

'Look at them,' agreed Manfred. 'We have our own private army.' The snowball fight had mostly ceased. A few vendettas were being exacted but, for the most part, spirits were high, and everyone felt like brothers in arms. Sensing this, Erich rose to his feet. A hush developed among the boys when they saw him. He put his hands on his waist and stood with his feet shoulder width apart in an unconscious imitation of their leader.

'Let's invade France,' roared Erich; his arm shot aloft. The boys bellowed in agreement.

In all the fun and excitement, Manfred had completely forgotten his father was nearby. He caught a glimpse of him in the distance. He looked at the melee impassively. Then he climbed into a police car and drove away. For a moment Manfred was glad that he'd left. Then an emptiness descended on him. He realised he would have liked his father to join in. But then perhaps his position militated against such frivolity.

His father had never exhibited any sign of playfulness with Manfred, even as a child. Yes, he remembered moments when his father seemed to be enjoying himself. But superficiality made him uncomfortable. He was not a light-hearted person. He was the chief of police, and he was now irrelevant.

Chapter Fifteen

28ᵗʰ December, 1938

Manfred looked out of his window. The early morning light reflected off the snow and blinded him momentarily. The sky was steel-grey, heavy with snow. Soon the cloud would unburden itself, and the air would become white. Back to bed, thought Manfred. Just as he was about to turn and bury himself in the warm embrace of the blankets, he caught a glimpse of Nina Kruger sitting in the square with a friend. She was the prettiest girl in the class. Her long blonde hair was tied in a ponytail and plaited. Clear blue eyes hid beneath impossibly long eyelashes. All the boys wanted to court her, but her father refused to let them anywhere near the house.

In a matter of a few minutes, Manfred was dressed and outside. He walked towards the main square patting down his hair. He half jogged, half walked towards them finally slowing down as he neared his quarry. Manfred walked past the seat, pretending not to notice the two girls, hoping they would shout over to him.

They didn't.

He walked into a shop named 'Geschäft Ladenburg', a large grocery store that sold everything, as far as Manfred could tell. The owner, Herr Weber, appeared and looked with stern kindness at his young customer. Manfred perused the confectionery. A moment of inspiration struck. He bought three bars of the second most expensive chocolate. Exiting the shop, he set off in the direction of the two girls. He put on what he hoped was his best smile and walked with an increasing sense of dread towards them. He heard their laughter, just, over the sound of his own heart beating. His smile had started too early, he scolded himself. It already felt strained, like the legs of a long-distance runner entering the home straight. Would they notice? Of course they would. Girls could smell fear in a boy like a shark could smell blood.

'Happy Christmas,' said Manfred, a little surprised and relieved at how strong his voice sounded. He held out the chocolate like he was going to stab them. The two girls seemed to pull back fearfully. Confidence crashed once more.

'For us?' asked Nina's friend when it dawned on her what he was holding. The few seconds that it had taken for her to comprehend what Manfred was offering were probably the worst of his life.

'Of course,' replied Manfred, uncertain whether a smile or nonchalance was the best course of action. 'I don't see any other beautiful ladies around.'

Someone shoot me, thought Manfred. Did I really say that? He felt faint with mortification.

Both girls giggled not at the wit so much as the gaucheness of the approach and obvious terror in Manfred's eyes. Neither girl considered the tall blond-haired boy before them at all bad looking. In fact, he was one of the most handsome boys from the school. He was often discussed among the girls but rarely with great enthusiasm. That he was quiet they did not mind. Good-looking, obviously. But there was something in his manner, an uncertainty, an awkwardness that made his company difficult. One felt uneasy with him. He was still a boy and they wanted more.

This was the case now. The two girls waited to see if he had anything fresh to offer beyond the chocolate and a nervous smile. This was a problem because Manfred was right out of ideas on what to do now. A part of him wished Erich was here; he was better with girls. Having a sister seemed to make him understand how to talk to this alien breed.

Manfred, as he stood there looking down at the two girls, who were now smiling to one another conspiratorially, felt lost. Finally, he asked, 'How was your Christmas?'

But the moment had gone. It was too late. Several seconds too late. It was obvious he was struggling, and they had simply lost interest in him. Again.

Katrine said hers was very good and thanked him. Nina didn't bother saying anything. It was a dismissal. He didn't know much about the opposite sex, but he knew when someone was closing a conversation off. He had enough experience with his mother. He wished them a good day and he returned to his house, his face burning hot in the chill morning air.

After lunch, Manfred made his way over to Erich's house. The earlier humiliation still seared his mind. It was time to have a man-to-man conversation with his friend and understand how Erich managed to be on such good terms with so many girls. As much as he liked his friend, he was no Aryan ideal. Shorter by at least five centimetres, he was not fat but certainly stocky. He had a confident air about him that made him good company for both sexes.

Along the way he passed the old house of Professor Kahn. He stopped for a moment as he realised new people were moving in. It had remained unoccupied for over three years since Kahn had been arrested.

A strange day. A day he would never forget. This was not because it was a teacher. In Manfred's experience, teachers came and went. Nor because it was someone he quite liked. No, the circumstances were as bizarre as they were sudden. Manfred's mind went back three years.

Spring 1935

Out of the classroom window, Manfred could see the cornflowers blooming like a purple sea, the wind creating ripples on the surface that broke outward like tiny waves. As he gazed through the window, he saw a grey-brown Opel Olympia drawing up outside the school. Two men stepped out from the car. The driver was a short no-nonsense type. He wore a raincoat and a fedora. The second man was taller, fair-haired and walked with a distinct limp. Manfred guessed he would have been old enough to have fought in the war. Their arrival caused a stir in the class and Professor Kahn had to work hard to regain the attention of the pupils.

The class continued for another ten minutes but the whispered hum did not subside. All the boys were certain the two new arrivals were members of the Gestapo. Why had they come to the school? Manfred soon found out.

A few minutes before the end of the class, the headmaster of the school knocked on the door and then entered. The class immediately stopped what they were doing and rose from their seats as if one body.

'Herr Professor,' said the headmaster. 'Come with me.' It was an order, curt and contemptuous, like he was speaking to an errant pupil. Turning to the class he said, 'Class, sit down. Wait here in silence until the bell and then leave for your next class.'

Kahn and the headmaster left the classroom. A minute later, the class rushed over to the window, scrambling to get a view. They watched Kahn being led away by the two men. The car drove off in a hurry.

'Did you see that?' exclaimed one pupil. 'His wife was in the car, too.'

'I know. I saw Julia Kahn there also,' said one of the girls, referring to the young daughter of the Kahn's.

'It's the Gestapo, no question,' said Erich, voicing everyone's thoughts at that moment.

The class returned to their seats but moments later a voice said, 'Look! There's another car.'

Several boys left their seats and went to the window. It was another Opel Olympia. A man in a trench coat stepped out from the back. He walked in through the front entrance.

'More Gestapo by the look of things,' said one boy. By now the whole class was balanced precariously by the window, fascinated by the events.

Moments later the man stormed out shouting at the head teacher who was following him. The class was stunned. They had never seen their head teacher looking so meek. It felt like he was now the naughty schoolboy. Manfred wasn't sure if he was enjoying the spectacle or uncomfortable with the fact that he did not understand what was happening. In fact, the whole class was wondering the same thing.

'What's happening?' asked a girl, a little fearfully. The car door slammed shut and within seconds roared away from the school. Manfred glanced at Erich, who merely shrugged.

A new teacher arrived the next day. The fate of Professor Kahn was never mentioned again. To talk of the professor openly was to risk punishment; everyone understood this. Manfred felt uneasy about the arrest. Although no one spoke of Kahn in public, in private the boys came up with ever more viciously implausible theories on why Kahn had been arrested and the mystery of the two cars.

One boy blamed him for the murder of a local SS man that had taken place a day earlier. Manfred almost laughed when he heard that. Whatever Professor Kahn was, he was certainly no murderer. But Manfred remained silent and let the stories career wildly along. All the boys knew the real reason why he had been taken. It was as obvious as it was simple. Except for the second car. No one could explain this mystery.

Professor Kahn was a Jew. Across Germany it was well known that the Jews were being rounded up and deported. This was all that had happened. Nothing to be excited about. However, Manfred remained uneasy. He had liked Professor Kahn. His last thought of Kahn as he left the group to return home that night was the look exchanged between him and Diana Landau a few years previously.

Manfred stood and watched the house from a distance. Workmen moved furniture from a lorry while other men arranged things inside. A man and a woman appeared. Both seemed to be about the same age as his own father and mother. Then a young girl appeared. She was about thirteen, perhaps older. Manfred smiled and thought about how she might look in a few years. Quite something, he concluded. Before he became too conspicuous, he decided to continue his journey. It was also too cold to be standing still. Better to keep moving. Slowly, he felt some semblance of circulation return.

The snow underfoot was beginning to turn icy, and he made his way carefully along the footpath to avoid falling. As he walked home, he saw a car accident. There was ice on the road. A small lorry failed to stop in time and bumped lightly into the car in front. A few passers-by stopped to look.

The man in the lorry got out. He was small, middle-aged and quite wiry. From the car a younger man got out. He was irate and began yelling at the lorry driver, who held his hands up to apologise. The younger man was having none of it, though. He pushed the older man and then hit him. The lorry driver collapsed to the ground. The passers-by shouted at the younger man to stop, and he began to remonstrate with them also. Then he heard screams.

Manfred pulled his coat up around his neck and walked on.

Chapter Sixteen

January, 1938

The world, it seemed, was covered in perfect white. The snow lay thick on the ground shining brightly in the morning sun. The shatter-brittle silence in the wood was broken by the delighted screams of young boys, at first a few and then many. All were bare-chested in the numbing cold yet delighted to be so. Their roars were a release, a yell of defiance against the elements. They would not submit. They would not be seen to acquiesce to its icy tendrils. Onwards they ran, every step a triumph of their will over themselves and Mother Nature.

Manfred and Erich followed along behind the group. They were responsible for the village group. At this moment they were happy to trail behind. It always interested them when the parents of the children urged them to 'tire the boys out'. It was a universal desire, it seemed to Manfred and Erich, that parents wished their children to be in a permanent state of exhaustion. The mystery was never explained to them. Their job was to follow orders.

They reached the brook and the group stopped. It was a small clearing and the boys filled most of it. Erich leapt onto a log and shouted, 'Jogging on the spot for one minute.'

Almost as one body they did as they were ordered. Erich encouraged them, through insults and coaxing, to go faster and faster. For the next half hour, the two dozen boys were led through a series of exercises, finishing off with a particular favourite.

'We'll finish now with a competition,' announced Erich. This brought a loud cheer from the boys. He reached into one of the two bags that he and Manfred had carried with them. From the bag he extracted a wooden club.

'We are going to see who can throw the gren… sorry, I mean club.' This brought another loud cheer and Erich had to wave his arms to quieten them. 'I mean, wooden club,' shouted Erich over the noise.

Manfred began to hand out the clubs. One by one the boys launched the clubs into an open space on the other side of the brook. Each new extension to the distance was greeted by cheers. Anyone falling short was met with good-natured abuse. At the end the boy who had won stepped forward to be met with acclaim from the rest of the group. Neither Manfred nor Erich, as the eldest at seventeen, participated.

'What is your name?' asked Manfred of the fourteen-year-old boy who had stepped forward. He was obviously new.

'Heinrich Mayer,' responded the boy. Manfred shook his hand. The boy could barely be described so. He was as tall as Manfred and equally well made.

'Congratulations, Heinrich, and welcome to our group.'

'Thank you, sir,' replied Heinrich.

It was the first time anyone had called him, sir. To the rest of the boys in the group he was just Manfred or Manny. He liked the sound of it.

The three boys who had fallen shortest in the competition were delegated to go and collect the clubs, while the rest of the boys sang songs. When the three boys returned, Manfred shouted, 'Right, boys, last one back to the hall is a rotten egg.'

Cheers greeted this order, and the boys tore off in the direction of the town. It was two miles away.

The meeting broke up an hour later and the boys went their separate ways. Manfred joined Heinrich as they were heading the same direction. The two boys chatted amiably, white vapour coming from their mouths, cloaking their faces. They trudged through the snow, both wearing their Hitler Youth uniforms, both saluting young boys who saw them.

'That was an impressive throw back there. You've obviously had practice,' observed Manfred.

'Yes,' replied Heinrich, 'I was a member of a Hitler Youth group in Dortmund before we moved here.'

'I imagine that was a bigger group,' laughed Manfred. 'We're probably a bit small for you.'

Heinrich shook his head. 'No, I like it here. It's very friendly. But yes, the other group was very large, and I certainly was nowhere near being the best at throwing. There were some very big boys in that group.'

'What does your father do?' asked Manfred.

'He works for the government,' answered Heinrich, after a moment of hesitation.

Manfred noted the hesitation and did not ask anything more on the topic. Instead, he responded by saying that his father was the head of police. Heinrich looked at him and nodded. There was something in the look that was unaccountable to Manfred. It was almost as if Heinrich knew this. Any further thought of this was ended when they arrived at his new friend's house. It was the same house once occupied by Professor Kahn. Heinrich saw the look in Manfred's eyes.

'You knew the previous owner?' asked Heinrich.

Manfred was about to say yes when he changed his mind, replying instead, 'I was passing a few days ago when I saw the lorry outside and the people moving furniture. I didn't realise it was you.'

The door to the house opened and a man in his early fifties stepped out. He was taller than Heinrich and very lean. His suit was clearly expensive, and he held himself with the confidence of authority. He smiled when he saw Heinrich.

'You've finished.'

'Yes, Father, this is Manfred. He's the group leader.'

'Hello, Herr Mayer,' said Manfred.

'Hello, Manfred.' He appraised Manfred for a moment and appeared to like what he saw. Manfred held the eye of the older man. They were of a similar height. The handshake was firm.

'Are you still at school, young man?'

'Yes, Herr Mayer, but I finish this summer.'

'What will you do then?'

Manfred hesitated a moment before saying, 'My father and mother would like me to attend the university in Heidelberg.'

The older man looked at him shrewdly and then said, 'I sense this is not your wish.'

'I wish only to please my family and make them proud,' replied Manfred carefully, aware of the older man's eyes on him.

Mayer nodded approvingly and Manfred breathed a sigh of relief inside. 'Good answer, young man. It is the duty of every son and daughter to make their family proud of them. I think you will.'

Of course, he would say this, thought Manfred. He had been brought up to understand, painfully sometimes, the difference between right and wrong, obedience and disobedience. Yet Germany was going through something extraordinary. A rebirth. The youth were

110

becoming a powerful force in the country. No longer did the older generation seek to beat respect into them. In his uniform, looking this man in the eye, Manfred felt as if he was an equal. It was no illusion. Only later did he see that it was a delusion. His mind and his heart had been betrayed equally thanks to men such as Mayer.

'Thank you, Herr Mayer.'

Manfred left them at this point and went back towards his house. He didn't see, from the upstairs window, a face looking down and following him until he was out of sight.

Chapter Seventeen

September, 1939

Manfred sat in the dining room of the Mayer family. The only sound was the clink of cutlery on porcelain. It felt so much like his own home. The room was decorated sparsely. Heavy oak furniture, supporting two large silver candelabra, was about as far as the family stretched for ornamentation. There was a large picture, the only one in the room. It was of the Führer. This was, perhaps, the only difference noted by Manfred from his own house. The family also had a maid. Marita had been with the family for years according to Mayer. Centuries more like, thought Manfred.

Manfred had become a frequent guest in the house over recent months as his friendship with Heinrich grew. Mayer was happy that his son had developed a group of friends that he approved of and encouraged Manfred in particular. There was something of the mentor in Manfred, which he quickly recognised. The arrangement suited Manfred as well. It gave him a chance to get to know Heinrich's sister Anja. With something approaching joy, he noted the arrangement seemed to be welcomed by Anja, too. Although she was fifteen, the age gap was immaterial. Manfred was prepared to play a longer game.

The conversation around the table inevitably turned to the one topic uppermost in the minds of every family in the country.

'They will declare war. Both France and Britain. They have to, or they are even more dissolute than I thought,' declared Mayer as coffee was served.

Frau Mayer and Anja looked at one another unhappily. Manfred noticed this and decided against becoming too ardent in favour of such an event. Fortunately, Heinrich was eager to declare his readiness.

'I hope they do. We'll show them. They couldn't beat us last time, they won't this.'

This seemed to please his father, who smiled indulgently. Mayer turned to Manfred and asked, 'What do you think, young man?'

Manfred thought for a moment and said, 'I hope they will see sense. The Führer does not seek war. He just wants what is rightfully ours.' He looked Mayer in the eyes as he said this. The older man nodded but it was difficult to read if this was in approval. Manfred continued. 'War will demand a high price of our country. I do not underestimate our enemies or their determination. But they shouldn't make the mistake of underestimating us. If the time comes for war, they will find us ready. I will be ready.'

Throughout, Manfred's voice was soft, steady. Unlike Heinrich, there was neither stridency nor certainty as he spoke, just a quiet determination. When he finished, he glanced at Frau Mayer. Then he turned to Anja; her eyes were red. Finally, he looked at Mayer.

From the drawing room he could hear the wireless playing music. Manfred recognised it as the prelude to 'Lohingren'. There was purity in the melody, a nobility that made Manfred's heart swell.

Mayer continued to look at Manfred and then slowly he lifted his hand and held it out to the young man before him. They shook hands. Finally, he spoke.

'Well said, young man. The future of Germany is safe, I know, because we have young men like you to carry the vision of our Führer forward.'

Manfred looked at Mayer and realised something had been decided. He would tell his father that he was not going to the university. It was a conversation he had avoided for too long. The time spent with Mayer had shown him where his heart lay. Over the previous months Mayer had never asked him directly what he wanted to do but, in conversation and without words, Manfred had revealed himself all too clearly to the older man.

'What will you do?' asked Mayer, after a short pause. He emphasised 'you'.

Manfred looked at him and said simply, 'I would like to join the army.'

From the corner of his eye, Manfred could see Anja looking down. But his eyes were on her father.

'Have you told your family?' asked Mayer.

Manfred shook his head and admitted, 'I don't know how to. My father wants me to go to the university. His heart is set on this.'

'I can understand,' said Mayer. 'But it is your life, and you must decide what is best for you. I can help you if you wish. I have many contacts. Someone like you, Manfred, could be moved towards officer training quite quickly. More quickly than you imagine. You're smart and I think you have leadership qualities. I've watched you with the boys.'

'Thank you, Herr Mayer. It would be a dream for me to do this.'

'Have you given any thought to which branch of the armed services you would like to join?'

* * *

It was late in the evening when Manfred returned to the family house. His mother was in the drawing room but did not look up from her book when he entered. Manfred looked at her for a moment. Finally, she turned away from her book.

'Do you want something?'

There was vagueness in her voice. Uncertainty. She seemed to be lost. More and more these days a fog surrounded Frau Brehme. She seemed to have little will or energy to find her way through it.

'Where's Father?'

'Your father?' She looked confused for a moment and then said, 'I heard some noise from the room over there,' indicating his father's office. She looked at Manfred to see if the answer meant anything before returning to her book.

Manfred left the room and his footsteps echoed along the wooden corridor. He knocked and waited for a reply.

'Enter.'

Manfred walked into the room. His father glanced up from the large wooden desk. He had taken to wearing spectacles. He looked over the rim of his glasses and said, 'You're back late. You seem to be spending a lot of time at the Mayer house.'

'Yes, Father, they invited me for dinner.'

Manfred stood still and there was a brief silence. They looked at one another and then his father asked, 'What do you want, Manfred?'

Manfred looked his father directly in the eye and said, 'I want to join the army, Father.'

Brehme took off his glasses and looked at his son. There was neither shock nor anger. If anything, it seemed to Manfred, there was resignation. Or recognition of the inevitable. The only sound in the room was the clock ticking. Manfred waited for his father to reply.

'May I ask why you don't want to go to university?'

'There's no point, Father. There will be a war. We both know this. The fatherland will want me to fight. It is better I join now and can, at least, influence where I go and what I do.'

Brehme nodded but did not look happy.

'Has Mayer put you up to this?' There was anger now.

'No, Father. It's my decision.' His voice was barely audible.

'Decision?' Now a hint of contempt.

'Yes, Father. Decision.' Manfred walked forward and stared back at his father daring him to raise an objection. It was a fight that his father must know was unwinnable.

'I knew a lot of boys your age who went to fight last time, Manfred. Most never came back. Those that did were never the same. You think that war is glorious. It's not. Trust me, I know.'

How? wondered Manfred. You didn't fight. There may have been a look on Manfred's face but suddenly Brehme stood up and roared at his son, 'Get out!'

Manfred reddened and then spun around, walking out of the room, slamming the door behind him. He walked into the library and switched on the wireless. It was the news. For the first few moments, Manfred was too angry to hear what the announcer was saying. Then, as he calmed, he heard the word 'war'. He stopped and turned up the volume. The voice of the announcer was mocking as he revealed that Germany was now at war. Manfred collapsed into the seat. His heart began to beat rapidly, and his breathing became laboured.

The door to the library opened. It was his mother. She looked at Manfred and said, 'Oh, it's you. I thought it was your father.'

'We're at war, Mother.'

'Who with?'

'Britain, France. They've just announced,' said Manfred, glancing at the wireless.

116

His mother did not seem to register what he was saying. Her face a mask, impenetrable, or perhaps, uncaring. Manfred couldn't decide. Later he knew.

'I see,' she said absently. 'Have you eaten?'

Manfred looked at his mother with incredulity. He then answered slowly, 'Did you hear what I said?'

'Yes, we're at war. It happened before I think.'

'Mother, I'm going to join the army. I'm going to fight. Do you understand?'

Frau Brehme looked at her son. Her face was a mask, neither approval nor disapproval. She nodded and left the room. This was no fit of pique or anger. Manfred stood alone; the announcer on the wireless had stopped and music was playing. It was the Horst Wessel Lied. Manfred sat down and listened.

For the last time, the call to arms is sounded!
For the fight, we all stand prepared!
Already Hitler's banners fly over all streets.
The time of bondage will last but a little while now!

Part 5: Britain 1941

Chapter Eighteen

Little Gloston: January, 1941

Henry Cavendish stood up from his table and looked at the young men sat with him. There were around a dozen of them, none older than twenty-five, all destined to leave the village at the weekend to join a branch of the military. The war had come to Little Gloston, and it was going to extract its toll.

Henry looked up and down the table in the entrance hall where they had enjoyed a five-course meal. All of them were familiar to him. He had seen them all grow up. The Shaw brothers sat closest, the Gissing brothers at the other end of the great table. There were other sets of brothers also. Some of the young men before him would not return. He felt an emptiness as he thought about his own wife and the loss she had experienced as a young girl in the previous war. Beside him, Jane looked up. Her eyes were brimming with tears.

Robert was also with them. He was back from his boarding school for the Christmas holidays. Whether it was the nature of the evening or the time at the school, Henry knew not, but there was a solemnity and a seriousness in his young boy that reflected the mood of the evening.

Much to Henry's surprise, Sarah had asked to attend the meal. He'd initially been unsure. As much as he worshipped his little girl, for little girl she always would be to him, he recognised something of his old manner in her: a stand-offishness. Growing up was its own journey. He looked at her and wondered what she must be thinking. He had no idea. She was sometimes enigmatic, often distant, always polite but rarely warm. To see her beauty and innocence among young men who would soon lose any trace of their own made his heart break in a hundred ways. Soon their country would train them to kill with impunity and efficiency. Beside her sat Lord Augustus Browning, son of a friend, and a friend of Sarah's in particular.

'Gentlemen,' said Henry, which caused some amusement among the audience, considerably relaxing the mood. 'I do mean gentlemen. I have watched you grow over these years into young men that your parents, any parent, in fact, would be proud of. You will leave us now to go off and fight a war you did not cause, against men who care not for liberty or justice or freedom, only conquest. You will take with you the burden of our fears and in return you offer us the promise of your life. A bad bargain, yes, but know this: you are fighting for something greater than yourself or your town or even your family. This is a fight for freedom. It is a fight you must win. Take with you our gratitude for your steadfastness, our prayers for your survival and the love that we feel for all of you. For you are also our family. I toast your success but most of all I toast your return, safe into the arms of the people who love you.'

The young men cheered Henry and made the toast. Danny clapped enthusiastically and looked across the table at where Sarah Cavendish was sitting. She was looking directly at him. Normally when he saw her, she looked away or pretended not to notice him. This time she continued to look at him. Danny wanted to tear his eyes away but could not. Finally, the sound of clapping ebbed away, and the moment was broken. On an impulse, Danny stood up and looked around the table.

'Thank you, sir, for inviting us to this supper. I think I speak for every man here when I say how special this evening has been. It's an honour to represent the village in this fight. We stand united against the tyranny that threatens our country, our village, and our families. As you say, sir, we have grown up together and yes, we are family. He today who sheds his blood with me shall be my brother.' This brought cheers from all the assembled audience and a knowing look from Henry Cavendish. Danny continued. 'We are not the first men from the village to go off to war, but I hope, earnestly, we are the last. I toast our country, our village and our families.'

The room rang to the sound of 'Hear, hear.' After the toast, Henry looked at Danny and said, 'Well done, young man. Whenever this business is finished, and you come back, I pray, I want to talk to you about your future. But there's much to do, I know.'

Danny nodded; there was a small matter of survival. He risked a glance at Sarah again. She had risen from the table and had gone to speak to one of the servants. Robert tugged at his arm and congratulated him on his response to his father. They chatted for a while about his school. As they did so, Danny saw Sarah and her mother slip out from the entrance hall into another room, to leave the guests to their talk of war.

Danny glanced at the young lord in front of him, who was now chatting to Lord Cavendish. Age had not made him any friendlier. Danny wondered what Sarah could possibly see in him. His character was evident in the perpetual sneer that the young lord took to be required from someone of his station when with people he clearly felt were inferior.

'Danny,' called Henry. 'Please let me introduce you to Lord Augustus.'

Sarah's friend seemed less than pleased by this. Danny tried to remain neutral and walked over. The two shook hands as Henry explained who Danny was.

'Pleased to meet you, I'm sure,' said Augustus. Henry looked at him as he said this. Was there a hint of amusement on his face? It was difficult to know sometimes with Lord Cavendish. Of late, Danny had begun to realise that he was a man who had a wicked sense of humour, but this was not always made obvious to the target of his amusement. Danny was becoming more adept at reading the signs.

'I'm pleased to see you again, sir,' said Danny with a grin. 'You've been a frequent visitor over the years if I remember correctly.'

'Indeed,' said Augustus, mildly flattered to be remembered.

Henry glanced at Danny. This was unusual, even from Danny. Although he was very familiar with the staff at the Hall, he was usually more reserved when speaking to the family. At this moment, Danny seemed to be a different person.

'I think I speak for the rest of the village when I say how grateful we are that you should honour us with your company at this moment,' said Danny.

The young man looked at him warily. For a moment Danny wondered if he'd pushed things too far. It would be mortifying to have to apologise.

'Of course, it's important we should be here to support our men,' said the young lord carefully. Danny could not decide if it was due to a suspicion that he was being mocked or something else. A moment later he knew. 'Of course, when the time comes, I will step forward to be counted,' said Augustus.

'I hope it will be over before then, sir,' replied Danny. He wasn't joking now. He glanced at Lord Cavendish, but his eyes were fixed on his son.

'I hope you're right, Danny. I hope you're right,' said Henry. His voice trailed off. Danny turned to look at young Robert Cavendish, who was standing enjoying a joke with the Gissing brothers. Augustus, meanwhile, stared down at his drink. Perhaps the enormity of what lay ahead had become clearer: a realisation that the tide sweeping these young men out into a stormy sea would one day claim him. A moment of silence followed, then Henry nodded to Danny. They both turned to join the other young men of the village. Just as Danny was about to move, he felt a hand on his arm. It was Augustus. He was holding his hand out. Danny was surprised initially. He stopped and stared at him; it was no more than a moment, and then he shook the proffered hand. They parted immediately; Danny joined his friends; Augustus left the room.

All too soon, it was time to go. The men left together as they had arrived, in a group. Henry left them for a moment. A few moments later he reappeared with Jane and Sarah to bid farewell to their guests. Danny and the men walked past the Cavendish family who were all standing in a line, shaking hands. Two women emerged from a nearby room. There was music playing from a wireless. Danny recognised Al Bowlly's voice. He was singing 'The Very Thought of You'. Danny sang along inside his mind. Its sweet melancholy caressed his senses. He took a deep breath, straightened his back and marched forward with a smile on his face.

Henry and Jane both said goodbye and thanks to Danny. Robert was about to say the same when Danny ruffled his hair and pretended to dig him in the stomach. This suited Robert better. He was not one for farewells. Sarah was the last in the line. Danny stopped for a moment and was about to say something until she shook her head imperceptibly. They shook hands in silence. Of Lord Augustus there was no sign.

The cold air hit Danny like a freight train. He walked ahead with Bert Gissing and Tom. None of them looked back.

Chapter Nineteen

Just after dawn, two days later, the young men re-assembled in the centre of the village with their families. The sky was orange and purple and there was a freshness about the air. Despite the hour, the whole village was awake and standing in the square to bid farewell to sons and, in Beth Owen's case, a husband. A bus was waiting to take the men to Lincoln where they would catch a train down to London to enlist. All had passed their medical a week previously and been certified fit to join His Majesty's Armed Forces.

Danny and Tom hugged their parents as they started boarding the bus. Kate's emotions were running wild at the prospect of both her boys leaving to join up. She looked at each of them with tear-filled eyes. Pride mixed with fear as she held them tightly. Stan shook first Tom's and then Danny's hand. He couldn't say anything. What was there to say? He knew what they were going to face. There were no words adequate to the demand of articulating his love, his pride and his fears. Then, much to the surprise of his sons, he hugged first Tom and then Danny. His grip was strong but so was the love he felt and had never been able to express to them. He released Danny and looked away. So too did Danny. He didn't want to see his father's tears or, perhaps, he didn't want his father to see his.

Minutes later the bus set off. Danny cast his eyes in the direction of Cavendish Hall. He saw Henry Cavendish, on horseback, join the road and he trotted alongside the bus. Danny acknowledged him and then the bus picked up speed and drove off towards the next village.

The journey took just over two hours as the bus stopped several times to take other men to enlist. Danny sat with Tom and soon became the centre of the banter on the bus between the rival villages. It was full-bodied and a foretaste of what life would be like in a barracks. Danny threw himself into combat with enthusiasm.

'The Germans are for it. Once they see the Little Gloston boys they'll climb right back in their tanks and head home,' said one wag at the back.

Danny shouted back, 'One look at you Branston boys will be enough. Jerry'll think anyone that ugly's got nothing to lose anyway.'

'Your mother didn't say that last night,' came the reply.

'She was probably fast asleep because you'd bored her so much.'

There were songs, too. 'Pack Up Your Troubles', 'Kiss Me Goodnight, Sergeant Major' and the recent hit, 'Hang Out the Washing on the Siegfried Line'. The whole bus gave a rousing rendition of 'A Long Way to Tipperary'. Everyone was in a good mood: excited, expectant and elated to be part of something so important.

It's a long way to Tipperary
It's a long way to go.
It's a long way to Tipperary
To the sweetest girl I know!
Goodbye Piccadilly
Farewell Leicester Square!

128

It's a long, long way to Tipperary
But my heart's right there.

The songs and the banter kept the mood up for the rest of the trip and by late morning all of the men had reached Lincoln in good spirits.

The train station was mobbed. Similar scenes played out to those from the villages. Danny and his brother took a train compartment with Bob and the Gissing brothers. Another half an hour and the train set off towards London's Kings Cross. From there the young men would split up and head to different basic training barracks in the south. Danny's group was destined to go to Caterham in Surrey.

As the train set off, an older man looked in on the carriage.

'I say, do you have room here for one more?' he asked.

'Yes, of course, make yourself at home,' said Danny expansively.

The man stepped into the carriage and hoisted his bag on the overhead shelf. The village boys looked at him as he sat down. Dressed in a suit and tie, wearing a clipped moustache, he had the look of a local bank manager.

Danny spoke on behalf of the boys and introduced all of them. The man seemed unimpressed and desirous to be anywhere else; however, with innate good manners he replied, 'My name is Carruthers. Are you chaps all from the same town?'

'Yes,' replied Danny and told Carruthers where they were from.

'I've heard of it but never been. I'm from Lincoln. I must confess, I don't know why I've been called up. It seems a frightful mistake. I manage a shoe factory. I would have thought a profession such as mine would have been held back.'

Danny suppressed a smile and was tempted to take the rise out of their fellow passenger. But he realised quickly that he was merely displaying outwardly the nervousness that they all felt but could not reveal. In fact, each of the boys would probably have taken a bullet before admitting any kind of fear for the future. This was particularly true in front of the friends they had grown up with, fought against and played with over the course of their lives.

A few moments later, the carriage door was opened by another man. He was a little older than the boys and seemed very ill at ease.

'Is there room here, chaps?'

'Yes,' chorused the carriage with the notable exception of Carruthers.

'My name's Harn,' said the young man.

The rest of the journey to London was taken up with the grousing from Carruthers and his ardent desire to speak to someone in command to set them straight on the mistake from the Ministry. A look from Danny stopped any ribbing from the other boys. None gave him a bad penny for his likelihood of success. Harn said little on the journey but seemed sympathetic to the situation Carruthers found himself in. His rare contributions to the conversation revealed him to be cynical rather than a moaner like Carruthers.

The boys were glued to the window as the train travelled through London. Overhead they could see barrage balloons so large they seemed to block out the sun. They looked at one another grimly. The war was coming closer. They disembarked at King's Cross station.

'It's big,' commented Hugh Gissing. There was no denying the accuracy of this statement. Carruthers had been to London before, and they happily followed him. He led them to the underground station, and they made their way to London Bridge. As there was half an hour before their train to Caterham departed, most took a stroll outside the station to see the city. There were sandbags all around the entrance. The street was mobbed with people, many in uniform: police, air wardens and army. Danny and Tom looked at each other.

'Different world,' said Tom.

Not just a different world, thought Danny. A terrifying one. The sandbags, the barrage balloons, the heavy presence of uniformed men and women was suffocating. He had never been to London before but everything he'd read spoke of a city with an extraordinary history. But now, standing on the street he saw and felt the fear of a city at war.

The train to the barracks was due to depart in ten minutes. With some relief Danny trotted back down the steps into the station. His feelings about what he had seen were mixed. The first sight of London had been disappointing. But he also wanted to come back and see the city properly: experience it. The first opportunity he could manage, he promised himself he would return.

Around ten hours after their departure from the village, the boys were met at Caterham train station by a man who introduced himself as Corporal Lawrence. The last part of their journey was made on a three-ton truck that took them to the army barracks. It was late afternoon. Despite being summer the sky overhead was distinctly unseasonable. At the gates they were greeted by a burly sergeant, who waved them through dismissively.

The new recruits looked at one another as the truck drove into the centre of the camp. It finally came to a stop. One by one they hopped out. The corporal hopped out of the driver's cab and quickly lined them up into three ranks of ten.

'Follow me,' ordered the corporal. He seemed to know what he was about. So, they followed him. Danny looked at Lawrence. He was perhaps three or four years older than him, but he was already a man. Alongside him, Danny felt that he and his friends were like little boys. This would change. Part of him welcomed this. Another part, he knew, feared the responsibility that adulthood would bring. Danny glanced down at the rolled-up sleeves of the corporal. He was wearing a strange looking watch.

'Mickey Mouse,' said Corporal Lawrence, spying the direction of Danny's gaze. He held the watch up for Danny and Bob to see. Their grins turned to laughter when Lawrence added, 'It's a reminder of the army I've joined.'

The new recruits walked towards the barracks in something that was never going to be mistaken for close order drill.

'I thought it was supposed to be hot here,' said Bob.

'Why do you say that? asked Bert Gissing.

'Because we're nearer the equator, you big lug,' came the reply.

The group laughed and Bob earned a not unfriendly biff around the head from Bert's cap.

'Not very welcoming weather,' whispered Tom to Danny. He was clearly a little nervous as they walked into the camp. The group was directed towards a large hut, accompanied by a sergeant who looked unimpressed with the new intake.

'I doubt the welcome will be any better inside.'

The men made their way to the Quartermaster Store. It was a large thin hut, an Ali Baba's cave of army equipment. Behind the counter were dozens of shelves stacked with boots and army uniforms. Along the counter were army men waiting to hand out the kit.

One by one the men marched down the counter collecting first their kit bag and then the uniform, based on the quartermaster staff's assessment of their needs. This evaluation often caused much amusement and irritation as the results were, invariably, a combination of too-small boots and over-sized uniforms.

They also received items of equipment from mess tins to a brush.

Danny looked at this implement with much confusion. Carruthers smiled and whispered, 'Clothes brush.'

Danny nodded his thanks. The final item they collected acted to sharpen each man's sense of where he was and what his new life would entail. It was a bayonet. Danny felt his heart miss a beat as he was handed the weapon. It may have been excitement, but Danny knew it was also fear. The reality of the war descended on him like a cloud. Moments later he was handed a broomstick.

'What's this?' asked Danny, bemused.

'What does it look like?'

'A broomstick?'

'You're a genius, move along.'

Danny stood where he was, looking dumbly at the broomstick. Then he looked at the quartermaster.

'No Lee Enfield?'

'All in good time. We're a bit low. Now move along.'

After the visit to the quartermaster, the group marched across the parade ground, fully laden, to the brick building at the other side. All around they could see other recruits dressed in PT gear jogging in groups, stretching, doing jumping jacks. Barked orders echoed around the square.

The corporal directed them towards their barrack room. It was a long room with two dozen iron beds in two rows. The boys selected beds near one another. There were already half a dozen men in the room lying on the beds. The windows were open to allow the smell of men to escape. It was an effort in vain. Danny grinned at Tom.

'I never realised how much the smoke at the forge covered the smell of sweat,' said Danny. Tom laughed and told him to speak for himself.

The proximity of the beds was more of an issue for some of the others. Carruthers moved his hand between the ends of the bed as if measuring the distance. He shook his head and made another mental note to bring to the attention of the commanding officer.

'I don't want to be near someone who snores,' announced Bob. Half a dozen pillows were thrown at him in response, even from folk who didn't know him.

'What time do they serve breakfast in bed?' asked Danny to no one in particular.

This brought a few laughs from some of the others. A few came and introduced themselves and before long a group of strangers were laughing and joking as if they'd been friends for a long time. Only Carruthers and Harn were out of sorts with their new accommodation. Most of the others, like Danny and his friends, were young, all in their early twenties. Carruthers, older and skinnier, was out of place because of his age. This was a young man's war. It wasn't for those who were soft. Harn seemed like a man who had skipped the chaos of youth and landed straight into the disenchantment of adulthood.

'My God, there are no sheets,' said a shocked Carruthers. The others laughed until they realised he wasn't joking. He added, 'I'm going to speak to the commanding officer.' He meant it, too.

Danny turned away and rolled his eyes to the rest of the group. A few sympathetic smiles greeted Danny. The other grouser added his thoughts also.

'I agree. Complete shambles, if you ask me.'

'No one did,' said Arthur, a stocky Londoner, managing to speak while maintaining a cigarette sticking resolutely to his bottom lip. He was probably the oldest in the group aside from Carruthers. Older but harder. He had a friendly face and a smile hung ready on his lips but there was an unmistakable solidity about him. Harn looked at him darkly but added nothing else.

Danny asked Arthur, 'You been here long?'

'Arrived a couple of days ago. Haven't really done much, only just had my uniform. You arrived just in time for that. Like a bloody tent, it is.'

'Who's the tailor?' laughed Danny looking at the ill-fitting costume sported by the Londoner.

'A chap in Saville Row,' replied Arthur, quick as a flash. 'I can get you his address if you like?'

'Thanks,' replied Danny. 'Do you think he can do it blue? I'm not sure green works with my hair.'

'I'm not sure any bleedin' colour would work with your hair. Now, take mine,' replied Arthur, removing his cap to reveal a bald pate. The rest of the barracks collapsed laughing, including Carruthers, and the exchange quickly established the pair as the jokers in the platoon. They were still laughing when there was a new arrival.

Arthur was the first to stop laughing. His face changed in a moment. Danny saw the change and looked round. The new entrant to the barracks was a sergeant. Danny immediately leapt to his feet followed by his companions.

The sergeant looked with undisguised contempt at the new intake. His hair was close-cropped. He was short but his wiry frame made him seem taller. His most prominent features were his eyes, which were small and contained an air of menace. Slowly he picked his way along the centre aisle, eyes straight ahead. There was no other sound in the room aside from his footsteps on the wooden boards.

Once the sergeant reached the end of the barracks, his back to Danny, Arthur glanced at him and rolled his eyes. A quick shake of the head followed and told Danny all he needed to know. The sergeant turned around again and resumed his silent inspection. When he was back at the entrance, he spoke.

'My name is O'Dowd. You'll see by my stripes that I am a sergeant,' said O'Dowd with something approaching a sneer. 'This means it is my job to turn a bunch of duds like you into…' The rest was left unsaid as another man entered the room. O'Dowd immediately stood up straight and barked 'Ten-shun.'

Although none of the new recruits had experienced the military, whether it was nature, or exposure to films, the recruits leapt to their feet and stood to attention. They were unsure of who had just entered but it was certainly clear that it was someone of rank.

The captain entered the barrack room and followed the same route down the aisle of beds. He said nothing. He stopped halfway and then returned to stand beside O'Dowd.

'New recruits, sir,' barked O'Dowd. Danny wondered if communication in his new place of work was conducted entirely along these lines. It seemed ludicrous. Thankfully the new arrival also found it a chore.

'Stand at ease, men.'

The new recruits took that quite literally and adopted postures that would not have been out of place in a pub at closing times. This seemed to enrage O'Dowd but amuse the captain. He turned to O'Dowd and asked, 'Can you show them what I mean?'

O'Dowd strode forward angrily and said, 'When you hear the order "Stand at Ease", you stand as follows. Feet twelve inches apart and arms straight.' He demonstrated the position and the rest of the barracks followed suit.

Finally standing at ease in the army sense, the new captain introduced himself.

'I'm Captain Budd. I won't try to get names now. Get changed and then at six make your way over to the dining hall.'

Indicating Arthur, he added, 'Perry will show you where to go. All I can say about the food is that you'll get used to it.'

136

The men laughed at this and stood to attention on O'Dowd's order as both he and the captain left the barrack room. When they had gone, Danny turned to Arthur and asked, 'What are they like?'

'Well, you've seen Sergeant O'Dowd. Trust me, he doesn't improve on acquaintance. We call him "Sod" because that's exactly what he is. The other sergeants are a tough lot; he's just plain nasty if you ask me. Captain Budd seems all right. Typical upper class mind you. Definitely not one of us.' Danny and the others nodded, grateful to have some advance intelligence on their situation.

The uniform proved to be every bit as ill-fitting as he supposed it would be but at least the boots seemed to fit. A few of the others were already grumbling about this.

'Don't worry,' advised Arthur. 'They'll change anything that obviously doesn't fit. Why do you think I look so good?'

They were still laughing as they crossed the parade ground towards the dining hall. Inside they fell into a long queue for the food. With an efficiency that could almost have been military, the queue moved relatively quickly. When Danny saw what they were getting and how it was served, it explained a lot.

A white watery mound landed on Danny's tin plate followed by something green and black that looked like it had been hauled from the bottom of a pond. The final item had the colour and texture of a turd.

'What is it?' asked Danny.

The man serving turned to another man and said, 'He wants to know what it is.'

In a mock French accent, the man said, 'Tell him it is beef-bugger-off.'

'Thanks. Where do I find the red wine?'

He walked on before the two men behind the counter could add anything else to their initial two-word riposte.

'You do get used to it,' said Arthur tucking in. So, Danny and the others did likewise. Only Carruthers seemed to be completely put out. After picking away at his food for a minute he stood up angrily and marched out of the dining room. The others from the barrack room saw him leave and they looked at one another.

'Looks like he's going to see the captain,' said Arthur. 'I give him three minutes.'

In fact, it was closer to five before the ashen-faced Carruthers returned to his seat. By then the mush had been nicked by some of the others. He looked at the empty plate and his face fell further.

'Serves him right,' whispered Arthur. 'We're in the army now and that's that. Ain't no one better than anyone else, and that includes the officers. A German bullet does the same damage to them as it does to us.'

Chapter Twenty

Caterham Army Barracks, Surrey: January, 1941

By ten in the evening, they were all in the dormitory sitting on their beds waiting for lights out. Arthur, as ever, had a cigarette stuck to his bottom lip. A few of the other recruits gathered around his and Danny's beds.

'We'll be here for six weeks, boys. So, no snoring.'

'What happens then?'

Arthur glanced at the clock and stubbed out his cigarette. 'Then we're separated off to the units we'll join for another six weeks of training, then look out, Jerry. Get ready, you can set your alarm by old Sod.'

Just as he said this Sergeant O'Dowd strode into the barrack room. Arthur winked to the group raising a few smiles. All of the recruits stood to attention beside their beds. O'Dowd was carrying paper bags wrapped up in string. He walked down the aisle handing out one of these packages to each man.

'What are these for, sir?' asked Bob.

'It's sergeant, not sir. They're for you to put your civvy clothes in

139

and send home.' When he'd finished, he took out a notebook and said, 'Now, I want your names.' The roll collection took a few minutes. When it was finished, O'Dowd left them with a warning that lights would be out in five minutes.

Tom glanced at Danny to tell him to look at their friend Bob. Danny glanced over. Bob was sitting on the bed staring at the paper and string. The Gissing brothers had also seen their friend and looked concerned.

'What's up, Bob?' asked Tom.

Bob shook his head and said, 'I can't do this, boys. I can't. I should be at home with Beth.' He held the paper and string tightly, scrunching it in frustration. Tom put a hand on his shoulder. There was nothing to be said. He glanced at his brother. Danny punched him lightly on the arm. Words would have sounded as hollow to Danny as they would to his friend. Bob had married. Tom was engaged to Rosie. Across the way, Bert Gissing was also doing a strong line with a young woman from a neighbouring village.

Danny realised at that moment that war was fought by the whole country, not just the men at the front.

Training began in earnest at six thirty the next morning. A bugle echoed across the barracks and O'Dowd burst into the room shouting at the recruits and banging his stick on the end of the beds. A few of the late risers were tumbled unceremoniously from what, moments earlier, had been a disrupted sleep.

To begin with, it was mainly drill parades and lectures. The new recruits were treated to talks on a variety of topics from life in the army and grenade throwing to instructions on the opposite sex.

'When will we get to train with live ones?' asked Arthur at the end of the lecture. This brought a burst of laughter from the men and from Budd before he dismissed them. The men liked Budd. He knew when to let the men have a release and when to step in with a rebuke.

Drill parades were run by the corporals and sergeants for each platoon. The square bashing and rifle drill required perfection in execution. Failure to do so was rewarded with punishment as Carruthers discovered when he had to run around the enormous parade ground holding the rifle over his head. He collapsed after a couple of laps.

With each passing day in the first week, Bob's mood grew increasingly dark. This was not helped by his friendship with Harn. At the end of each exercise, they would take themselves off for a chat and a smoke. Danny looked on with feelings of both sorrow and helplessness. The physical nature of the training was not a problem for him or Tom and the Gissing brothers. Like them, Bob was a bit larger but lacked their height for the weight to be distributed. This made things especially tough for him. O'Dowd soon picked up on Bob's discomfort. He took delight in picking on the weaker members in the platoon.

Despite his initial reluctance and his lack of physicality, Carruthers was beginning to win over the rest of the members in the group. O'Dowd's bullying meant the others were now on his side and more likely to help him as training toughened with each day. In fact, each morning started in a routine fashion.

Bugle call at six thirty would be greeted with groans all around, but Carruthers always took it further. He was a particularly light sleeper.

'I'm not sure I had more than two hours' sleep with all the snoring,' he complained. This was greeted with the usual sympathy. However, by this point, Carruthers was as impervious to the insults as the other recruits were to his grousing. In fact, it was a sport enjoyed by both assailants and target. Taking the rise out of Carruthers gave the men a chance to blow off steam. Carruthers, by now, seemed

141

to enjoy the catharsis of giving vent to his feelings albeit in entirely unconcerned company.

One morning Carruthers had the room in stitches with his musical criticism of the bugler.

'I'm convinced the bugler is blowing the wrong notes. I definitely heard a C which should have been an F. Has anyone else noticed?'

No one had but they were laughing too much to point this out.

The first day at the rifle range was a welcome break from the monotony of parade ground drill, PT, and the droning lectures. Captain Budd made an appearance at the range. Up until then he had only seen them during the occasional lecture and the odd meal when he would ask them how they found the food. Carruthers always spoke negatively about it, but he was in the minority with Harn on this subject.

O'Dowd stood before them with the Lee Enfield rifle. He demonstrated with an economy of movement.

'In order to take the bolt out, you push forward the safety catch with the thumb of the right hand.' Get on with it, thought Danny. I just want to shoot something. Preferably you.

The demonstration ended when the new recruits were told to partner up and lay down in front of the open range. Each was given ammunition and ordered to load their weapons. This was done with varying degrees of incompetence, but the Little Gloston boys had no problems. Guns and hunting were a part of everyday life in the village and their capability with the weapons was soon apparent. Budd came over to them and commented on their accuracy.

'Good shooting, men. I see you've done this before. Carry on.'

They had done it before but not for such an extended period. By the end of the rifle range practice, most were sporting blisters on their trigger fingers. Carruthers and some of the slower learners were better off as they had not been so rapid in their firing. This caused some good-natured banter from the older man.

'If you were as useless as me then you wouldn't be in such agony. Only yourself to blame, really.'

'Jerry'll be shaking in his jackboots when he comes across you,' laughed Arthur.

'I prefer not to blast away like a child with a pop gun, personally,' replied Carruthers with exaggerated superiority.

'It's not what your missus told me last night,' said Arthur.

'You're lucky she was so interested,' replied Carruthers amid the laughter.

With each day, as the group became more confident together, Bob's temper became increasingly frayed. He finally snapped at O'Dowd on the fourth afternoon on the parade ground as his hat dropped off his head by accident. As he bent to pick it up, O'Dowd shouted at him.

'Stand still until I tell you to pick it up.'

Bob lost his cool and suggested that O'Dowd pick it up himself. The language he used in this suggestion, quite apart from the act of responding, caused the sergeant to storm over to Bob. His face was inches away.

'What did you say, Owen?'

Bob, realising he had spoken unwisely, remained silent.

'Cat got your tongue?' continued O'Dowd, now enjoying the humiliation. 'Well, I think you can take yourself over there and start running with the gun over your head. Go on, hop it.'

Bob had no choice but to do as he was told. A minute later, in full view of all the recruits, Bob was running around the parade ground. His lack of fitness and his anger meant he burned up energy fast. Within fifteen minutes he had collapsed. Rather than allow him to recuperate, O'Dowd ordered him to clean the toilets. He missed the evening meal as a result. However, the other boys smuggled some rations to him when he came into the barracks later that evening, still grumbling.

'Cheer up, Bob,' said Hugh Gissing. 'We've saved you some food.'

'Thanks,' said Bob, clearly embarrassed. 'I hate that man, boys. I hate him.'

'Steady, Bob,' counselled Danny. 'Don't do anything stupid.'

'Don't you worry,' replied Bob grimly, before tearing into the food.

Next morning the recruits were woken, as usual, and they stumbled blindly out from their beds.

'I don't know why they start us so early,' grumbled Carruthers. 'Another hour in bed wouldn't make much difference.' He shut up as soon as O'Dowd entered the barrack room shouting for them to get up.

Their initial parade ground foot drill was followed by breakfast and then a lecture on field craft. Danny was fascinated by the lectures in a way that many of his fellow recruits were not. He often brought a paper pad and made copious notes. This brought a good degree of ribbing from his brother and the two Gissing brothers.

'Hark at him,' said Bert Gissing.

'Teacher's pet,' added Tom. The image of Danny being swatted across the back of his head by Mrs Grout flitted through his mind. The memory made Tom smile. She had never beaten the mischief from him nor his curiosity. That same boy, a couple of years later, would read Shakespeare at night.

'We'll see who's laughing when Jerry is shooting the arse off you, and you don't know which direction to run.'

'I'll take cover behind you while you're reading the stars, Danny-boy,' said Arthur holding his arm aloft towards the heavens.

The rest of the morning was to be taken up with close combat without bayonets. Tom and Danny grinned at one another. Another interested spectator was Captain Budd. His interest in parade ground drilling tended to be only slightly above that of the men under his leadership. The indefatigable O'Dowd seemed to the only one who liked the endless drilling.

Inevitably, Bob and Harn were the first two recruits to be asked to grapple with O'Dowd. Despite years of training with Danny, Bob didn't last long. Harn hit the ground with an almighty wallop and stayed down for a minute in agony. There was little sympathy from either sergeant, commanding officer, or the rest of the recruits.

Finally, Danny was asked up. For the previous few minutes, he had studied O'Dowd closely. It was clear the sergeant knew how to wrestle. However, his age and size, calculated Danny, would count against him. But Danny knew better than to be complacent and the two men circled one another warily. Whether it was instinct or just observation of Danny over the previous week, O'Dowd knew this would be a different proposition. It wasn't just Danny's height and physique. There was a look in the eye that O'Dowd recognised. The kid had a quiet confidence.

Looking on, the rest of the recruits and Captain Budd sensed this was a more evenly matched bout. Previously there had been a lot of noise and good-natured banter. Now there was silence save for the distant orders from the parade ground. A few initial feints from both men were easily dismissed and then finally they came together. An initial attempt to throw Danny was narrowly beaten off and they stepped back again.

O'Dowd, after four demonstrations already, was beginning to pant. He knew Danny was stronger. He now realised Danny also had technique. Sweat rolled down his face and, for the first time in front of a recruit, he felt fear. He dismissed this quickly. He'd seen too much in his life and he'd dealt with bigger problems than Danny Shaw.

O'Dowd's small eyes narrowed, and Danny braced himself for the next attack. Seconds later it was all over. O'Dowd lay on the ground. He bounced up immediately and attacked Danny again, almost catching him unawares. For another minute the two men were locked in battle and then, once again, the sergeant was lying on his back. Budd applauded the two men as O'Dowd rose to his feet.

'Who showed you how to do that?' asked Budd.

'My dad,' replied Danny, mopping his brow. He was sweating profusely. To be fair to O'Dowd, he'd given him quite a fight. A few years younger or a few pounds heavier and it might have been Danny on the ground.

Budd nodded and asked Danny, 'He was in the other lot?'

'Yes, sir.'

Turning to Tom Shaw, Budd asked, 'Are you equally proficient?'

'Yes, sir,' replied Tom.

Budd nodded and looked at O'Dowd. He pointed to the Shaw brothers and said, 'Sergeant, split the men into two groups. Detail these two men to take over the unarmed close combat training.'

'Yes, sir,' barked O'Dowd. Once Budd had left the men, he glared at Danny and said, 'I'll get you back for this, Shaw.'

Danny returned his gaze. Another few weeks and they'd be gone. There was no point in starting anything now. Instead he merely nodded, then turned away to organise his group of men.

Chapter Twenty-One

Caterham Army Barracks, Surrey: February, 1941

It was a light punch on the arm. Danny was awake in an instant and bolted upright. Carruthers was by his bed. Danny looked at him in confusion because it was still night outside. When Danny's eyes found their focus, he saw it was after two in the morning.

'What do you want?' whispered Danny.

'Your friend and Harn. They've just sneaked out of the barracks,' whispered Carruthers. 'I think they're deserting.'

This was alarming. Danny rose from his bed and went to the window. It was dark outside, but the moon was quite bright. Initially, they could see nothing; then Carruthers pointed to a hut around forty yards away. It was just about possible to make out Bob and Harn.

'Christ almighty,' said Danny. 'Come on.'

They picked up their boots and ran to the door. Slipping into their boots quickly, they ran over to where the two men were hiding. Both were waiting for the guard at the gate to be changed. This usually took place at two.

He and Carruthers arrived at the doorway where the two men lay hidden in the shadows.

'What the hell do you think you're doing?'

'Mind your own business, Shaw,' snarled Harn. Bob said nothing; he looked mortified.

'You're going home, aren't you?' said Carruthers.

'What if we are, Danny? We shouldn't be here,' responded Bob.

'Nor should I,' pointed out Carruthers. 'I have a wife, a family and a good job.'

'Come with us,' sneered Harn.

Carruthers almost recoiled physically at the thought. Then he said, 'I'm here now. I'll make the best of it.'

'Get away will you,' said Bob sharply. He was becoming increasingly uncomfortable by the second.

'We're only trying to help,' said Carruthers trying to reason with them.

'Leave us alone,' said Harn, pushing Carruthers sharply on the shoulder.

This angered Danny and he grabbed Harn by his lapels. 'Enough of that. He's trying to make you see reason. None of us want to be in the army.'

'You volunteered,' said Bob sulkily, like a child trying to excuse bad behaviour.

'It doesn't mean I want to be here. There's a job to be done. If I could go home tomorrow, I would. C'mon, this is madness. Come back to the barracks and we'll say nothing about this to anyone.'

It was clear that Bob was now torn. His distressed face tore at Danny.

'What's wrong, Bob?'

Tears were streaming down Bob's face. 'It's Beth. She's pregnant. I don't want my child to be an orphan.'

Danny grabbed both of Bob's arms. His heart felt like it would explode. How would he have reacted in similar circumstances? Duty demanded he stay and fight, but Danny recognised a higher duty to the country. This was a fight for survival. The last two years had brought a human cost to the country. A black cloud of death hung in the air. No one was immune from its effects. No one was excused from sacrificing their time or, indeed, their life for the cause of survival. But Danny was not there to police his friend. He released Bob's arms.

'It's up to you, Bob. They'll come after you. They'll put you in prison. Is that any better for Beth and the child?'

'Leave him alone, Shaw. He's a big boy. He can do what he wants.'

Danny realised the opposite was true, but he had no time or desire to reason with Harn. He looked at Bob and shrugged.

'Fine, Bob, you decide.' He turned to Carruthers and said, 'Let's go back. It's their look out.'

Carruthers was troubled by this, but Danny gave a curt nod. If they stayed any longer, they would get caught and O'Dowd would certainly not believe their story. The two men turned and walked back to the barracks. A few seconds later they heard steps behind them. It was Bob.

'Bloody hell,' was all Bob could say.

Danny glanced back at Harn. He was already darting towards another hut, nearer the entrance.

'Damn fool,' said Danny following Bob and Carruthers back into the building.

This left the group with a problem. Harn's departure was unlikely to succeed. He would almost certainly be caught. It was a question of how long. In Danny's view, this affected them all. Carruthers was thinking along similar lines.

'If they catch him, he'll say we knew all about it. This makes us complicit.'

'I know,' replied Danny grimly. However, the thought of going to either O'Dowd or the captain appalled him. Finally, he said, 'Bob, you get to bed. Whatever happens, deny everything. I'll go to Budd and tell him about Harn.'

'I'll come with you,' said Carruthers. Seeing Danny was about to object, he put his hand up.

'Don't. We should go now.'

Bob looked like he would also join them, until Danny all but frog marched him to his bed.

'All right, all right, I'm going,' he whispered.

A few minutes later Danny and Carruthers were dressed and walking along the parade ground to the sergeant's quarters. They walked inside and found O'Dowd's room. It was well after two and they expected he would be somewhat displeased.

'Here goes,' said Danny, knocking on the door. There was no response. Danny looked at Carruthers. 'Should I go in?'

'No, I wouldn't advise it.'

'Afraid "old Sod" might be in a nightdress with the captain?'

Carruthers looked shocked by this suggestion and not amused. This made Danny's grin even wider. A lot of things went on in the countryside. Nobody necessarily approved but nor did they speak of it. They were obviously a bit primmer in the city.

Danny rapped the door again, only louder. This time they could hear noise from inside. Danny knocked again and whispered loudly, 'Sergeant, wake up.'

The door opened and O'Dowd's face poked through angrily. 'What the hell do you think …?'

'Sergeant, it's Harn,' said Carruthers. His clipped tones brought

O'Dowd to a standstill. He knew immediately what the problem was.

'Wait here.' Less than a minute later O'Dowd was at the door again, in his uniform, trying to put his boots on without socks.

They made their way quickly out of the sergeant's quarters over to the senior officer's room. A similar episode ensued as they notified Captain Budd. By now ten minutes had elapsed. The next step, led by Budd, was to inform the gate of Harn's actions.

'We need to organise a small detail of troops to go to the bus and train stations. He won't get very far.' He turned to Danny and Carruthers. 'You two return to your barracks. Thank you for telling us. You did the right thing.'

The two men returned to bed. Carruthers glanced at Danny. 'Your friend may still have problems.'

'I know, bloody fool,' said Danny grim-faced. 'Harn will point the finger at him, all right.' With this unhappy thought, Danny fell asleep as soon as his head hit the pillow.

The next morning the barracks was blissfully unaware of the previous night's events until someone noticed the absence of Harn.

'He's done a bunk.'

Carruthers and Danny looked at one another and with a shake of the head they decided not to say anything on the topic. Bob looked at them remorsefully but remained silent. He knew there would soon be hell to pay but the fact he had stayed would count in his favour.

O'Dowd made their life a misery as usual in the morning, but no mention was made of the affair. Around mid-morning, Budd appeared at the drill and whispered to O'Dowd.

'We need three men for a task. Carruthers, Shaw and Owen fall out.'

'Lucky sods,' said Arthur, out of the side of his mouth, to Danny.

151

The three men followed Budd towards the senior officers' mess. They walked along the corridor to the office of the commanding officer. Budd gave a quick rap on the door and walked in. The commanding officer looked up from his desk. Colonel Foster was a man closer to seventy than sixty. Had this inconvenient war not come along, he would have been enjoying a well-earned retirement in Dorset.

The thought of this saddened him immensely. What saddened him even more was the necessity of sending these young men off to a war that he'd hoped would never happen again. The men liked him although his appearances were rare.

'Sir,' said Budd. 'This is Shaw and Carruthers. They alerted us to the absence of Harn. This is Owen. According to Harn, Owen tried to accompany him.'

Foster looked first at Bob. He was not unsympathetic in his manner, and he asked simply, 'Is this true?'

'Yes, sir,' replied Bob, despite the advice of Danny.

'You returned though,' continued Foster.

'Yes, sir.' Bob glanced at Danny and Carruthers as he said this.

Foster turned his attention to the two other men and then looked back to Bob.

'Why did you want to leave?' asked Foster. Bob explained the situation with his wife. Foster listened intently. When Bob had finished, he asked, 'What age are you?'

'Nineteen, sir.'

Foster shook his head and felt such sadness. He remembered hundreds of faces like Bob's that he'd commanded once. Most were buried in the fields of Flanders. He remembered the cruelty with which the army had treated those who had suffered from the natural fear any sensible person would feel.

'How did you gentlemen come to be involved?' Foster had now turned to Danny and Carruthers.

'I'm a light sleeper, sir,' said Carruthers.

'You're fortunate, Carruthers. This may save your life one day.'

Carruthers smiled for a moment and then related what had happened. When he had finished, Foster asked them what they had done to prevent Harn from leaving.

Danny answered this time. 'We tried to persuade him, sir. He wasn't having it. Bob came with us, but we let Harn go.'

'Why?'

And there it was: the key question that Danny had been wrestling with since he'd woken up. Danny took a moment and then answered truthfully. 'Bob's my friend. I would have battered him rather than see him go. Harn, sir, is not what you'd call a friend. If we'd started a ruck, it would have woken the camp and we'd have been in the same situation here anyway.'

This was the best Danny could come up with in the situation but even he felt the chances of it working were remote. Now, he realised in surprise, they were all culpable to a greater or lesser degree in Harn's AWOL.

The silence in the office once Danny had finished was overpowering. It was almost palpable. Foster glanced at Budd and then back to the three men.

'Harn was caught last night at the train station. This would not have happened so quickly without your timely intelligence. However, had you acted in the way you acted towards your friend, it need not have happened at all,' said Foster to Danny and Carruthers.

Turning his attention to Bob, he said, 'Nobody chooses to go to war unless they are a damn fool. You are no different from any man

153

here. You have no more right to avoid war than any other man. You are not a special case, Owen. Remember that. I sympathise with your situation but remember, many men like you have already given their lives against this tyranny. Many more will. It's likely some of the men in your barracks will die. If I could stop that happening, I would. I can't. All I can do is make sure that you and the rest of these young men are trained to such a degree that your chances of survival are greater. I want that you all be inculcated with the values and the esprit de corps that ensure that you work effectively together. This is how we will defeat the Nazis.'

The three men stood to attention, eyes ahead as the colonel spoke. With each word, Bob's shame increased. Danny suspected this was the case and felt deeply for his friend. Paradoxically, he also began to feel something else. It wasn't for another year before he could identify what the feeling was. By then he was in the middle of desert, dust and death. The feeling was love. Love for his friends and for his fellow recruits.

Foster had paused to let his words sink in. He could see they were having the intended effect.

'Harn will be given fourteen days detention. We'll let him out. No doubt he'll try again. This time alone. He may succeed, who knows? If not, we'll repeat the process. We'll probably try and post him elsewhere after that. No doubt, in return, we shall receive someone else just like him.'

The three men waited for their punishment, for they were all, by now, convinced this was where things were heading.

'You three men,' said Foster, pausing for a moment while he looked each in the eye. They were all very different, he thought. Carruthers, older, weedy, and yet as likely to make a good soldier as anyone; Owen, stouter, so young to be at war, so young to be married. What madness. And then Shaw. The one they all had hopes for. An officer in the making; the only person who did not realise this was him.

'You three men,' repeated Foster, 'are dismissed.'

Chapter Twenty-Two

Caterham Army Barracks: March, 1941

Change was in the air. Flowers were beginning to bud. Birds were reappearing in the trees. The sound of dawn was no longer silence or rain battering the parade ground. The heat of summer was just around the corner. Danny didn't care. He was enjoying army life but, at the same time, as he looked forward to the changes he knew would soon occur, he felt trepidation.

It was now six weeks since their arrival at the barracks. Route marches were the only occasions any of them had been in the outside world over this period. Captain Budd made a rare appearance at the parade ground accompanied by O'Dowd. The sergeant looked even less happy than normal.

The platoon immediately stood to attention, but Budd quickly made them stand at ease. He then gave them the news they had been looking forward to for days.

'Gentlemen, you will doubtless be aware that at this stage of your training some of you will be leaving and some will stay on. Your basic training has finished. The next six weeks of your instruction will be specific to the branch of the army where you will be headed. This will be revealed tomorrow. The good news is that tonight you will be permitted to leave the barracks and go out into town. I suspect this is more likely to be a pub than a museum.'

This was greeted with laughter by the men. Budd laughed along with them.

'I don't blame you. However, I hope that you can enjoy a well-earned drink while remembering something tremendously important now. You are British soldiers. We hold ourselves to a high level of account. Do nothing that will let yourself, your comrades, or your regiment down. The locals will be very welcoming. Do not take advantage of their goodwill. I hope my meaning is clear. Others will follow you and they will also want to be able to have a drink in town without encountering ill will or anger. Sergeant O'Dowd will now hand out your passes.'

He broke off for a moment. Overhead, he and the rest of the recruits could hear the low moan of plane engines. Everyone looked up. The training had included plane identification. They were closer now; the distinctive, malevolent cackle overhead and the underside, made these planes instantly recognisable.

'Messerschmitt,' said Budd. Three planes flew past, too high to take a pot shot at from where they were. A minute later the sound of the planes was a distant murmur, but the ack-ack had started.

'Give 'em hell, boys,' shouted Arthur. This set off a chorus of shouts of encouragement to the gunners. Budd looked on. He was smiling but his mood was bittersweet. Somewhere between the pride he felt for the transformation of the men before him was a sadness at what they would face. He avoided trying to get to know the men personally. This was a factory for recruits. Most of them came in callow youths. They left as men. Many of them were going to their deaths. Budd knew this and it saddened him greatly. Every night he had to console himself with the same thought: there was a job to do.

The platoon broke up. Danny walked with Arthur and his friends to the barracks. Tom said quietly, 'I thought that had all finished.' He was referring to the Battle of Britain which had ended the previous year.

'I know,' replied Bob. 'We gave them a hiding.' He wanted to believe it was true. They all did. Otherwise, what was the point?

Five thirty came. Danny was joined by his friends from the village as well as Carruthers and Arthur.

'Don't you two cramp our style,' warned Hugh Gissing to the two older men as they climbed onto the bus bound for Guildford, the nearby town.

'If my dog looked like you, mate,' replied Arthur, 'I'd shave its arse and teach it to walk backwards.'

Even Hugh laughed at this, and the bus set off into town. They arrived half an hour later in the centre. It was a nice spring evening, and still quite bright. All around were army personnel. All around the army were young women walking in groups.

'I think I'm in heaven,' said Bert Gissing as a couple of teenage girls walked past the group. 'This place can't be real.' Above their heads, the sound of music emanated from a flat. It was Al Bowlly. He was waltzing in a dream. So was Danny. He looked around him with something approaching awe.

Until this moment he had not realised how limited his life had been. He had accepted the monotony of life at the forge and lived vicariously through the books in the Cavendish library. But Guildford seemed the promise of something else. Another type of life. He glanced at Tom. Their eyes met and they smiled.

'Bit different from Little Gloston,' said Tom.

'Just a bit,' agreed Danny. 'C'mon, let's go.'

They strolled along the high street, saluting back to people who saluted them. Children seemed to be fascinated by soldiers and they stopped time and time again to speak to star-struck young-sters. By now the boys had worked out that many of the kids had older sisters and they made extra efforts with the boys who were accompanied by young women.

'Look at this,' said Danny, pointing to a photographer's shop, "Arnott's Photographs". 'Do you fancy getting a team photograph?'

The boys looked at one another and then Carruthers said, 'Well I'm game.' That appeared to swing the doubters and moments later they were climbing a narrow staircase to a small studio. Danny knocked on the door and they all trooped in. The photographer in question was a young woman, in her mid-twenties.

'Hello,' she said introducing herself, 'I'm Lucy Arnott. What can I do for you?'

Politeness constrained a more truthful answer from the boys.

'We'd like a team photograph, please,' said Danny. 'And indi-vidual ones. Then if you can send prints to our home addresses, please.'

'Certainly,' said Lucy, leading the men to a studio behind the counter. The studio was small, but they were able to line up in two rows before a plain grey backdrop. Lucy apologised for the basic set up.

'There's a war on.'

For the next ten minutes Lucy took photographs of the boys. It would have taken less time, but the amount of jesting interrupted the poses. At one point, Lucy threatened to insist they all stayed out of the studio while the individual shots were being taken. The behaviour improved.

The session completed, they left the studio and returned to the high street.

'She was all right,' commented Arthur.

This brought a predictably ribald response as, to a man, the others pointed out his marital status.

'Can still look, can't I?' pointed out Arthur. 'Anyway,' he continued, 'when you reach the elevated state of happiness that me and the missus have ...' The rest was left unsaid as the everyone began to hurl abuse in Arthur's direction. He concluded, 'I was just saying she's a nice girl. You lot could do worse, and knowing you, probably will.'

'I'm not sure I want to go back,' announced Tom when they found a pub that wasn't already packed with boys from the barracks they had left. The girls, the sun, the feeling of freedom was in stark contrast to the monotony of life in the barracks. Like Danny, he recognised how limited his life had been thus far. The presence of so many attractive young women also made him think about his own Rosie. She was his first and only sweetheart. It was the way of things in the village. They were engaged and talking of marriage before he left. Now, he was not so sure.

He watched Danny make his way to the bar. Danny had to walk sideways through the throng of army men, dodging occasionally as someone carrying three or four beers in their hands required right of way. It took a few minutes to be served. This was unusual in his experience. So different to the village. He ordered half pints of bitter. Bert materialised from nowhere to help him; they brought the drinks outside, where the group had stationed themselves to have a better view of the girls. The young women of the town were on their own form of parade ground. Conversation was muted as they drank the freedom down in huge gulps.

'How long have you old men been married, anyway?' asked Danny after a while.

Carruthers raised his eyebrow and looked at Danny in mock seriousness. Then he admitted, 'Fourteen years now, no, fifteen in July.'

'What about you Arthur?' asked Hugh.

'You won't laugh?' asked Arthur. He was met by the inevitable response, which started him off too. 'Eighteen years, next year.'

'Bloody hell,' said Danny. 'You must have married late.'

'Get out of it,' laughed Arthur, smacking Danny on the arm.

Then he heard it again. That song. Al Bowlly was singing 'The Very Thought of You.'

Arthur noticed the change in Danny's features as they all listened. He nudged Tom in the ribs and his eyes asked a question. Tom shrugged, bemused. Soon the others were singing along. As the song ended they all surrounded Danny and crooned the words to him, laughing as they did.

The evening wore on. Their number diminished as a few of them went in search of dancing and female companions. The remaining boys were Danny, Bob, Carruthers and Arthur. All were in a jolly mood bolstered by half pints of cheerfulness. The singsong in the pub was in full cry as the pianist and singer led the crowd in 'If You Were the Only Girl in the World.'

Closing time saw the boys troop back towards the bus stop. When they reached it, they saw a hundred other recruits waiting for a bus that would barely take fifty.

'Bloody hell,' said Danny, giving voice to everyone's thoughts. 'How far is it to Caterham?'

161

'Thirty miles at least,' said Arthur, with his heart sinking.

'This is ridiculous,' said Carruthers, 'Why on earth don't the army have something organised?'

'Army? Organised?' replied Arthur. 'Where have you been for the last two months?'

As he said this, a lorry came past, and then stopped suddenly. Sitting in the front passenger seat was Tom, grinning broadly.

'Hello boys, bit of a walk by the looks of things,' he shouted. 'You'd better get in.'

Danny noticed that there was a young woman sitting between Tom and an older man, who was driving. It was Lucy, the photographer they'd met earlier. He gave Tom the thumbs up, and he ran around to the back and hopped on with the other lads. Inside the back of the van were the two Gissing brothers. Both looked like they'd had such a great evening they would bitterly regret it the next morning. Bert was semi-conscious; Hugh out for the count.

When they arrived back at the camp, they carried the Gissing boys into the barracks and undressed them. Along the way Tom related how their night had gone.

'We met up with three girls leaving the park. They were heading into the town to a dance. We asked where it was taking place and they suggested we join them. It suited them because they were getting a bit tired of fending off some of our lot. They said we were more polite. Have to thank Bert for that. He remembered to take off his cap when we met them.'

Danny knocked Tom's cap off as he said this.

'Anyway, the dance was at the church hall and there was no alcohol. The two boys here were about to leave when I saw Lucy. She told us there was a secret bar at the front, outside. The vicar had no idea. Well, maybe by the end of the night he did. By then,

Bert and Hugh were five sheets to the wind, but we managed to get them away before it became too obvious.'

'What's the story with Lucy?' asked Danny with a grin.

This time, Danny had his cap knocked off by Tom who said, 'You're too young yet.' This amused Arthur and Carruthers immensely.

Chapter Twenty-Three

Sergeant O'Dowd relished this day on many levels. He would be rid of the latest batch of recruits. They would become someone else's problem. A new lot would arrive in the next few days. New people to bully. He was looking forward to it immensely. There was a fundamental problem with the training the army was giving to each new bunch of recruits. They became soldiers. A unit. A brotherhood who looked out for one another. After six weeks they were a tougher, more resourceful and more confident bunch of men. In less jaundiced eyes, this would have been considered a success. In O'Dowd's, it was a disaster.

With each passing week their fear of him diminished as their effectiveness grew. O'Dowd's opportunities for bullying them decreased exponentially. The one glowing exception to this was their first pass. Time after time it presented untold opportunities to mete out one last dose of punishment. In this regard, the last day was usually one of double joy for O'Dowd.

The morning was predictably bad for most of the whole platoon. The Gissing brothers knew they were in big trouble, which was unlikely to be mitigated by the fact that this was the day when the platoon would break up. The platoon scrambled onto the parade ground like a wave crashing against the cliff: uncontrolled, arbitrary and compelling in equal measure.

O'Dowd looked at the riches in front of him and almost did not know where to begin. This was the mother lode. Like an ivory poacher stumbling across the mythical elephant's graveyard, he walked along the line, almost licking his lips in anticipation as he slowly identified potential victims. Finally, he returned to the centre standing directly in front of the platoon. With a bark that resembled a growl, O'Dowd began the drill.

'Ten-shun.'

The platoon's movement had all the silken precision of an inebriated elephant which, many still were. In particular, the Gissing brothers were almost a day late in completing their drill. Neither cared much. Both had long accepted the inevitable and made little effort to keep in time or stem the giggles. O'Dowd lost no time in picking them and many others out for their appearance and sent them out running around the parade ground, rifle in air. One by one the runners and riders fell by the wayside. After ten minutes of drilling, barely half of the platoon was left, although Danny and his friends were still at the races.

This was very disappointing for O'Dowd, still smarting from his humiliation in the unarmed combat. Danny had adroitly managed to avoid upsetting the highly upsettable sergeant. As a result, aside from extra duty peeling potatoes or night watch, Danny had escaped any direct confrontation.

After half an hour of drilling, there were few still running. Most had offered up a sacrifice to Dionysus by the side of the parade ground. This provided much amusement to those of a more temperate disposition. It also offered potential rewards to those running a book on the field. O'Dowd was delighted with his handiwork and made a few bob in the process from the other sergeants.

The pantomime was brought to an abrupt conclusion as Budd arrived at the parade. He looked on with amusement at the carnage. However, he recognised the cause and decided to put everyone out of their misery. The recruits returned to the barracks to await details of their next posting.

As they trooped back, the whole parade ground stopped for a few moments and looked up. Overhead a Spitfire appeared and then another and then another. There was a rumble in the distance. The parade ground, to a man, began to cheer the RAF as they went to engage the enemy. The dog fight was too far distant to see, but the sound would live with Danny.

The men went inside to await details of their posting. Within twenty minutes a call came from the parade ground, and the men poured out of the barracks to see two planes returning, both Spitfires. Once more the recruits cheered but the sound died down as they realised there was no third plane. Danny and the rest of the men took off their hats. They looked at one another and then continued back to the barracks in silence.

One by one the men in the room received news of their posting. Tom and the Gissing's were to join an infantry regiment. Carruthers was to join signalling in the Artillery. Bob, Arthur and Danny were to join the Royal Tank Regiment. This meant they would be posted initially to Tidworth for further training before being garrisoned in nearby Thursley.

When they had all received details of their posting, they met back at the barracks. Danny was happy with his news. He had wanted to join a tank regiment. Tom was less pleased. He had also wanted to be in a tank.

166

'Lucky buggers,' said Tom with a grin. 'You get to ride into battle. We've got to bleedin' walk.'

'Nice big targets for Jerry though,' pointed out Bert.

'True enough,' agreed Tom. Looking towards Carruthers, Tom said, 'You've got the cushiest number of the lot.'

'They clearly recognise officer class, chaps,' responded Carruthers, grinning.

Tom and the rest laughed at this before Hugh pointed out the one salient fact to their friend.

'Remind me of your rank, Private Carruthers.'

'Temporary, old chap. Cream always rises to the top. They'll see sense soon.'

'Like they saw sense in calling you up to start with. Don't hold your breath, mate,' said Arthur. 'More chance of Hitler wearing a dress and taking up with a bloke.

'How do you know that he doesn't already?' asked Hugh.

'I hadn't thought of that.'

Early afternoon and the group gathered on the parade ground for the last time. There was a genuine sense of sadness at the parting of the ways. Danny shook the hands of the Gissing brothers and grinned.

'Who'd have thought, boys?'

'I know, Danny,' replied Bert. 'I hope you give Jerry as hard a time as you gave me all those years ago. We'll win in no time.'

Hugh grinned also. 'Do you know, Danny, in all the years I never got to throw you? It never rankled, though. However, just this once.' At that moment he pushed Danny, who fell back over Tom, who was kneeling behind him. Arthur caught him before he fell to the ground.

The whole group broke into cheers and then laughter, none more so than Danny. Arthur gently lowered him to the ground. A few other recruits came over to see the source of the hilarity. One was O'Dowd. He glared at Danny and ordered him to stand to attention. All the recruits did so.

He walked around all of them with silent malevolence. Then he said, 'You can laugh now but you'll change your tune when the bullets are flying.' And then he walked away. It was the last they ever saw of him.

'Always so sunny, isn't he?' said Arthur.

Tom was the last to step on to the three-ton truck that was to take them to the station. He looked at his younger brother.

'I guess this is it then, kid.'

'Looks like it,' replied Danny. His breathing had suddenly become laboured such was the weight in his chest.

'Come here,' said Tom, putting his brother in a bear hug. This brought good-natured wolf whistles from the truck. In turn the two brothers gave a time-honoured gesture by way of response.

'Look after yourself,' said Danny, finally.

'You, too.'

'Head down.'

Tom hopped up into the truck. Moments later it was on its way to the train station and then it would be a short stop to war. Danny wanted desperately to be alone. The public nature of the farewell was not what he wanted. There was so much more he had wanted to say but realised, given the opportunity, he wouldn't have said it. Nor would Tom. It wasn't necessary. He felt a pat on the back and then another. Bob looked at him with sympathy as did Arthur and Carruthers.

'Don't worry, Danny. Tom will be all right. Just you see,' said Bob.

Danny nodded and turned to watch the truck drive away into

the distance and then it was out of sight. He turned and walked back towards the barracks to collect his bag and the rest of his gear. The truck taking the recruits to the Tidworth garrison was making ready.

Chapter Twenty-Four

Tidworth Army Barracks, Wiltshire: March, 1941

The truck reached the crest of a hill giving Danny his first view of Tidworth. The valley below seemed to be dotted by dozens of large daisies lined up in neat rows. As the truck neared the camp, he saw they were medium-sized tents. This was to be his home for the next six weeks. The village came into view, but it was dwarfed in size by the area taken up by the garrison.

'Bloody hell,' complained Arthur. 'Don't tell me we're roughing it.'

'Looks like it,' said Bob glumly. The barracks at Caterham now seemed like a luxury hotel in comparison to the garrison they were approaching.

'Do you think there's even a NAAFI?' asked Bob.

'Can't afford to eat there anyway,' replied Arthur.

They passed one young lady on a bike, who smiled and waved at the truck.

'Not so bad really,' said Bob.

'Yeah, could get used to it I suppose,' agreed Arthur. Danny grinned at the two of them and rolled his eyes.

The sign outside the camp read: Royal Tank Regiment (RTR), Tidworth. The truck rolled past the sign and past a corporal standing guard at the gates and into the camp and the twenty recruits debouched from the back of the truck. Danny looked up at the clear blue sky and the shining sun. He felt excited at what lay ahead but also apprehensive. He missed having Tom around. His ready grin made him a reassuring presence and not just for Danny, either. His manner was more passive than Danny's, but he was well liked by all.

'What do you reckon then, Danny-boy?'

'We'll soon find out, Arthur. Tell you what. Although, I've never been here before …'

'You've never been anywhere, yokel,' said Arthur quick as a flash.

'It's like Little Gloston,' said Bob, finishing Danny's thought. 'I know what you're thinking.'

Around them the silence of the garrison was broken only by orders being barked in the distance and the sound of birds singing. Arthur mimicked shooting one of the birds.

'You're evil, you know that?' said Danny grinning.

'No, just a city boy who likes his sleep. I suspect we won't get any more of it here than at the other hotel.'

A sergeant came over to the group and they instinctively formed themselves into ranks.

'Well done, boys,' said the sergeant sardonically. 'Let's see how sharp you are after a ten-mile route march. Right turn, and quick march.'

The group jogged over to a large wooden hut where they were registered and assigned tents. The registration process did not last long and, after depositing their belongings, they were back on the parade ground. The sergeant tried his best to sound mean-spirited but after O'Dowd who, to Danny and his friends, seemed a genuinely nasty piece of work, this man came across as the very incarnation of nonchalance.

The initial inspection came off with no casualties. The sergeant, whose name was Sykes, resumed his 'pep' talk. It was a beautiful September day, and the heat of the afternoon was having its impact on him. Sweat poured off his forehead, as it did for all of them.

'I don't know what kind of summer camp you've just come from, but this is the army now and there'll be no more shirking. Reveille is at six am, and I'll have you drilling and polishing until lights out.'

Sykes continued mining a similar furrow for another few minutes before realising, in the warm sun, his heart wasn't in it. Nor were the hearts of the soldiers if their bored expressions were anything to go by. He decided to make an ordered retreat.

'Any questions?'

'Sergeant Sykes, sir,' called out Danny immediately.

Sykes looked at Danny and said, 'Name?'

'Shaw, Sergeant Sykes.'

'Proceed.'

'Can we see a tank?'

This struck Sykes as a reasonable question given the fact that they were a tank regiment. It also struck him how rarely new recruits ever asked. However, in the past there had been no tanks with which to practise. Since last August, there had been an influx of several A9s and A13s. The RTR had, if not an embarrassment of riches, then at least a few good tanks to give the new recruits the first-hand experience they would need.

A few minutes later Corporal Coldrick was detailed to provide a brief tour of the garrison. Unlike many of the NCOs they had encountered, Coldrick seemed to have more sympathy with the new lot, and a sense of humour.

'You're very lucky, you know. We've just had a fresh bunch of tanks delivered. This is good news and bad news for you. The good news is you'll get a chance to ride in them and learn how they work.'

'What's the bad news?'

'You won't be allowed to drive any. You'll be like kids standing outside the sweetie shop,' guffawed Coldrick. 'And don't even think about trying to sneak into one and taking it for a spin. Trust me, it won't be jankers for you. It'll be an all-expenses paid trip to Aldershot for a month or two.'

Danny frowned and turned to Arthur for an explanation.

'The glasshouse. It's where they sent Harn,' answered Arthur.

Then it dawned on Danny. He'd heard about the glasshouse before but not shown much interest. Not a place to visit, he decided. They'd never seen Harn again. Nobody talked about him. Nobody missed him.

They marched down to an open area away from the tents. Finally, the tanks appeared like giant green reptiles hidden behind the white cotton of the bivouacs. There were half a dozen sitting stationary in a line. As they were walking towards them, Coldrick explained the differences.

'These are what you call cruiser tanks. And, no, I ain't talking about your holidays in Skegness.'

This lightened the mood although Danny could feel butterflies in his stomach as he neared the two beasts. He tried to imagine himself inside. He also tried to imagine what it would be like to face the larger and more powerful Panzer tanks the Germans were reputed to possess.

'The A9 is on the left. These boys are pretty nippy. While the Germans are crunching their tanks into reverse gear, we can take a pot shot or two at them and be back in time for a cuppa by the time they start moving.'

'Assuming we can get near enough,' whispered Arthur. Danny frowned and looked at Arthur, a question in his eyes. Arthur pointed to the gun. 'Not very big, is it?'

Danny smirked and glanced down at Arthur's crotch. Arthur began to laugh and said, 'I've had no complaints.'

'Oi, what are you two gabbing on about?' shouted Coldrick, noticing the exchange between the two men.

'Looking at your gun, Corporal Coldrick. Not the biggest.'

Coldrick grew more serious. He pointed to the two guns and said, 'Actually, you're not far wrong. Both the A9 and the A13 have a two-pounder which is thirty-seven millimetres. But the new Honeys match up better to the Panzers. They also have their eighty-eights. These anti-tank guns can take you out from nearly a mile away. You'll have to ask the powers that be as to why we are using smaller, more mobile tanks and not big ones like Jerry uses. These cruisers are meant to be used for quick engagements. In, out and then on your bike. Bit like you with your missus. There's another type of tank called a 'Mathilda'. That's an infantry tank. It's heavier because the armour is thicker. No Jerry shell will get through it.'

'You mean Jerry shells can pierce this, Corporal Coldrick?' This was Danny, asking the question that was now very much on everyone's mind.

Coldrick nodded and then smiled. 'It will if you stand still and let them shoot at you long enough. The idea with this, boy, is you shoot while you're on the move. You'll notice they also come with machine guns. That's for dealing with infantry.'

'Do these tanks stop bullets?' asked Danny.

'You really don't fancy being shot at do you, son?'

'Not if I can help it,' laughed Danny. Coldrick laughed also.

'Sensible lad,' replied Coldrick. The group was now gathered around the lighter A9. Coldrick pointed to the armour and said, 'In answer to your question, the A9 has fourteen-millimetre-thick armour. The A13 has thirty. Won't stop a shell but both will stop rifle shots, so you're better off than those boys in the infantry. Anyone want to go inside?'

There was a chorus of yeses. Arthur stepped forward and climbed up the side and went in through the turret. A voice from inside said, 'Lumme, I've been inside bigger things than this.'

This brought a predictably ribald response from the other men. One or two others were also climbing in through the turret.

'See if you can move the two machine guns at the front,' ordered Coldrick. There were cheers when the men managed this. Over the next twenty minutes the men climbed into the tank and inspected what was likely to be their future workplace.

Danny, meanwhile, walked around the outside of both tanks. Coldrick looked at Danny, who was inspecting the tank with fascination. Normally the new lot were keen to climb inside and play. They were like children with a new toy. Danny was clearly appraising the tank. He walked over to Danny.

'What are you looking at?'

'I used to be a blacksmith,' said Danny, tapping the armour of the tank and listening to the sound it made. He ran his fingers over the rivets.

'What do you see?'

'It feels, I know this will sound strange, but it feels thin.' Danny ducked down and looked at the wheels and the tracks.

'If one of those rivets gets a direct hit, it shatters and turns all of you into mincemeat.'

'So, we keep moving.'

'Now you're getting it, son,' responded the corporal.

'How fast does this go?' asked Danny.

'About twenty-four miles per hour on a flat road.'

'How fast are the Panzers?' probed Danny.

'Similar but these would work better on hilly terrain. We're a lot lighter than the Panzers. Our suspension is also better off road.'

Danny stood up and looked at Coldrick. His face was grim.

'So, you're telling me that their tanks are just as quick as ours on the flat and they can outgun us.'

'That's about the size of it.'

Danny shook his head but remained silent. Coldrick looked at him and asked, 'What's your name, son?'

'Shaw, Corporal Coldrick.'

'You're Shaw,' said Coldrick. Danny wasn't sure what to make of the fact his name seemed to be known. 'What age are you?'

'Nineteen, Corporal.'

Coldrick looked at Danny for a moment and then wandered off to see how the other men were getting on. Danny, meantime, crawled underneath the tank. It was very narrow, and he came out again after checking the underside armour. It seemed unlikely anyone would be foolhardy enough to attack in this manner although mines would be a worry. A few of the others noticed Danny's more rigorous inspection and laughed.

'Afraid of closed spaces, Danny?' shouted one wag.

'Only if they're anywhere near your arse,' responded Danny. 'I'd rather take my chances with Jerry out in the open with a target painted on my chest.'

Danny hopped up onto the front of the A9 and then levered himself through the turret into the tank. His first thought as his feet hit the floor was its size. The tank was meant to have up to six men, but Danny couldn't for the life of him see how that would work in such a confined space.

Arthur was still inside. He looked up at Danny from his position at the machine gun and said, 'What do you think.'

Danny was far from happy and pointed to the gun. 'Like taking a water pistol to a gunfight.'

'You reckon?' said Arthur. Danny nodded in response. He pulled himself out of the A9 and jumped down to see the second cruiser, the A13. His hopes were not much higher for this. It was plain to Danny, even without seeing the Panzers, that they were badly outmatched. The experience of France suggested that the manoeuvrability strategy had been of limited effectiveness, notwithstanding the success at Arras. The excitement he had felt earlier on the way over was gradually evaporating. In its place was a sense of dread, a fear for the future. As he examined his own feelings, he realised it was based on trust. Or a lack of trust in the army command.

His father's experience in the Great War remained locked inside his mind. On the few occasions Danny and Tom had tried to talk to him about it, Stan had closed the conversation down. Therefore, Danny sought other sources to understand better the conflict his father had been engaged in. The conclusions from the books he studied in the library at Cavendish Hall were unanimous. The British and French had been poorly led. With increasing certainty, Danny realised that the lessons from the war had been learned better by the defeated country than by the visitors. He was the last to jump down from the inspection of the tanks.

'Cheer up,' said Coldrick. 'It's not that bad.'

Danny looked at him and said quietly, 'I think it is.'

Coldrick didn't disagree.

Part 6: Germany 1941

Chapter Twenty-Five

Ladenburg (nr. Heidelberg): January, 1941

The road was virtually empty. The snow didn't help, of course, but someone had done a good job of clearing it to the sides. The brightness made it an uncomfortable drive. Despite the ice, the police car sped along the main road towards Heidelberg without any problems. Manfred and his father said little on the journey. Each lost in his own thoughts. Neither was prepared to be the first to share them.

Manfred felt excited and scared. He was prepared to admit as much to himself. A part of him would have liked to have told his father. Another part rebelled at the idea. It had never been that kind of relationship. Instead, their bond was based on obedience. Manfred had been a good boy insofar as he had rarely rebelled. As far as Brehme was concerned, he had fulfilled his role as a father.

'Look,' said Brehme, pointing to the sky.

'Messerschmitt,' replied Manfred. Neither said anything as they looked at the plane make manoeuvres in the sky.

'Yes,' confirmed his father. 'Look at it go. England will have trouble against those.'

'I know,' said Manfred, smiling, happy to talk about something. 'One day we'll have fighters powered by jets, Father. Can you imagine?'

'Really? Are these things possible?'

'It's possible. I'm sure our scientists will find a way. Then watch. The Luftwaffe will rule the skies. I mean, you can't kill what you can't catch.'

They continued along the road driving past large fields filled with cattle. Manfred gazed at them.

'The Kramer farm,' said Brehme.

'I wonder what it's like to be so rich,' said Manfred in wonder. 'Do they have any daughters?'

Brehme turned to his son and laughed. Then he realised Manfred wasn't joking. Well, at least he was thinking in the right way. He was thinking of life after this bloody unnecessary war. He felt the anger rise within him. A bloody unnecessary war.

The grey sky began to lift. With the appearance of blue the atmosphere in the car lightened considerably. There was little point in being angry with Manfred. While he might have felt frustrated with the situation that had provoked his son to volunteer, and there was no question he could not avoid feeling disappointment that the boy was not shrewder in his choices, at the very least he respected him for standing up and being counted.

Manfred felt elation sweep through him as they crossed the bridge into the town of Heidelberg. All around were young men and women: students. And army. Manfred saw his father looking at him.

'You're absolutely sure?'

'Yes, Father. I'm sure,' confirmed Manfred.

They arrived at the train station and parked. The two men jogged from the car into the relative warmth of the station. Brehme left his son for a moment to confirm the correct platform. He came back from the guard and updated Manfred.

'Plenty of time,' said Brehme.

'Yes.'

All around there were young men accompanied by their parents. All were probably destined to go to the same training camp as Manfred. Brehme looked around at the scene and then glanced at his son. The partings were universally consistent: the fathers standing awkwardly as the mothers embraced their sons, often in tears.

'Son, your mother …' Brehme started to say but Manfred held his hand up.

'I know, Father. I know.'

'She's not well.'

'I know. I'm sorry, Father,' said Manfred. He realised he felt guilty. For the first time he thought about his father alone with his mother. The lines on his father's face were drawn tight. He was ageing and Manfred had only just noticed for the first time. There was worry too. Whether it was for him or his mother he knew not. The sorrow gave way to irritation. He wanted to be away now. Away from that house. Away from the repressive atmosphere. How he had hated it.

The excitement he felt now confirmed the rightness of his decision. He wanted his father to leave him. But his father stood there stupidly, just looking at his son.

Manfred knew he was desperate to say something. However, eighteen years of giving orders, of discipline and obedience, are not easily overcome. Peter Brehme looked at Manfred. He wanted his son to give an opening that would allow him to say what was in his heart. The rage in Manfred died away. Perhaps it was time to forgive. He held out his hand to his father. Brehme looked down and held out his hand to shake with sadness in his eyes.

Then Manfred pulled his father towards him, and they hugged. It was just a moment, but years of castigation disintegrated. Brehme pulled back with tears in his eyes. He turned away and rushed to the car.

Manfred watched him go and then spun around to face the rest of the station. He felt faintly embarrassed. But then he saw that all around him, parents were hugging the young men who, like him, were going to war. He picked up his bags and walked to the platform. People had started boarding already. He walked along the train and found an empty carriage.

Within a few minutes he was joined by several other young men. They were all a similar age. The train bumped forward to the sound of silence in the carriage. Manfred smiled at the awkwardness. He knew about this. But he felt so excited that it could not be contained any longer.

'Where are you heading to, anywhere nice?' he asked the rest of the carriage. He had a grin on his face because the answer was obvious. Everyone smiled and soon they were talking about themselves and the future.

Matthias Klug was the oldest at twenty-one. He'd left the university two terms before graduation. Manfred looked at him and wondered why. He was tall. Very tall, in fact. The growth of flesh had easily been outstripped by the lengthening of his bones. He was skinny and bespectacled, with mousey hair. This was a long way from being the Aryan ideal. But his warm smile and unusually self-deprecating manner soon won over the carriage.

Lothar Lenz was the youngest at seventeen. He was also the biggest. His stocky build, powerful arms and youth proclaimed vitality and strength. He had left school the previous year to apprentice with his father as a mechanic. Lothar was quiet and clearly felt a little overawed by the boys around him. But it was clear there was a good humour with the youngster and a quiet confidence based on his unquestionable physicality. No one had messed him around in a very long time.

The other passenger in the carriage was the same age as Manfred, Gerhardt Kroos. The two boys recognised one another. Each had played football in local teams and had played against one another throughout the years.

Gerhardt was the most confident of the three but, when he spoke, he also proved to be the most interesting. After half an hour of travel he mentioned casually, 'I have a friend at this camp we're going to. Well, I gather he's just left. Anyway, I've heard from his family what it will be like.'

'Go on,' shouted the other boys in unison.

'Well, it's a bit like Hitler Youth.' He laughed as did the others. He didn't need to add how much tougher it would be. 'We drill, we read maps, they teach us field craft, and weapons training, a lot of weapons training, in fact. In this respect we've been preparing for this for years, if you think about it.' This made the boys cheer as it was what they were most looking forward to.

'On arrival we'll be put into a room where we meet the rest of our gruppe and our Gruppenfuhrer. They're formidable people. Our sergeant and commander also come. The commander gives us a lecture on the German army and its role in our society.'

'Boring,' commented Lothar, which raised more smiles.

'Then comes the training. The instructors are usually people who fought in the last war. This is good because they'll know what it's like, but I gather they push you really hard over the sixteen weeks.'

Manfred chipped in at this point. 'I read other armies only train for ten or twelve weeks. We have the best training in the world.' The boys smiled and felt better on hearing this.

Gerhardt continued. 'My friend says training is planned down to the hour. At first, we drill on how to wear the uniforms; then we do lots of running. We run in all weathers, I might add. We're taught proper map reading, and reporting, how to do range estimation, target description. Each of us is treated like a leader in our own right.' The others nodded, completely absorbed in Gerhardt's explanation.

'We're expected to stay neat and tidy always. The rooms are inspected regularly for cleanliness. Not just our room, either. They expect us to have spotless rifles and clean uniforms. Our uniforms are white by the way.' This brought groans.

'Probably because we are virgins,' said Manfred laughing.

'Speak for yourself,' chipped in Lothar, which made everyone smile.

'They won't stay that way, I hear. They'll be grey by the end of training even with all the cleaning,' finished Gerhardt.

The three-hour journey passed easily as all four shared their background and where they wanted to be posted. Lothar, due to his training as a mechanic, had already been earmarked to join the Panzergrenadier division.

'I've asked to join them, too,' said Manfred.

'Fantastic,' said Lothar, 'maybe we will train together. And what about you?' asked Lothar turning to the other two boys.

Gerhardt and Matthias both shrugged. Neither had given much thought to what would happen after basic training. The conversation turned towards the merits of the different arms of the military: the Luftwaffe, the Kriegsmarine and the Deutsches Heer with its various subdivisions. The idea of being with the Panzers began to grow in Gerhardt's mind.

'Why do you want to be in a tank?' asked Gerhardt, smiling. 'Do you like the idea of all that armour around you?'

186

'Damn right,' replied Manfred, which caused the whole carriage to burst out laughing.

'Good plan, actually,' said Matthias, thoughtfully. 'Perhaps I might do the same. Better than being in the infantry and walking into machine-gun fire.'

Gerhardt looked at Matthias. The reality of where they were going and what it would mean suddenly became very real. The four boys became quiet. Just at that moment they went through a tunnel. The boys laughed. Nervously.

Chapter Twenty-Six

Reinsehlen Camp, Lower Saxony, Germany: January, 1941

The room was filled with around twenty other young men. All were around the same age as Manfred and his train companions. Aside from the recruits, the room was mostly empty of furniture save for one large photograph of the Führer and an enormous Nazi flag draped from the high ceiling. Everyone looked happy to be there, which meant they were probably as frightened as Manfred. They stood rigid to attention. All eyes stared straight ahead like soldiers in a toy army. They were alone, waiting for the arrival of their section commander. They didn't have to wait long.

The door opened and in walked one of the shortest men Manfred had ever seen. He was hardly the Aryan ideal with his dark, close-cropped hair, bow legs and bull neck. He had a look in his eyes that Manfred associated with Nazi authority. Anger.

In fact, his eyes were virtually popping with rage as if he'd just received a carpeting from his commanding officer and was about to dish out some revenge on the people before him.

Manfred's assessment was directionally correct but did not come close to the intensity of the next hour. Based on the talk, or rant, it seemed that Drexler, for he was so named, hated young people, life and the enemy, in roughly that order. Manfred risked a glance at Gerhardt, who was standing beside him towards the back of the group. Gerhardt saw Manfred look and half smiled. Seconds later, Drexler ripped through the assembled men to stand in front of Gerhardt, his face inches away.

'Is something amusing you?' shouted the diminutive dictator.

'No, sir,' said Gerhardt, eyes focused somewhere in the direction of Berlin.

With a swift lateral movement Drexler was standing in a similar proximity to Manfred. He roared at Manfred, 'What was so funny?'

Flecks of spittle sprayed over Manfred's face. He didn't blink. Drexler's was tomato-red, except for the prominent blue veins around his eyes. The eyes. Clear blue and full of a hatred that Manfred had never witnessed before, even in the most sadistic of his teachers, and there had been quite a few. But with this anger there was also something familiar and reassuring.

As quickly as Manfred had felt afraid and uncomfortable, he realised this was what he had been living with all his life. Only more concentrated. The next sixteen weeks were to prepare him and the rest of the group for life and death situations. All at once Manfred regretted his immaturity and resolved to become the best he could be.

'Nothing, sir,' said Manfred in a clear voice.

Drexler glared at both boys. He pointed at both. 'You, you. I will keep an eye on.'

Seconds later, Drexler was standing at the front of the group lecturing them on the importance of obedience. The message was clear. They had now to forget the carefree days of youth. Rebellion would not only be considered intolerable, it would be punished forcefully.

The more Drexler spoke, the more Manfred felt at home. He knew this world. It was his world.

As the group left the room, Manfred took a risk and went to Drexler.

'Herr Commander, I apologise for my actions. I wish to be punished, sir.'

Drexler looked at Manfred in surprise. His eyes narrowed in suspicion, and he said, 'Do you?'

'Yes, sir. I must learn a lesson.'

Moments later Gerhardt was standing beside Manfred. 'Sir, I wish to be punished also.'

Drexler nodded to a subordinate. Manfred and Gerhardt were led out of the room to another room where the other young men were being measured for uniforms. As Gerhardt had correctly forecast, the uniforms were white. They were both handed backpacks and told to put them on. Manfred's first thought was it weighed a ton. He later found out it was around thirty-six kilograms. He glanced at Gerhardt, who smiled ruefully. Their first day was not going as they would have liked.

After they received their uniforms and pack, the same subordinate took Manfred and Gerhardt to the parade ground. They lined up together.

'I am Sergeant Haag. Over the next sixteen weeks you will grow to hate me.'

One look at Haag and Manfred felt inclined to agree. There was, whether intentionally or not, a sly malevolence about this man that was absent from Drexler. With Drexler what you saw was a good summary of the man. Haag seemed an altogether different prospect.

Manfred resolved to be particularly careful when around him. His arm swept around the parade ground. It was the size of six football pitches.

190

'While your fellow recruits are eating, you will run around the outer perimeter of this parade ground. You do not stop.'

The two set off running. It was around six in the evening and the light was beginning to fade. It was bitterly cold, but Manfred knew the running would soon warm him up. He and Gerhardt ran alongside one another.

'Not too fast, my friend,' warned Gerhardt. 'No talking either. They do not set a time limit. We run until we collapse. This is how they do it.'

'I'm sorry, Gerhardt. It was my fault,' said Manfred.

'Enough,' replied Gerhardt.

After the first lap, Manfred could feel the straps chafing against his shoulders. He had certainly warmed up and the breath was already clouding around his face. His face was set in stone. He would not give in. Nor would Gerhardt. The two of them plodded on, lap after lap.

Around an hour later, many of their fellow recruits came out to see them. This had been a direct order from Drexler. Word had spread in the base of a punishment, and they were joined by other recruits who were in the latter stages of their training.

Both Manfred and Gerhardt were suffering agonies that breeched every threshold of pain. Their shoulders were red raw from the weight of the packs. Their backs were also aching, and the muscles at the front of their legs felt like water. The only sound on the parade was of their steps and their breathing. Manfred no longer felt human. It was as if his mind and his spirit had evacuated his body only to be pulled back by the pain of each step.

Another half hour passed. Many of the assembled audience were in shock. This was now beyond punishment. It was torture. For these men, teachers, accountants, factory workers, shop keepers, it was a new level of brutality they had never witnessed before. The silence

191

became a murmur as the two staggered on, no longer jogging. They're feet dragged drunkenly on the parade ground.

'Quiet,' screamed Drexler, as the murmur had grown louder.

And on the two boys went until finally Manfred collapsed on the ground. Gerhardt, himself on the point of collapse, stopped to help his companion up. Once up, they continued for another lap. By now they were barely moving forward. Their bodies were awash with sweat. Both tried to gulp in large quantities of air but the weight on their backs and their lungs restricted their airways. The pain from the straps was now unendurable.

Within a few metres of one another they both collapsed unconscious. Drexler glanced at his wristwatch and raised his eyebrows to Haag. With some disgust he saw a half smile on his subordinate's face.

'Bring them in. Take them directly to the doctor. Make sure they are hydrated. Don't feed them.'

Chapter Twenty-Seven

Manfred and Gerhardt were woken up by the sound of a tray clattering and cutlery clanging against the floor. They were in beds alongside one another in the hospital attached to the training camp. Manfred glanced at Gerhardt.

'I think I'm paralysed. I'll never move these legs again.'

Gerhardt threw his head back and laughed. 'Me too. I'm in agony.'

A male orderly brought each of them a small breakfast of porridge. He told them that they had twenty minutes and then they would have to vacate the beds.

Twenty minutes later, both men levered themselves off the beds and stepped gingerly onto the floor. On the table beside them were their uniforms, now laundered after the night before.

'Nice service here,' remarked Manfred.

'The food could be better,' pointed out Gerhardt.

'True, and I didn't think much of the waitress,' said Manfred indicating the returning orderly. Both men laughed and then grimaced as they tried to put their uniforms on. This was proving a difficult task with bodies that ached like hell.

'I know,' said Manfred, 'I'll help you.'

'You've been a great help already,' replied Gerhardt.

Manfred stifled a laugh as Haag arrived.

'Hurry up you two. The commander wants to see you immediately.'

Haag stood and waited as the two boys tried to move their devastated bodies towards the exit.

'Not so smart now, are you?' commented Haag, laughing mirthlessly.

Manfred glanced a warning at Gerhardt. A blink of the eye was his acknowledgement. A few minutes later they made their way slowly to the office of the section commander. Drexler sat behind his desk. Haag joined him to one side. The two men looked at the boys. Haag's face had a half smile, but Drexler looked angry, as usual.

Like everything else they had seen in the training camp, furnishings and décor were minimal. Drexler's office contained two photographs. One was a standard portrait of the Führer. It was very large and behind his desk. It was almost as if Drexler didn't want to have to look at him. Another photograph was on the wall to the side. An army battalion was lined up in three rows. It was the first thing Manfred saw when he entered. A small inscription underneath read, August 1914. Manfred glanced back at Drexler.

Drexler was about fifty years of age. He might have been older, probably not younger. It was hard to tell. His hair was closely cropped. Lines marked his face like trenches. They rose vertically on his cheeks, looped around his eyes, and continued horizontally on his forehead. There were no laugh lines. A life lived without joy etched on the face of a man without pity.

The two men stood in front of Drexler who eyed both. They were dying to sit down. It was clear Drexler understood this and seemed intent on dishing out yet more torture.

'Sore?' he asked piteously.

'Wiser, sir,' replied Manfred. It was a risk, but Manfred was too sore to care.

Drexler looked at him suspiciously but said nothing. Finally, he stood and walked up to each man. He looked at them, deep into their eyes. It was as if he wanted to reach into their souls. There was a ruthlessness in his eyes, or was it something else? Manfred was still too young to understand lies, truth and everything in between.

Now, standing before this man, he thought he saw something else. It was no longer just anger. The eyes no longer had that mad intensity, the hatred. If pushed, Manfred would have described the look on Drexler's face as one of curiosity.

'Your uniforms are very clean,' said Drexler. This much was obvious. They were spotless. Neither Manfred nor Gerhardt had given any thought to this. Instead, they glanced at one another in confusion. 'Yes, the magic laundry fairies cleaned them for you while you slept,' continued Drexler.

Gerhardt was the first to realise. He said, 'Who should we thank, sir?'

'Your friends were up until midnight cleaning and drying them. Perhaps you should thank them,' answered Drexler. There was a faint shake of his head as if in disbelief.

The two men looked at one another guiltily. They owed Mattias and Lothar one.

'Yes, sir,' chorused both men.

Drexler walked behind them and then back round to his desk. He sat down and picked up some sheets of paper. Without looking at them he said, 'Dismissed.'

Manfred and Gerhardt hauled their carcasses out of the room. Haag followed them out of the office. They walked towards the barracks.

'You were lucky there,' said Haag as they arrived at the barracks. 'But I will be watching you. Trust me. You so much as take half a

195

step out of line and I'll have you back on that parade ground faster than you can say "heil".'

'What happened?' asked Lothar as he and the three others walked towards the main hall.

Manfred told them about what had prompted the punishment. Neither Matthias nor Lothar would listen to any thanks from their grateful companions. When they arrived at the hall, Manfred's heart sank when he realised there were no seats. They would have to stand. He was already on the point of collapsing again. The beads of sweat on Gerhardt's forehead suggested he, too, would not last much longer.

The colonel of the camp stood before them on a small stage. Draped behind him were large red flags with swastikas. He looked out across the several hundred men that comprised the entire camp. The opening of the talk was a welcome to the new recruits, if welcome it was. There was little in the manner of the black-uniformed man that suggested hospitality would be the order of the day. He opened with a short observation about the German army and its role in German society.

The speech lasted half an hour. The colonel spoke without notes but with great passion. Manfred would have been bored by the end had he not been in such agony. His legs had locked into position. He feared moving a muscle, lest he be singled out again.

At the end of the speech, much to his amazement, a reference was made to him and Gerhardt, although their names and the relative recency of their arrival were not mentioned. The colonel reminded all about the importance of discipline and how infractions would be punished.

Afterwards, as they left the hall, Manfred could feel the glances of other men on him as he limped beside Lothar. Matthias, meanwhile, was surreptitiously helping Gerhardt. The rest of the morning was given over to lectures on how the next sixteen weeks would progress. Each of the discipline heads explained the scope of the training and the expectations.

Much to Manfred's surprise, the lecture by Drexler was oddly moving. It was less about a specific discipline and more a philosophical reflection on the nature and brutality of war. He left no one under any illusion about what they were being trained to do. They would become killers.

With each lecture, it was clear that Matthias was becoming increasingly glum. After one break, Matthias spoke to Manfred about his worries.

'This is a mistake. I should never have come,' admitted Matthias.

'Why not? You'll be fine,' reassured Manfred.

Matthias shook his head sadly.

'Look at me. I couldn't have done what you and Gerhardt did last night. You know that one of the men here told me that this has happened a few times. No one has lasted longer than an hour. You two were out there for much longer. One guy only lasted ten minutes. That would be me. Even assuming I could carry that damn pack, I would have been crying on the ground in no time. Everyone here thinks you're both supermen.'

'The pack wasn't that bad,' lied Manfred. 'Thirty kilos or so.'

'Thirty-six, you idiot,' corrected Matthias, with a rueful smile.

'We'll look after you,' said Manfred.

'I'm not sure that's a good idea. This camp isn't about brotherhood, it's Darwinian.'

Manfred looked confused for a moment.

'Survival of the fittest,' clarified Matthias. 'Before they started burning books, I read a lot.'

'Probably best to keep that to yourself. I know what you mean.

Charles Darwin. I don't think our leaders like to think of good-looking Germans like you, Matthias, being descended from apes.'

'My arms are long enough.'

This seemed to relax him a little, but it was clear that he was worried. Manfred felt for his new friend. He had every reason to be concerned. All around him he saw young men like himself, hunger in their eyes and full of youthful vigour, itching to burn off their energy in as violent a way as they were allowed. Very few people looked like Matthias. Few sounded like him. Manfred wondered how long it would be before the likes of Haag started to pick on the weaker men.

The rest of the morning was given over to drill in the parade ground. Manfred and Gerhardt were excused and allowed to return to the hospital section for their injuries to receive further treatment.

Lunch was the main meal of the day. All the soldiers went to the dining hall to eat at 1230 hours. This gave the four companions a chance to catch up properly following the previous evening. Lothar confirmed what Matthias had said about their epic effort. Gerhardt, like Manfred, was too sore all over to care much. A few men came over and congratulated the pair, shaking their heads at the same time in disbelief.

'My God, that was extraordinary,' said one young man. He had also been on the train the previous day but in a different carriage.

'I'm Dassler. Fred Dassler. I saw you yesterday on the train.' Fred was joined by another boy, of seventeen. 'This is Willi. He's from Heidelberg also.'

'Hello,' said Willi, clearly a bit nervous of being with the older boys, especially two celebrities like Manfred and Gerhardt. The six chatted through lunch that lasted an hour. Then all the recruits re-assembled on the parade square. The parade was taken by platoon sergeants.

'Not many officers around,' observed Gerhardt in the square.

A voice from behind said, 'They do that. They want to teach you how to survive without officers wiping your arse for you.'

Gerhardt glanced behind and saw a big man with a gap-toothed smile.

'Thanks, my friend. Good to know.' Gerhardt glanced at Manfred. 'You hear that?'

'Interesting,' said Manfred. 'They want us to obey automatically but they also expect us to be independent.'

'Indeed,' said Gerhardt, nodding.

After an easy drill, the new recruits were taken to the shooting range and given instruction on firearms proficiency. Most of the young men were familiar with guns, and even Matthias showed fluency on loading and reloading that belied how he looked. He grinned sheepishly at Manfred.

'I'm not completely useless.'

He then proceeded to knock out half a dozen bullseyes in as many shots. By the end of the shooting practice, Manfred was matching Matthias bull for bull.

The men trooped home wearily from the rifle range. Gerhardt walked slowly with his new friends.

'Did you hear the sounds from further down the range?'

'Yes, machine guns. I can't wait,' said Lothar. 'I can't hit the side of a barn door with the rifles. The machine gun is what I need. No messing there – rat, tat, tat, tat,' mimicked their friend. The group laughed.

It was early evening now. This was the time for cleaning. First, the uniforms were cleaned followed by the rifles and the machine guns. Finally, the room itself had to be made spotless. They assembled for the evening meal at 1830 hours. It was relatively light, but the evening was not over yet. After the evening meal the recruits were expected to polish their boots then make sure their area in the barracks was clean and would pass inspection.

After having spent the first night in hospital beds, Manfred and Gerhardt found the new beds much less to their liking; they did little to ease their aching muscles.

'Boys, I mean it,' said Gerhardt. 'We have to defeat the British quickly. I'm not sure if my body can take these beds for long.'

Around him the group laughed but the rest of the young men in the barracks, unaware of the joke, told them to keep quiet. Lights were out by eleven on their second day at the camp.

Chapter Twenty-Eight

Reinsehlen Camp, Lower Saxony, Germany: March, 1941

Just after five the next morning the men were woken and told to get ready. Over the next sixteen weeks the pattern stayed the same. The men washed and shaved and made ready for the morning run of five kilometres. In the first week, Manfred and Gerhardt joined Matthias among the stragglers. Lothar also found it a strain, but then again, as his friends pointed out, he had more to carry with him. This was usually responded to with a punch on the arm. Even when he did it lightly it could still be painful. Matthias never made this mistake. He was fighting his own battle with his body. His inability to progress physically was being noticed.

Haag seemed to delight in picking on Matthias and often forced him to skip breakfast to run a further two kilometres. It seemed as if Haag was on a mission to break the young student. The other boys smuggled some bread for him to eat from their own allowance.

Breakfast consisted of coffee and bread. It followed the run just before seven. As grateful as Matthias was to his friends, the strain was growing worse for him by the day. His friends felt powerless to do anything about the bullying from Haag. Even his exemplary performance on the rifle range with pistol, rifle or machine gun was not enough to offset his physical limitations.

As the weeks progressed, Manfred and Gerhardt overcame their initial physical discomfort and rose to the top by virtue of their natural athleticism and an awareness, from Gerhardt's original intelligence, of what the instructors were looking for in their recruits. Both young men were natural leaders. This was borne from their experience in the Hitler Youth. They stood out among the recruits of their intake and even among the wider body of men.

Aside from the physical side, both excelled at the weapons training which consisted of firing artillery, throwing grenades and dozens of hours at the rifle range. They mastered the techniques related to mortar bombing and the use of artillery. Their experience in the Hitler Youth of map reading, the use of compass and squares, understanding eight figure grid references and how, generally, to orient themselves meant they were soon followed, quite literally, by the rest of the recruits.

Both responded well to the German army approach of training all men to a rank above themselves. Gerhardt explained one evening why this was so.

'Think about it,' he said. 'We are going to war. Officers are as likely to die as we are. It makes sense that there will be promotion in the field. They'll need men who are ready to make the transition quickly.'

'While you're waiting for the call to be Field Marshall, Gerhardt, can you get me a coffee?' asked Manfred. The group burst out laughing and, seconds later, Manfred found himself buried in Gerhardt's armpit and receiving a half a dozen rabbit punches. He was chortling too much to feel any pain. To be fair, the power of the punches was diminished by the fact that Gerhardt was laughing even harder than the others.

When Gerhardt had finished inflicting retribution on his friend, Manfred patted down his hair and grinned.

'Your armpit smells like a milkmaid's …'

Manfred's precise anatomical simile was drowned out by the group's pointed and all too accurate query as to how Manfred would know, exactly.

Confirmation of their status came six weeks into their training when both were called into Drexler's office. This was the first time their section commander had spoken to them since the incident on the first day. Gerhardt looked at Manfred when the order came.

'What now?'

Manfred shrugged. 'Let's find out.' The two men rushed to the office and knocked on the door.

'Enter.'

They marched in and stood to attention. Drexler rose from his seat and stood in front of them. For the next minute there was silence.

Finally, Drexler said, 'I've been watching the two of you over the last six weeks. You've done well. I'm recommending that you each lead a small gruppe in the upcoming divisional exercises.'

'Yes, sir,' chorused both men, straining hard to contain their delight.

Drexler nodded and then dismissed them. He walked over to the wall and looked at the photograph of his old battalion. He was sitting at the front. His height made it pointless placing him anywhere else. His eyes ran along the ranks of the men. They were all so young, just like the boys he'd just dismissed. Cannon fodder all. Ordered to commit suicide in the thousands. He could still name most of them: Klaus, Hans, the Seeler twins. The list went on in his head.

All dead.

Tears welled in his eyes. Every time he stood in front of this photograph, he swore an oath he would never send any man into battle as badly unprepared as he had been. All his men would be ready for what faced them. They would be stronger, smarter and readier than the men they faced. The rage within him rose and then died away. He returned to his desk and preparations for the exercises ahead.

Chapter Twenty-Nine

A steady beat of rain on the tin roof greeted Manfred on the morning of the company exercise. He'd barely managed any sleep. In preparation for the day ahead, a battery of artillery had boomed nearby all through the night. By the time the recruits had risen and made ready, they were all as sleep deprived as Manfred. And there was no breakfast.

'Did you sleep much?' asked Manfred to Gerhardt.

'No. You?' replied Gerhardt groggily.

'I did, no problem,' said Lothar with a big grin. He was set upon immediately by the other two; all three of them laughed like kids.

After they were washed and dressed, the recruits jogged two kilometres to the 'battlefield'. Their first view, when they reached the crest of a hill, was of an enormous, open plain. It stretched for a couple of kilometres. In the distance they could see hills and trees. At the end was an escarpment rising to reveal battlements.

Although mostly flat, the plain was not featureless. There was plenty of cover on the plain. Several ditches ran like scars along the landscape. They looked like they had been created by previous attackers. Small clumps of trees, studiously avoided by the artillery, dotted the landscape. As you got closer to the escarpment, there were a few knolls which meant any approach to the defender's area was a tremendous challenge. The 'defenders' area was protected with barbed wire. The landscape was also pitted with holes from field guns, providing additional cover for attacker or defender.

The recruits who had been in training for six weeks or longer were the participants. They were split into attackers and defenders. Disappointingly, Manfred and Gerhardt found themselves on opposing sides, each leading their own gruppe from their intake.

The artillery continued their bombardment firing real ammunition. At a point just before they took up positions, this changed to blanks. The bombardment continued, however, causing the ground to feel like it was shaking under their feet. The sound and the impact of the shells set everyone on edge. As they took up positions, the noise level seemed to blast out its own greeting.

The exercise began. All at once Manfred could hear the crack of gunfire as the recruits began to fire their machine guns and rifle blanks at an imaginary enemy.

Manfred watched as groups of men rushed forward, flinging themselves flat when artillery fire whistled overhead. Officials wearing white armbands were dotted around the battlefield. They would appear from time to time and order some men off the range designated 'killed in action'.

Manfred observed all of this. He quickly recognised the futility of a frontal attack. He ordered his men together and pointed to a nearby field on the other side of a fence over a kilometre away.

'We'll go around their flank and attack their rear.'

'Can we do this?' asked Matthias, shocked. It felt as if they were cheating.

Manfred looked down at a sheet of paper in his hand. His orders. He looked back at Matthias and ripped up the sheet. Then he smiled.

'We're doing it. And yes, my friend, we're going to cheat if we must. Who's with me?'

This cheered everyone up. A row of grins creased the faces of everyone. This was more like it. They could break the rules with impunity or march to their death like sheep. Surely this folly lay buried in the mud of Verdun, Passchendaele and a hundred other battlefields.

Manfred's gruppe waited for a particularly heavy barrage of fire and then he led them away from the main field towards a large clump of trees on the outer perimeter. Peeping between the trees they could see a wooden fence. The trees provided cover for Manfred's group and they were soon lost in the chaos of war. Scaling the small wooden fence was a simple matter.

'Are you sure about this?'

This was Matthias again. He was now less worried about cheating than the obvious smell emanating from the field. The rest of the men laughed. All were now feeling slightly more sympathetic towards Matthias. This was high risk with the added disadvantage that it looked very much like the field had recently been spread with manure. The ripe farmyard smell of cows and pigs permeated the air.

'Look,' pointed out Manfred, 'the enemy barrage is too heavy. Do you want to be hauled off the field before we even have a chance to engage the enemy?'

The silent reaction told its own story.

'Fine,' continued Manfred. 'We will roll over and over on the ground in order to reach a new assault position. Yes, you'll get a little dirty. Follow me.'

With that, he flung himself onto the dung covering the field and began to roll over and over. With rifles pressed between their knees, tight to their chests they rolled, cursing and swearing as they went. The escarpment was half a kilometre ahead. Behind it lay 'the enemy'.

To reach them they had to scale the small farm fence then climb the rock face. This would take them to the rear of the defence position.

Manfred led the way. For the next fifteen minutes they crawled through the mud, the mulch and the manure. The rain persisted, beating down on their tin helmets with a metronomic pulse. The conditions made progress slow. However, pointed out Manfred to his comrades, it would provide a distraction for their enemy. This was partly out of hope, and partly out of a desire to keep their spirits up.

They finally arrived at the perimeter fence closest to the defender encampment. One by one they hopped over the fence and sprinted towards the escarpment, praying they would not be seen.

Scaling the rock face presented a separate challenge. Although it was no more than seven or eight metres in height, Matthias still looked at it with a degree of anxiety. Manfred, as leader, selected himself to go first.

The first few minutes at the base of the escarpment was spent looking for a route that might be scalable. Finally, he identified what he hoped was the safest approach. He felt nervous, however. By now he was acutely aware that they were in a great position, far in advance of his other comrades. But they had cheated. There would be consequences, he felt sure. And then there was the escarpment which seemed more like a cliff every time he looked up. Now, there was a real risk of injury if he fell. And if anyone fell, he knew it would be his responsibility. Manfred felt very nervous.

The rock face was solid. Manfred put the gun over his back and began the ascent. The main problem was less the availability of footholds than the weather conditions. He whispered down to his companions, 'Be careful. It's every bit as slippery as it looks.'

Manfred made his way up carefully, rock by rock, foothold by foothold. After a few minutes he reached the top. He leaned over the edge and used his rifle to help pull up the men following him.

* * *

From a vantage point at the headquarters of the attackers, Drexler, standing with the colonel, observed the action through his binoculars with a smile on his face. He pointed out what was happening to the colonel and soon all the senior soldiers were watching in fascination at the flanking move led by Manfred.

'Very good,' commented the colonel. 'Who is leading those boys?'

'Brehme, sir,' replied Drexler. 'If you remember, he was one of the boys that ran for nearly two hours on the parade ground.'

'Ah yes, I remember him. Interesting, isn't it? Every two or three months someone has the same idea. Until then we see these boys get mown down like sheep going to slaughter. Keep an eye on him, Drexler.'

'I am, sir,' confirmed Drexler.

Manfred's platoon made good progress up the escarpment. Within a few minutes they arrived at the top. Matthias was the last to attempt the ascent. His first effort was humiliating. He fell within the first two metres. Manfred was frustrated by this but, equally, recognised his friend was trying his best. He ordered the man in front of Matthias to stay on the ridge which ran along the middle of the rockface. It presented a good foothold and allowed the man to help Matthias by giving him a rifle to hold on to. At the top of the escarpment, the rest of the men and Manfred could see the defenders rear a few hundred metres up ahead. Between them and the defenders lay a clump of trees.

'Make for the trees, they'll give us cover,' whispered Manfred, before realising there was no point in doing so given the noise of shelling half a kilometre away. 'You all smell by the way.' It was true; their uniforms were encrusted with foul-smelling filth from the field.

'Good camouflage, sir,' pointed out Willi.

Sir.

Willi had said 'sir'. Manfred liked the sound of it and silently thanked Willi for his unintended praise. He and the other recruits began to crawl laterally at first and then forward. There was at least one hundred metres of open space before they reached the trees.

The spirits of the group were raised when Matthias finally appeared at the top of the rockface and crawled forward to meet them.

'Sorry for keeping you waiting. Have we captured them yet?'

The group laughed and then started to progress towards the clump of trees. It took a little over five minutes to cover the distance.

'Nearly there,' said Manfred. 'Keep your heads down.'

Once the clump of trees was directly between Manfred and the defence position, Manfred and the rest of the men stood up and sprinted for cover. All of them, around twenty, were now out in the open.

A few metres from the trees, and still out in the open ground, around a dozen defenders stepped out from the clump and pointed their rifles at Manfred. The group was led by a familiar face.

'Hello, my friend,' said Gerhardt with a smile. 'Going anywhere in particular?'

Manfred's face fell when he saw who it was. Just behind Gerhardt was Lothar. His grin, if anything, was even wider. Then, with a rueful smile, Manfred said, 'How did you guess?'

'Disobey orders? Catch the enemy unaware? I'd have done the same so I guessed that you would try to do the same. Oh, and give us your weapons and put your hands up.'

At this point two officials arrived to confirm the capture. They led the recruits towards the front of the defence position. A few minutes later, the two groups of boys became visible to the raised platform from the front of the field where the exercise was taking place.

* * *

'That's interesting, Drexler. Have you seen?' asked the colonel.

'No. What, Herr Colonel?'

'Your young man has been caught. He's a prisoner of war.'

There was a ripple of noise from the officers as they began to observe the captives being led to the front of the defence to join the other prisoners of war.

Drexler trained his field glasses on the defence position. After a few moments he said, 'Interesting. I wonder who thought to defend the rear position.'

'Indeed. This is the first time that attack has failed,' replied the colonel.

Drexler continued to scan the two gruppes. His gaze fixed on Gerhardt and he let out a laugh.

'What's wrong?' asked the colonel lowering his glasses and looking at Drexler.

'You're not going to believe this, sir.'

The boys returned to barracks stinking from the manure-encrusted uniforms. Everyone in the finished exercise was now aware of what had happened. Manfred's group were the main body of official prisoners, although a few stragglers had also made it to the escarpment. It had been a bad day for the attackers. Almost all the attackers had been designated 'killed'. When they reached the platform where the senior officers were situated, there was a spontaneous burst of applause for the two groups from the other recruits. It lasted for a short period before the colonel raised his hand and demanded silence.

'Gentlemen, this is your first experience of combat. I have no doubt you found it exciting, thrilling even. The fire in your bellies was real, the desire to crush the enemy so strong it was almost palpable,' said the colonel. He surveyed the young men in silence for a few moments.

'Yes, we have watched it all from our position here. We saw examples of great bravery from the attackers. At the same time, we saw stupidity on a grand scale. Too many of you gave your 'lives' cheaply. When real bullets and bombs are flying, you will act differently. If you do not, you will die. It's as simple as that.'

The colonel turned to Drexler and asked if there was anything else. Drexler shook his head, and they dismissed the recruits. All had to jog back to the training centre a few kilometres away.

'You can put your hands down, Manfred,' whispered Gerhardt. This brought a laugh from all those around, none more so than Manfred.

The rain beat down on Manfred's face as he jogged alongside Gerhardt. His mood veered wildly between pride in the reaction of all to their audacious tilt at the defenders and frustration at their defeat. His one consolation was that it was Gerhardt who had proved their undoing, but the failure rankled.

'I can't believe you guessed, Gerhardt. It's killing me.'

'I'm not sure we've heard the end of it, though. I disobeyed my orders to do it.'

'Me, too.'

They looked at each other and both erupted into laughter. Alongside them, the other participants looked at them in bewilderment.

'Yes,' continued Gerhardt when he had recovered his composure. 'I left a detachment to defend our position and took a group of men to the clump myself. It was a strange feeling. We waited over an hour for you. We had no idea if you'd come.'

'My God, I had no idea,' replied Manfred.

'Some of the guys were unhappy but Lothar was great. He threatened them.'

Lothar, who was jogging ahead, turned around and grinned.

212

'I was hoping to break some heads, but they came around to Gerhardt's way of thinking.'

'Probably didn't want you to sit on them,' said Gerhardt.

'Splat,' said Manfred with a grin.

They were all required to wash and get cleaned before their evening meal. The exercises had lasted all day, which meant no one had eaten since the morning. All were ravenous. However, as Manfred and Gerhardt made their way to the dining hall, Haag came over towards them.

'Don't like the look of this,' whispered Manfred.

'Follow me,' ordered Haag. It wasn't a request, and he didn't look very happy.

The two friends glanced at one another as they headed towards the colonel's office. A sharp knock at the door and then Haag entered. The colonel sat behind a large oak desk. To his side was Drexler. This was the first time the two boys had seen the office. It was much larger than Drexler's office and it was more lavishly furnished. Aside from the standard portrait of the Führer, there were a dozen framed photographs around the office with the colonel standing beside leading Nazi figures including Hitler himself.

Both men looked serious. Manfred and Gerhardt felt a sense of foreboding. They had already been punished; a further infraction might spell the end of their army careers. The thought of returning home in shame seemed real at that moment.

Manfred felt his breathing become constricted. The beat of his heart seemed to be louder than the clock on the wall. Finally, the colonel addressed them.

'Do you know what these are?' he asked.

The two boys looked down.

'Yes, Herr Colonel,' they said in unison.

'Tell me,' ordered the colonel.

'Written orders, Herr Colonel.'

'Correct. They are your written orders.' He handed two small sheets to Manfred and Gerhardt. 'Read them to me.'

Manfred glanced at Gerhardt then began to read: 'Support the main thrust of platoon C. Stay in reserve until C make breakthrough, then pivot around to centre and support main army.' He looked up when he had finished and then turned to Gerhardt.

'Defend the forward redoubt,' began Gerhardt. 'Stop enemy advance. Defend to last man.' He looked up at the two senior officers.

The colonel spoke again.

'Simple instructions, don't you agree? Yet you both deliberately disobeyed your orders. To do so on a battlefield risks immediate court marshal and summary execution. In this training centre it means being expelled. I don't need to tell you the kind of shame that this will bring on you and your families.'

Manfred felt his heart sinking. He could barely keep his eyes on the colonel. By now he was finding it very difficult to breathe.

'What shall we do with them?' asked the colonel, turning to Drexler.

'I would like to know what they have to say for themselves, Colonel, sir.'

'Very well,' came the reply.

Manfred turned to Gerhardt, who raised his eyebrows. Taking a deep breath, Manfred began to speak.

'We started to follow the orders but observed quickly that the frontal attack was against a heavily defended position. Without tank and air support it was, in fact, suicidal. The two tanks were, as you know, supporting the attack on the western perimeter. I felt that a better option for us was to seek a way around their flank and catch them by surprise with a rear attack. I ordered my men to march two kilometres east and make our way through the neighbouring field …'

'Through shit, I believe,' pointed out Drexler. Manfred looked at Drexler. Was there the ghost of a smile?

'Through manure. We almost managed to reach the defenders' base but were intercepted,' finished Manfred.

Both senior officers turned to Gerhardt.

Gerhardt cleared his throat nervously. Then he glanced at Manfred and said, 'I have known Brehme for many years. We played football against one another in Heidelberg.'

'Is this relevant?' asked Drexler irritably.

'Yes, sir. Brehme was captain of a team we played often. I observed back then that he was a leader on the field and a smart tactician. He was able to change things around when they were not working. Which was usually the case. We were a much better team.'

'Get on with it,' ordered Drexler irritably.

'I suspected that Brehme would quickly see the folly of a frontal attack. This seems like a relic from the last war. We're not stupid Tommies,' added Gerhardt.

'For the last time,' ordered Drexler in exasperation.

'I knew Brehme would throw away the rule book. I took some men to survey our rear, believing it to be a potential weakness in our defence. By that I mean our rear was unguarded due to the assumption, a false one, that no one would be stupid enough to crawl through a neighbouring field, a couple of kilometres away from the battlefield, scale an escarpment and attack the rear position. I ordered my men to take a position in the trees that would give any attacker cover. However, the trees also gave us cover and a good view of any potential action from this angle.'

'You've explained your actions; how can you possibly justify disobeying orders?' asked Drexler.

'I believe it was von Moltke, sir,' said Manfred, 'who observed that no plan survives contact with the enemy. We had to adapt to the situation on the battlefield. To do anything else would have been suicide. My duty was to achieve the objective, not obey orders that were ill-conceived and impossible to execute.'

Manfred looked at the two senior officers. He spoke with passion and almost a trace of anger. He knew what he'd done was right and if the military were too stupid to see this then Germany was in trouble.

'Yet, you still failed.'

'Yes, sir,' agreed Manfred, but to his surprise, no less than to that of the two men addressing him, he continued. 'I failed because the person who stopped me also adapted his strategy to the battlefield situation rather than follow orders that were no longer relevant.'

Gerhardt glanced at Manfred. His first thought was that Manfred had gone too far but then he realised that perhaps their best strategy was now attack. He picked up the theme and developed it further.

'Brehme is correct, sir. In a battlefield situation, the army which has the flexibility to adapt to the situation will win. Far from having dull-witted order-takers marching like sheep to the slaughter ...'

'Kroos,' shouted Drexler. 'That is enough. Remember, you are addressing superior officers. Moderate your tone and language immediately.'

'Sorry, sir.' Gerhardt realised his mistake immediately. Before him were two men who had fought in the last war, who had followed such orders, probably without questioning them. Worse, they had probably given such orders themselves. He felt his face burning in shame.

'Enough,' said the colonel. 'I've heard quite enough of this. Both of you get out of the office. The section commander and I will discuss your fate.'

Manfred and Gerhardt saluted, spun around and left the office. They made sure that they were around the corner before they began to speak.

'Did we go too far?' asked Gerhardt.

'Not far enough, my friend,' replied Manfred. As they walked across the parade ground towards the dining hall, Gerhardt stopped. He looked at the building they were walking towards. Manfred stopped too and looked at him.

'What's wrong?'

'Nothing,' said Gerhardt, looking around. They both stood and looked at the large buildings of the training centre and the parade ground. Then he added, 'I'll miss this.'

'Me, too,' replied Manfred with a smile. 'We did the right thing, though. Whatever they may say.'

'Yes. We did.'

'What do you think, Rolf?' asked the colonel. 'Boys like that are dangerous. We both know this.'

'True, Klaus, but,' said Drexler looking around the office, 'before all of this, before you became a politician, I can remember a captain who didn't always do as he was told. I remember one time at Cambrai …'

'My goodness,' replied the colonel. 'Those tanks. We'd never seen the like before.'

'No, nor had our officers. They gave us orders, but they had no idea what they were doing. How could they? There were no orders on how to defend against them. No manuals to guide us then. We only had our wits, our initiative. We wouldn't be here if we'd obeyed those orders, Klaus, and you know it.'

The colonel looked up at Drexler and smiled. He lit a cigarette and inhaled slowly. 'I know, Rolf. But it's the same old story, isn't it? If we punish them, then morale will plummet; if we promote them and they turn out to be wilful, disobedient and dangerously stupid it will come back to haunt us. If we do nothing, then everyone will take it as carte blanche to disobey orders. And don't forget they've already been in trouble.'

'True. But my God, Klaus, they were nearly two hours running around that parade ground.'

'Extraordinary, I agree.' The colonel laughed bitterly and shook his head. 'Whatever we do my old friend, it's wrong.'

'Forget what you think you should do,' growled Drexler leaning over his colonel. He thumped his breast and fixed his eyes on a man he'd known for nearly thirty years. 'What's in here, Klaus? What is your heart telling you to do?'

Chapter Thirty

Reinsehlen Camp, Lower Saxony, Germany: April, 1941

Silence.

It was almost palpable, certainly pure and enough to put all the young recruits on edge. A barked order felt like a rock hurled into a calm pool. Several hundred recruits moved as one. The sound of their steps echoed like a clap of thunder in an Alpine valley. For the next few minutes, the recruits went through their drill. When it had finished, they stood to attention. All eyes stared straight ahead yet everyone was burning to look at the man inspecting them.

Sixteen weeks had passed since their arrival. This was their passing-out parade. Pride glowed through the eyes of the men in the square like a flame in the night sky. The colonel, followed by Drexler, walked along the ranks, accompanied by Erwin Rommel. He walked past Manfred. Rommel's visor cap Schirmmütze was below the eyeline of the two young men. Sadly, Rommel didn't stop but walked on. However, further up he stopped and spoke to Matthias.

'Where do you hope to serve, young man?' asked Rommel, looking up at the tall bespectacled young man.

'Panzer division, Herr General.'

Rommel nodded and walked on with the other officers. The parade ended and the new members of the German army retired to their quarters to await instruction on where they would be posted.

Manfred was joined by Gerhardt, Lothar, Matthias, Willi and Fred in the barracks. Each sat on a bed and they chatted for the hundredth time about the future.

'I can't believe you pitched for the Panzers, Matthias,' said Gerhardt throwing his cap at his friend.

'They'll never find a tank big enough to fit you,' added Manfred.

Matthias looked serious and said straight-faced, 'I think he recognised in me someone with the intelligence, the calmness under fire and the natural authority to command a tank.'

The group burst out laughing at this, as did Matthias, who clearly did not believe it himself.

'I'll be pissed off if I'm not in the Panzer division,' said Lothar.

'Will you go home?' asked Fred archly.

'Damn right I will,' said Lothar glumly.

'Maybe you'll get Luftwaffe, Lothar, although I can't imagine any plane getting off the ground with you on it,' said Gerhardt laughing. Lothar leapt on his friend and started pummelling him in the stomach. This only made Gerhardt imitate the sound of an aeroplane crashing. The sound of the laughter suddenly stopped but the two boys continued wrestling. Lothar finally felt someone tapping his back with a stick.

'What the h…?' said Lothar turning sharply.

Above him stood Haag. His face was twisted into a snarl. He glared at the two young men with an undisguised malevolence. Gerhardt and Lothar leapt up from the bed and stood to attention. The others had already done so.

Haag pointed his stick under the chin of Gerhardt and said, 'You.' He then turned around and tapped Manfred on the chest. 'And you. Come this way.'

Manfred and Gerhardt looked at one another. Memories of their earlier misdemeanours returned, and they followed Haag to the office of the colonel. It felt like déjà vu. Haag knocked on the door and then entered.

The surprise for both could not have been greater. Sitting in the place of the colonel was Rommel. Both men immediately saluted him. Rommel made a half-hearted salute back and then ushered them forward.

'Names?'

'Brehme, Herr General.'

'Kroos, Herr General.'

Rommel studied them for a few moments. Then he spoke. 'Have you any thoughts on where you would like to be posted?'

'Panzer division,' said the two in unison. They glanced at one another and tried hard not to smile.

'Popular today,' said Rommel sardonically. 'We'll see about that. For the moment I have been advised by two men, whose views I trust, that your behaviour over the last sixteen weeks merits another direction.'

Manfred felt his heart sink like a rock thrown into a pool. It was unfathomable to him how the sins of the last few weeks followed him around. Surely he'd proved his worth by now.

'You've both been recommended by these men to become Fahnenjunker. You know what this means?'

It took a moment for the news to sink in. The colonel and Drexler had just endorsed their advancement to officer training.

'Yes, Herr General,' replied the two men, barely able to suppress their desire to let out a cheer.

'Very good. You can return to your quarters. Thank you and congratulations,' said Rommel.

Manfred and Gerhardt turned and left the office followed by a very unhappy looking Haag. This was not helped by the wink to him, unseen by the senior officers, from Gerhardt as they left.

The three men inside the room looked at one another. A few moments later they heard a wild cheer from the two men, who thought they were out of range.

'They seem happy,' commented Rommel with a raised eyebrow.

'They should be, Erwin,' replied the colonel.

'How old are they, Klaus?'

'They are both nineteen, I believe,' replied the colonel.

Rommel shook his head and said, almost to himself, 'So young. Are you sure they're ready, Klaus?'

'You weren't much older, Erwin, when you were leading a platoon.'

'I didn't know what I was doing,' replied Rommel.

'Yes, you did, sir.'

This was Drexler. 'I'm still alive because of this.'

Chapter Thirty-One

Ladenburg (nr. Heidelberg): April, 1941

Peter Brehme looked at his son. The emotions he had held in check before could barely be contained now. His son. A junior officer, a Fahnenjunker. He stared at him in the doorway for a few moments and, tears brimming in his eyes he said, 'Herr Fahnenjunker.'

'Father,' said Manfred, grinning. Moments later his father hugged him tightly and pulled him inside lest his emotional display be observed.

'Let me look at you,' said Brehme. What he saw overcame him. His son. Tall, strong and now a man. The grey-green uniform clung to wide shoulders and made him seem like a young god. There was something about him now: a hardness that was not there before, steeliness in his blue eyes. He was no longer a boy and Peter Brehme could not have felt prouder.

'Why didn't you tell me you were coming? I would have come for you.'

Manfred laughed and then his face became more sombre. 'Mama,' said Manfred. It was neither a statement nor a question. It was an utterance of hope in expectation of an answer he did not want to hear. His father's body seemed to sag in an instant. He looked crestfallen. Beaten.

They walked through to the drawing room. The wireless was playing Parsifal. The song of the flower maidens. His mother was sitting by the fireside staring at the flames. She didn't stir.

'Renata,' said Brehme softly.

She looked up. Her eyes were empty. There was no recognition, no welcome, no happiness at seeing her son.

'Manfred is back. He's staying with us tonight. He's an officer now.'

'I'm training, Father,' corrected Manfred, trying to smile but desperately sad. He wanted to leave. There was nothing for him here. He felt the spirit and the happiness at being home slowly creep from his skin and dissolve into the void.

His mother smiled and said absently, 'Well done.' She could have been congratulating a friend's child.

Manfred glanced at his father and saw the sadness in his eyes. Renata Brehme returned her gaze to the fireplace and the two men left her alone.

'She just sits there all day. We barely speak now.'

'The doctors?'

'What do they know? It's what happened to your grandmother.'

'But so early?' replied Manfred, unable to take in the fact that a relatively young woman could slowly lose her mind to an old person's disease.

His father couldn't speak; the desolation was clear. They walked into the dining room. Leni smiled a welcome and complimented Manfred on his uniform. They spoke for a while as Manfred told him of life at the two training camps. Life at Hannover had been more technical and academic than his initial training spell. Both he and Gerhardt had struggled initially but finally found their feet.

'And now?'

'I will go to Munster, Father,' explained Manfred. 'The Panzertruppenschule is a school for the Panzer division. It will train me and other armour officers to operate Panzers. I will meet up with Gerhardt there. He wants to be in the Panzer division with me. I hope you meet him, Father. He's a great friend. We will spend twelve weeks in basic training. This will help familiarise us with the workings of the Panzers, and with the tactics to be used when commanding tanks in the field. When I graduate, Father, I will be promoted to Oberfähnrich and sent on field probation.'

Manfred's father beamed with joy as his son spoke. 'My word, son, you will make us very proud. I wish ...' Brehme left the rest unsaid. Manfred nodded and they drank their coffee to the sound of the clock in the kitchen and Wagner in the drawing room.

Manfred walked through the town, stopping often to receive the congratulations of many townspeople; some he knew, many he did not. The town was now full of uniforms. A grey-green sea of soldiers ready to sweep away the enemy but, for the moment, spending time with lovers, worried mothers and proud fathers. There were a few black uniforms also. Manfred made his way towards the Mayer household. As he did so, he saw a familiar face in an unfamiliar uniform.

'Erich,' he shouted.

Erich turned around and broke into a big grin. The two friends embraced and then stood back to look at one another.

'You made Fahnenjunker, Manny. I'm not surprised, my friend.'

'Thanks,' said Manfred looking at the black uniform of the Waffen-SS. Manfred was also unsurprised by this choice.

'When did you join?'

'Just before you left,' explained Erich. 'I couldn't say anything. I want to become an officer like you, but I'll have to spend a year in the ranks. Then, if they think me good enough, they'll send me to the Junkerschule near Munich.'

'They're bound to take you, Erich,' laughed Manfred.

'I hope so, but I am going to make sure there is no doubt,' said Erich, a knowing look on his face.

'How do you mean?' asked Manfred.

'I've been visiting your friend Mayer. He's well connected. I'm paying much attention to his daughter. You remember Anja?'

Manfred stopped walking and looked at Erich to see if he was joking. He wasn't. Manfred felt empty as he looked at his friend, his rival. A surge of hatred rose in his chest and then, as quickly as it came, it went, as he realised his friend was looking at him strangely.

'Is everything all right, Manny?'

'Fine. I was just on my way to Herr Mayer's house now.'

Erich looked at him and seemed to realise what had happened. He turned and said coldly, 'Me, too.'

The two walked side by side to the door of Mayer's house. Erich looked at Manfred and smiled suddenly. 'Hey do you remember …?

'Yes,' said Manfred. But the memory of what they had done disgusted him now. He wanted to obliterate that night and what had happened to Kahn from his mind.

Erich knocked on the door. It was answered by the family maid. She led the two friends into the drawing room. Mayer looked up and immediately set his newspaper down.

'Manfred,' he exclaimed in delight. 'This is a wonderful surprise.' He regarded the young man for a moment and then congratulated him on his advancement. 'I will call Anja. I'm sure she will be very happy to see you.'

226

Manfred sensed Erich was not so delighted by this. The two of them sat down as Mayer went to find his daughter. Before they had chatted easily but now there was silence between them. Both looked straight ahead at the door.

A few minutes later, the door opened. Anja burst in and looked excitedly at Manfred. She was clearly delighted by the visit.

'Manfred, I can't believe it.'

Manfred rose and she was able to look at him in his uniform. Erich rose more slowly. He may as well have not been in the room. He realised this with a surge of anger.

Manfred stared into the green eyes of Anja and realised he needed to say something, but his mind was spinning.

'I've been promoted,' he stammered at last.

'Father told me,' said Anja, oblivious to Manfred's nervousness.

'He's done well,' said Erich paternalistically. 'I knew he would, Anja. I'm proud of him.'

Manfred reddened slightly but not from embarrassment. It was anger. Erich was paying him a compliment and patronising him at the same time. At that moment he wanted to kill Erich. He wanted him out of the room so he could be alone with Anja.

They all sat down and Manfred had the chance to talk about his experience at the training camp. Erich listened, clearly unhappy at the turn of events. It seemed to Manfred that Anja was not interested in his friend. The thought that the two of them could have been sweethearts was more than he could bear. However, on this evidence, it did not seem to be the case. If anything, Anja's reaction to him suggested Erich was unwelcome. In one sense, he was glad to know the situation now, even if he knew it would also cause him to feel jealous while he was away at training. But his friendship with Erich was now under threat.

He and Erich tacitly agreed to leave the Mayer household at the same time. There had been no opportunity to speak to Anja alone, no chance to say what he was feeling or ask if he could write. This was frustrating and meant that Erich had a clear field until he returned from training. Manfred hoped his intuition was correct, that she was not interested in his friend. For a moment Manfred wondered if he could be so described now.

He looked once more at Anja. Her green eyes had become moist with sadness; the fragile beauty ripped Manfred's heart apart. How desperately he wanted to be with her. Anger welled up inside him. Anger towards his friend but, even more, towards the enemy that denied him what he so desperately wanted. He saw Erich looking at him. There was no mistaking the hint of triumph in his face.

Erich and Manfred had met as friends, but their parting was colder. Both sensed a shadow lay between them. This saddened Manfred but not as much as he thought it might. He knew that they had been growing apart for some time. Manfred had no problem with the SS. But it seemed to him that Erich had chosen the easy option. Was Erich trying to avoid the front line? He doubted if even the SS could avoid fighting, but it did offer the possibility for his friend to operate closer to home. This would potentially keep him near Anja and away from the fighting to come.

Manfred walked back towards his house. A light breeze blew in his face. He barely acknowledged the people saluting him. He couldn't wait to be back behind closed doors. And then he thought of his mother. Just one night, he thought. I can manage that. He pulled the coat up around his face and strode forward as if heading in to battle unarmed.

Chapter Thirty-Two

Munster, Lower Saxony: April, 1941

The train broke through a clump of trees and crossed over a bridge. The River Oertze roared below the bridge. Gerhardt and Manfred looked with excitement through the window at the small town of Munster coming into view. The town had one of the largest army garrisons in the country. This one was primarily dedicated to the Panzertruppenschule I, the tank training school. It would be their home for the next dozen weeks as the army educated them about the workings of a Panzer, and how to command tanks in the field.

Tanks were dotted around the field in front of the large white buildings. Manfred and Gerhardt's eyes were glued to these fearsome machines driving at speed across the countryside. They were dark in colour, which made them seem almost demonic. Soon they would receive their camouflage colours.

'My God, imagine facing those monsters,' exclaimed Manfred.

'I'm glad we're German,' replied Gerhardt laughing. 'I have never seen anything like them.'

The train pulled into the station and the two friends, along with other Fahnenjunkers, were met at the entrance by an elderly man wearing a uniform. Manfred glanced at Gerhardt and raised his eyebrows. The two friends smiled, and they followed the elderly man. Soon the group of twenty were on the back of the army truck and en route to the training camp.

Sergeant Krauss looked at the recruits. There was a faint smile on his lips. He turned to the tank beside him and patted the armour at the front.

'Tell me,' he asked, 'what do you feel when you look at this vehicle?'

A few of the recruits called out various thoughts: pride, awe, excitement. Manfred listened to them and then he said quietly, 'Fear.'

Krauss looked at the group and said, 'Who said that?' Manfred held his hand up. 'Step forward so I can see you.' Manfred did as he was ordered. Krauss walked up to him. 'Brehme, Sergeant Krauss.' He was standing to attention, eyes directly ahead.

'At ease,' said Krauss. He looked away from Manfred and to the rest of the group. Without saying anything else he walked along the line and back.

'Fear, he said, and he's right; the killing power of a tank is immense. Ours and theirs. Look at this Panzer Mark III. Not even our latest model. You're lucky. We've had a few arrive in Munster. This supersedes Panzers One and Two. Some of our boys are using Czech tanks. These aren't much better than machine guns on wheels. This will be your tank until the Mark IV is ready. You will get to know this tank. It will become your brother, your sister, your lover. It will become part of you.'

He hit the armour again with his stick. It made the sound of a dull clang rather than the light tinny sound of thin metal.

'You are lucky. This tank is the best. It's better than any other tank

230

you will face. This is twenty tonnes of beauty and death. It can hit tanks from a longer range.' He pointed to the gun. 'This is a fifty-millimetre gun. We will be shipping these out to North Africa soon. The tanks against you only have a thirty-seven-millimetre gun. Along with the thirty-millimetre-thick armour, it means they must be beside you before they can do any damage. Trust me, if the enemy gets that close to you then you deserve to die.'

This brought a few nervous laughs from the recruits.

'You will have stopped them by this point, or our eighty-eights will have done the job for you,' continued Krauss amidst the laughter. 'If not, you'll almost certainly be dead.'

This was said almost as an afterthought, but it worked in quietening down the recruits.

'Yes, these machines are deadly, and you should be scared. But think about this: the British know this too. They know in a straight fight, we win. So, they won't want a straight fight. They'll run, they'll hide, they'll do anything to avoid a firefight. This is our advantage. They will fear us. They will fear what these monsters can do. My friends, I am afraid of what these things can do. My job is to make you and these machines one. They must become an extension of you like your arm or your leg or, most importantly of all, your brain. Do you understand?'

'Yes, sir,' shouted the group as one.

Krauss looked at them and nodded slowly. Then after a few moments, when the only sounds Manfred could hear were the songs of birds, the beat of his heart and the breeze echoing in their ears, he added, 'Good. Because if you don't understand what I'm saying, then this monster, this death machine, this tank will become your coffin.'

Part 7: Britain 1941

Chapter Thirty-Three

Thursley, Surrey: April, 1941

The sun rose, apparently. Then it disappeared behind a cloud and refused to come out for the next few hours. Danny looked up disgustedly.

'British weather. What I'd give for a bit of sunshine.'

The time was coming when he would miss the grey-cold climate of his home. But that was the future.

'What'll we do today?' he asked no one in particular.

Arthur had been giving the matter some serious thought and proposed a solution. Danny grinned and suggested they should run it by Corporal Lawrence.

'Already have,' came the reply.

'And?'

The tank trundled slowly over the common. A head popped out from the turret. The reward for this foolhardy action was to feel the rain batter its face. Seconds later, the head disappeared back into the tank turret uttering an oath. Onwards the tank trundled, oblivious to the puddles and the mud.

'We should call the tank, "Pig". It bloody loves this weather,' said Arthur, wiping the rain off his face.

'You're not such a big fan of the rain, I take it?' replied Danny, down below. He was manning the machine gun but was likely to be unemployed unless the local deer came armed with anti-tank guns.

'No, I'm bleedin' not,' growled Arthur.

'We need the rain. How do things grow, otherwise?' pointed out Danny reasonably.

'Go on back to the sticks, country boy,' replied Arthur. The tank seemed to dive at that point into a large pothole. 'Bloody hell, what was that?'

He was told they were going through a ditch. The tank suddenly reared up again, throwing Arthur backwards, much to his chagrin. The laughter of the other men was as much sympathy as Arthur was ever going to get. He rubbed the back of his head and continued to grouse as they advanced.

There were five men in the tank. They were still in training, so roles were rotated each day. Three people sat in the compact turret of the A13. The commander, a gunner and the wireless operator.

'Are we nearing our objective?' shouted Arthur, who was the gunner. His position offered no hatch and his only view of what lay ahead was through the narrow aperture of his gun sight. As the tank bumped around so much, he had little idea of where they were.

'Why don't you get your arse up top and see for yourself?' shouted Corporal Phil Lawrence, who was the commander of the tank on this day. Lawrence, much to the delight of Danny and Arthur, had joined them at Thursley a couple of weeks previously having had a request to join the Royal Tank Regiment accepted.

'I did. It's too wet,' pointed out Arthur. 'What if we come across an Italian tank?'

236

This brought a volley of abuse from the boys below. Reluctantly, Arthur opened the turret again and looked out. The rain had eased off to a mild drizzle. Droplets fell from his steel helmet.

There was a shout from below, 'Well?'

'Just up ahead. I'll have to open the gate,' replied Arthur. He climbed out of the turret and opened a wooden farm gate originally intended to keep hostile cattle or sheep at bay. The tank followed Arthur through the gate onto a road. Across the field was their destination. It was a pub: the Fox and Hound.

Five men emerged from the top of the tank and jogged towards the pub.

'Do you think it's all right to leave it there?' asked Danny as he entered the pub.

'Leave it out,' said Arthur. 'Even Jerry wouldn't invade on a day like this. Mine's a bitter, as you asked.' The others laughed and called out their orders to Danny who strode towards the bar. The barmaid sized up Danny and turned her smile on full beam. She was probably twice Danny's age but that didn't matter, she thought. There had been plenty like Danny before. There would be again. She never could resist a man in uniform. She leaned forward giving Danny an eyeful of her ample bust.

'What can I do for you?'

Danny smiled and said, 'Your smile is enough, darling, but now that you mention it, five halves of bitter.'

'Cheeky, I've got my eye on you.'

'And I've got my eye on you, love,' said Danny with a wink. The other locals at the bar roared their approval at the exchange.

'Got a live one there, Mildred,' shouted one.

Danny brought the drinks back in two relays. 'Thanks for the help,' he said sardonically.

'Didn't want to cramp your style,' said Arthur.

Danny glanced back at Mildred and waved before turning back to his friends, and replied, 'More your generation, Arthur.'

A gentle clip round the back of the head was Danny's reward. The five comrades savoured their half pints. They knew that training was at an end. It was only a matter of time before they would be posted to a theatre of conflict. Opinions varied on where this would be.

'Greece,' said Lawrence. 'Has to be. They're an ally and they've been invaded. Unless we support them, how do we expect to get other allies?'

'Good point,' agreed Arthur. 'You should be a politician. They're the damn fools that took us out of Africa when we were minutes away from kicking the 'Eyeties' out. Now look.'

The two men looked at Danny. He was shaking his head in a manner they had grown used to and to respect.

'Looks like the child disagrees,' said Lawrence.

'He just wants to be playing with his toys,' continued Arthur.

Danny grinned. 'I like the big toy outside. Never had anything like that when I was growing up.'

'Let me know when you grow up,' said Arthur, as his six-foot-two friend collected the glasses and brought them back to the bar for a refill.

'Here, here,' said Lawrence, 'he's back on the pull.'

When Danny returned from the bar with another round, he looked at their eager faces and said, 'Yeah, it could be Greece but I'm with Arthur. It has to be North Africa.'

Lawrence looked glum. He knew the boys were right.

'We were all but home and dry there. It's like Stoke going one nil up and then pulling Stanley Matthews off because they think the game's over. We could have had Africa sorted and then dealt with bloody Greece. Old Adolf would have been surrounded on all sides.'

'He's no Denis Compton, though,' said Arthur puffing on his pipe.

'Who?' asked Lawrence.

'Matthews.'

'Get out of it,' replied Lawrence, a native of that jewel in the Midlands.

'I don't see Matthews coming in at number three for Surrey, any time soon,' guffawed Arthur.

Danny ignored Arthur and replied to Lawrence. 'Like it or not, we've not got enough men out there now. They need to cut Jerry off from all that oil.'

'Hark at him,' said Arthur. 'Fifteen weeks or so of training and he's a proper little general now.'

The other two men in the group who were around Danny's age remained quiet through all this nonsense. Jim Donnelly and Will Anderson sat looking on in silence. They were happy to listen to their fellow recruits. Donnelly was small in stature with a gap-toothed smile. He operated the radio while Anderson, a mechanic by trade, doubled on the machine gun and made repairs when the tank broke down, which was a frequent occurrence.

'You're quiet,' said Arthur, looking at Anderson. 'Is the tank all right?'

Anderson wiggled his hands to indicate that this was a fifty-fifty answer.

'What's wrong?' asked Danny.

'Engine sounded ropey back there,' said Anderson. 'I'll take a look when I finish this.'

'Great,' said Lawrence. 'Might have been an idea to say this before we parked the damn thing outside a pub.'

Arthur made a point of noisily slapping the palms of his hands on his face.

Late afternoon, the sky was still hidden under a black pall-like cloud. Bob Owen stood by the road leading into the barracks and watched several tanks pass him by. He looked at them with a sense of marvel and fear. Every night he had the same dream: his bullet-riddled body falling underneath the wheels of the tank. The crack of his bones would wake him up gasping for breath.

Nightmares aren't just for the night. Each passing day increased his sense of dread. Soon he would be inside one of these beasts. Facing him would be an enemy inside a better-made tank, intent on killing him. It was madness. How could any sane person step inside one of those death machines and drive happily towards certain death? He felt the tears sting his eyes as he looked at each tank. Quickly he wiped his eyes free of the incriminating evidence of his cowardice. He thought of Danny. Over the last few weeks, he found his envy of Danny turning more bitter.

There seemed to be no fear in his friend. Danny's nature, his character, had adapted to, rather than been changed by the training. Gone was the boy he had travelled down with. He seemed not so much a man, now, as manly. His natural gregariousness and good humour remained, but it was enhanced with a quiet assurance about what he was there to do and a confidence that he could do it. There was a certainty about his role in a tank, a wider understanding of tactics and a courage that remained beyond Bob's grasp.

Today, like every day since his arrival at the army training camp, Bob lived in dread that his fear would be perceived by his comrades. He would be seen for what he was: a coward. Unmanly. He had not yet managed to develop an independent life outside himself and assimilate his identity within the group. He was an outsider, and it was becoming more apparent by the day.

How could he face the enemy? How could he face the aggressive artillery fire, the deadly crack of bullets, the crushing terror of tanks when he could barely bring himself to be incarcerated in one during training? Rain began to fall gently creating rivulets running down his face. He stood looking out at the field with the tanks and the trucks arriving with soldiers from other camps. All around him men sprinted for cover from the rain.

'My bet is we'll be out there by summer,' said Arthur. His eyes were on Anderson, outside in the rain, looking at the engine of the A13.

'Out where?' asked Danny, smiling.

'Don't start that again,' replied Lawrence. 'I hope Will's all right.'

'Yeah, it's a bit wet out there,' noted Donnelly. Unlike the others, he was genuinely concerned for his friend's welfare.

'Who cares if he gets wet. It's the damn tank I want sorted,' laughed Lawrence. A minute later he saw Anderson give the thumbs up.

Lawrence nodded and looked at the rest of the boys. 'That's us. Come on we better move it.'

The journey back took place without incident. As they arrived, they saw several three tonners arriving with soldiers. Lawrence called down to Danny and Anderson below, 'Something's up. We've got company.'

'How do you mean?' asked Danny.

'Looks like the whole battalion is here.'

'Interesting,' responded Danny.

The tank pulled into the allotted space and the crew hopped out. The drizzle was making up its mind and becoming something heavier and even more unpleasant. Danny spotted Bob standing under a tree smoking a cigarette. He jogged over to his friend.

'Guarding the tanks?'

'Something like that,' replied Bob in a neutral, almost unrecognisable voice. They looked at one another. Bob was performing a role in front of his friend now. All the world is a stage, and Bob was acting a part. He wasn't a person any longer but a perspective. He hoped that the mask he showed would soon become his reality. He suspected it wouldn't. Danny would be the first to see this; perhaps he had already.

'What were you up to today?' asked Danny.

'Same thing you did yesterday. At the garage learning about ignition systems, crankshafts and clutch plates.'

'Exciting, wasn't it? You must be an expert now,' said Danny with a grin.

'All over it,' lied Bob.

Danny looked at the soldiers streaming between the trucks and the barracks. Something was in the offing.

'Do you know what's happening?'

Bob looked at Danny with a raised eyebrow; a sardonic smile spread over his face.

'Time to become heroes.'

Chapter Thirty-Four

Commanding Officer Lieutenant-Colonel Dinham Drew looked out at his men as they stood in ranks in the parade ground. The rain beat softly down on his black beret. He preferred to wear this when addressing the men even if it offered precious little protection against the British weather.

Drew was in his forties but would easily have passed for much older. His age stood in contrast to the youth of the men he commanded. He seemed like a father figure to the regiment: a father figure in the Victorian mould. Discipline was his guiding principle. Flouting army regulations, poor turn out on the parade ground, half-hearted drilling were routinely punished. This was not just a moral crusade; Drew believed discipline was a bulwark against fear, against incompetence and most importantly, weakness. It would save the lives of his men. Nothing mattered more to him than victory but at the least human cost.

For nearly a minute Drew said nothing. Danny was at the front and tried to read his face. He felt a shiver travel along his arm and down his back that had nothing to do with the rain. All around him stood the men of the RTR. To a man they were holding their breath.

The parade ground was eerily silent. Finally, Drew spoke in a voice that came not just from another caste but from another century.

'Are we all here?' he asked a staff officer at his side. The officer nodded.

'At ease, men. I called this meeting because I've got some news for you. I shan't beat about the bush. You may be hearing rumours that we are going abroad. This shouldn't be a surprise. We need you where it matters. For security reasons I can't say where, so don't ask. Put it this way, you won't be in England this Christmas. It's time to go to war. However, it does mean you can have embarkation leave of seven days. Married men first. They probably need it.'

'No, we don't,' shouted Arthur from the back.

Everyone laughed, including Drew.

'Be that as it may, details will be posted soon. This is it. This is what we've been training for. Jerry has been taking pot shots at us long enough. Now it's our turn. Good luck, men.'

And that was it. They were going to war. Danny turned to look at Bob. His friend was shivering in the rain. His face had turned white.

'I can't do this, Danny.'

Bob was shaking. Physically shaking. Danny wasn't sure what to say. The two friends were in Danny's tent. No one could hear what Bob was saying, his voice barely audible. Tears welled in Bob's eyes.

'I'll never survive. What'll happen to Beth? My baby?'

'Enough of this, Bob. I'll look after you. We'll all look after one another.'

'Haven't you been listening?' said Bob angrily. 'It's one thing to take on a bunch of Italians but the Germans are different. They killed my dad in the end. They'll kill me; wait'll you see.'

'No one's saying it'll be easy, but this is what the training is meant to do. You'll see when the time comes.'

Bob looked at Danny incredulously then shook his head. Danny waited for Bob to say something as he was out of ammunition on his own pep talk.

'Not sure you've been listening, Danny-boy. It's one thing to learn how to drive a tank, master its weapons and maintain them. But if you can only see eighty yards in front and the guns that you're up against can knock you out at eight hundred yards, or more if it's one of their anti-tank guns, then no amount of training will help. Do you understand? The odds are stacked against us making it through, Danny. It just takes one mistake from us or, more likely, a well-trained Jerry and we're buggered, mate. Well and truly buggered. We're cannon fodder, mate. That's all the likes of us are.'

This was difficult to argue with. Danny had also thought along similar lines but usually stopped himself before it became the kind of spiral downwards to a dark place where no light or prospect of escape existed. Bob was falling headlong into such a place, and he hadn't finished yet.

'You realise we have to be halfway up their arse before we can kill them. How the hell does that work? What do we do? Shout, "Oi, look over there," then calmly drive up and take a pot shot? Well, Danny, I can tell you it ain't that easy. They expect us to die. They expect us to keep going at them until our tanks are climbing over our dead bodies and the Jerry has run out of ammo. It will be just like the last war, trust me. They've learned nothing. I'm not having it, Danny.'

'Don't do anything silly, Bob.'

'Why not? Look what happened to Harn. He'll spend the war in a warm, comfy jail, just you see. But he'll live. They'll let him out. Sure, he'll have a bad name but who'll care? Who's the idiot here?'

'He won't live if Hitler wins, Bob.'

* * *

Lieutenant Greening assembled the men from his section which included Danny, Arthur and Bob. Greening was a former cavalry officer who had transferred to the RTR. Although he was nicknamed 'Lord' Greening by the men, he was well liked. In his late twenties, he radiated composure and competence. His wavy blonde hair and dandified appearance might have counted against him had he not proved himself fitter than the majority over assault courses, an expert marksman and a sympathetic leader.

He was accepted by old sweats in the battalion, the ones who had survived France and the Dunkirk evacuation. This was more than could be said for new arrivals such as Danny. They had yet to prove themselves. This meant they were either ignored or generally disregarded. Greening mingled easily with the men, making sure to have a word with everyone. He sat down with Danny and Arthur.

'Chaps, you've probably heard me chatting to the others by now. I won't add much to what old "Detention" has announced,' said Greening. This caused both men to laugh. Another reason to like Greening was his use of Colonel Drew's nickname. If anything, Drew was harder on his officers than on the men.

'Perry, as a married man, you'll be able to go on embarkation leave from tomorrow. As there are so few married men, Shaw, you can also go if you like. We just need to keep a balance of fifty-fifty going and staying. You and Owen can go back together if you like.'

Danny grinned and said, 'I might try London for a night. Never really been before, sir.'

Arthur replied, 'Here we go. I suppose you'll be looking for a place to stay?'

'Now that you mention it.'

'Told you,' said Arthur, looking at Greening.

'I'll leave you gentlemen then. You seem to have matters in hand.'

246

Greening left them to speak to Bob. Danny looked at his friend. Bob was laughing nervously with the lieutenant. He turned to Arthur and said, 'So you'll put me up then?'

'You can meet the missus and the family but one word. If you so much as look at my little girl, then it ain't Hitler you need worry about.'

Danny looked affronted. 'What kind of man do you take me for? She's only a child. I saw the picture of them.'

'That was taken four years ago,' said Arthur grimly.

'Oh,' said Danny. 'That would make her?'

'Sixteen. I'll be standing guard outside the room, sonny boy.'

'Leave it out, Arthur. I'll climb in through the window,' laughed Danny. He received a clip for his trouble, which only made him laugh more.

A few minutes later, Greening came back to Danny and Arthur. This was a surprise as both thought he had finished with them.

'Parry, Shaw,' said Greening, 'I was wondering if you would like to come with me for a few minutes. Where is Lawrence?' Danny called over to Phil Lawrence who was chatting to Jim Donnelly. Lawrence jogged over and the three men followed Greening.

As they walked, Greening talked about commonplace things. This was a surprise as Danny had thought the lieutenant wanted to talk to them about Bob. It was no secret in the section that Bob was on the very edge of his emotions.

It soon became apparent they were heading towards the officer's mess. Once inside, Greening led them down a long corridor towards the office of Colonel Drew. A quick knock on the door and then they entered an outer office. Two young secretaries had desks here. One of them told Greening to go on through.

Lieutenant-Colonel Drew glanced up as the men entered. He put his pen down and rose from his seat and walked around his desk.

'Stand at ease, men. So, you're Stan Shaw's boy.'

Danny nearly collapsed when he heard this.

'Yes, sir,' he stammered by way of reply.

'I knew him from the last lot. Good man. I've heard good things about you Shaw.' Danny said nothing but looked straight ahead. 'Corporal Lawrence, Private Perry, thank you for joining us also. I have some news for the three of you which may come as surprise and perhaps not a happy one.'

Drew looked at Danny and the two other men for a moment and then said, 'Well, as you've heard, we're pulling out soon. The last few weeks we've been assessing the men.'

Here it comes, thought Danny. It is about Bob, after all. It wasn't though.

'War is a terrible business,' said Drew. Danny was sure few would disagree. 'Many of our boys will die. We've trained you as best we can, but this is the reality. Our regiments in North Africa have had a bit of a tough time of late. We need to supplement them with men like you. I've agreed to transfer you over to the 6th Royal Tank Regiment as they need more tank men. This will not affect your leave, of course.'

Danny felt himself breathe a sigh of relief but then he thought of Bob. What would his friend say? The guilt began to envelop him. He'd promised Beth he'd look after Bob. Instead, he was going to be forced to abandon him.

'Sir, what about Private Owen?' asked Danny. 'We came down together from the same village.'

Did Drew's face cloud over? It was just a moment. A look. A slight shift in the body. The colonel nodded.

'Very well, Shaw. I shall see what I can do.'

Chapter Thirty-Five

London: April, 1941

Danny and Arthur walked along the platform at Waterloo Station together. It was mobbed. Hundreds of soldiers had also disembarked from the train and were being met by wives, sweethearts or family. All around them, soldiers were being embraced. The noise was deafening. People were shouting, women crying, men laughing, dogs barking. Danny swivelled around as he walked, unable to believe what he was hearing and seeing.

'Come along country boy, my Edith will be here somewhere,' said Arthur. Then he spotted his wife and pointed. 'There she is.'

Edith Perry was a woman in her mid-thirties. She seemed older than Arthur. When she saw Arthur, she ran towards him, and they embraced. Danny stood beside the couple awkwardly. Further up were two young girls that Danny guessed were Arthur's daughters. The eldest was unquestionably the one Arthur had mentioned. She and her sister, who was a year younger, seemed faintly embarrassed by the open affection displayed by their parents.

Finally, and a little reluctantly, they joined their parents and embraced. Then Arthur stood back and introduced Danny.

'Girls, this is my chum, Danny. Danny, this is my missus, Edith, but you can call her Mrs Perry.'

Edith punched Arthur gently on the arm and said, 'Don't you listen to him, Danny, come here.'

Moments later Danny was taken in a bear hug by Edith, and she was just as strong as she looked.

'This beautiful young woman,' said Arthur proudly, 'is Vera.'

Danny shook hands awkwardly with Vera. Arthur's daughter was the image of him but with her mother's height and robust build. She smiled at Danny, clearly pleased by what she saw. Danny caught a warning glance from Arthur, but it was done with a smile. Edith, however, had decided on first meeting that Danny was ideal son-in-law material.

Arthur's other daughter was Sally. She seemed to have more of her mother in her. Dark eyes and mousy hair. She was skinny and looked younger than her fifteen years. Danny grinned at both girls. He kept his compliments on the safe side of flattery but was more effusive in Edith's direction, which had Arthur rolling his eyes and his wife already planning the wedding.

'You can stay with us as long as you like, young man.'

'It'll just be the night, Mrs Perry.'

'You can cut out the Mrs for a start; don't you listen to Arthur. Call me Edith.'

'Thanks, Edith, just one night. I have to go back home and see my family,' replied Danny.

'So you should. I'm glad to hear that family is important to you,' said Edith and looked at Arthur meaningfully. Arthur was, of course, unaware of the significance of the comments. His face fell into that state of confusion most chaps feel when they realise their better half has communicated something of great importance and they are, as ever, on a completely different wavelength.

They walked along the concourse of the platform, dodging soldiers, family and porters. Outside the station, banked against the entrance, was the familiar sight of sandbags. The grey-iron sky was blotted by the barrage balloons of a city at war. Overhead they heard the low moan of plane engines. There was no siren, however. One of ours, thought Danny.

The bus ride to Lewisham took twenty minutes. It was mid-morning when Danny stepped into the Perry household. The house was a red-brick Victorian terrace house on a street with a few hundred others that looked identical.

'You'll have to kip on the settee,' said Arthur as they walked through the front gate.

'It'll be more comfortable than what I'm used to,' pointed out Danny.

'Ain't that the truth.'

Inside, the house was small but spotlessly clean and Danny was made to feel like one of the family. However, he also realised he was not one of the family and, having deposited his belongings, withdrew to go sightseeing in London. The two girls seemed disappointed by this news, as did Edith. Danny was amused by the smile of satisfaction on Arthur's face, though. He promised to be back in time for tea.

In truth, Danny was delighted to be free. He had not had a moment to himself in over four months. As badly as he wanted to see his family again, he had been looking forward to this afternoon for a long time.

He took a bus to Trafalgar Square. He'd seen photographs of the square, dominated by Nelson's column and the Landseer lions. His first sight of the square made his heart swell. He walked through past the column, scattering pigeons hither and thither. Service personnel, men and women, were all around him. He took a seat and happily watched the world pass around him.

It was early afternoon and he began to feel peckish. He'd hardly spent any money in his time at the various camps so, on a whim, he decided to treat himself. He walked past Charing Cross along the Strand in search of Simpson's. As he dodged his way along the crowded street, he was surprised to find that lots of people doffed their hats to him. Children came over and saluted him. He saluted back with a broad grin. After a five-minute walk, he finally found himself outside the restaurant.

Simpson's-in-the Strand had been visited by his father over twenty years before. It felt like a thing for him to do. He knew it was one of the oldest restaurants in London. He suspected it might also be one of the more expensive. He didn't care. Life was for living and the time left for him to do so had a huge question mark hanging over it.

The Strand was busy with cars, office workers and servicemen. Danny strolled along wide-eyed, past the Savoy and finally came across Simpson's. The archway with the chess mosaic was impressive. He'd been to restaurants in Lincoln, but nothing like this. If this was what it looked like outside, it made him nervous to think about the interior, the people, the serving staff even. He took a deep breath and entered. All at once he saw people look at him.

They nodded to him. And smiled.

The interior more than matched the entrance. The walls were wood-panelled, rather like those at Cavendish Hall. Descending gracefully from the ceiling were several chandeliers. All around the room were well-dressed people and officers from the different services. At first glance, there were few men from the ranks.

Not surprisingly the price of the food matched the décor. Danny gulped as he saw an attractive waitress come over, beating another waitress, he noted happily, in a race to his table. The young woman was about Danny's age, perhaps a little older. She wore her dark hair tied back in a bun and her black dress fit snugly over her slender frame. Accompanying the more than satisfactory appearance was a warm smile.

'Hello,' said the waitress, 'have you had a chance to choose something?'

Danny smiled up and said, 'Perhaps just a tea and a sandwich.'

He pointed to what he wanted. The waitress smiled knowingly and took the order. He felt his cheeks turn red as he thought about how cheap he must seem to her. Still, she hadn't appeared that snooty. Rather than worry about how he appeared, he decided to relax and enjoy his moment dining with his betters.

Around ten minutes later the waitress returned with a plate laden with sandwiches. Danny looked from the plate to the young woman in shock.

'Did I order all that?'

The waitress smiled and said, 'No, but you looked hungry.'

'Thank you,' said Danny, raising the tone of his voice slightly in query.

The waitress smiled and took Danny up on the implied invite to offer her name, 'Abigail. My friends call me Abby.'

'Thanks, Abby.'

'Are you around for long?' asked Abby.

'No, I'm heading home tomorrow for a few days, then back here next week. I'm on embarkation leave.'

Abby looked disappointed. So many men leaving to fight. It broke her heart to see them. All were so young: some her age, many younger. Something in her face must have registered her sadness.

'Bloody war,' said Danny.

'I know. Good luck.'

'Thanks, I'll be back next week. Wednesday. Will you be working?'

'Yes, maybe I'll see you?' said Abby before adding, 'I like dancing.'

Danny laughed. 'I need a good teacher.'

Chapter Thirty-Six

Little Gloston: April, 1941

Danny had written every week since leaving for army training. However, the rapidity of the news on embarkation had meant he'd not been able to write and tell his parents he was returning home. Telegrams were forbidden.

Mid-afternoon the next day, Danny found himself disembarking from the bus and walking towards the family cottage. Ahead he could see the orange glow of the forge. He could make out his father and Kate Shaw. It wasn't until he was a dozen yards from the front gate that his father registered his imminent arrival. His father stopped and stared at him. Danny stopped too. Then he broke into a grin. He could see his father struggling with his emotions. Stoicism won, just. He dropped the hammer he was holding onto the dusty floorboards and walked out of the forge.

'Kate, we have a visitor.'

'Who?' shouted a voice from inside the cottage.

'Come out and see for yourself, you lazy bint,' shouted Danny, standing against the garden gate.

A scream came from the kitchen and, moments later, Kate Shaw was running along the garden path, tears in her eyes. She nearly knocked Danny over in her eagerness to embrace him. Stan Shaw ambled over to them and put his arms around his wife and son. His stoicism finally crumbled when he saw the stripe. He looked his son in the eye and then the tears fell freely. White lines streaked his soot-soaked cheeks.

'Good to have you back, son,' said Stan, finally.

Danny cleared the plate and looked expectantly at his mother.

'Don't they feed you down there?' said his mother, laughing as she rose to replenish his plate.

'Army food?' said Danny querulously.

'Don't remind me,' said Stan. Danny eyed him for a moment hoping that his father would talk more about that time. Nothing was added, however. A refilled plate was put in front of Danny, and he polished it off eagerly.

'When did Tom leave?'

'Two weeks ago, but we still don't know where.'

'I haven't heard anything either. Most think we're going to North Africa.'

'Surely we've already beaten the Italians,' said Kate.

Danny and Stan exchanged a look and then Stan said, 'The Germans arrived; it changed things. It won't be over for a while.' There was no disguising the catch in his voice as he said this.

None of this helped Kate Shaw's mood. Danny sensed this and said, 'Don't worry, Mum. I'll be protected by an inch or two of armour.'

This seemed to make her happier, but Danny didn't need to look at his father to know this was hardly going to be enough against some of the big anti-tank guns they would face.

After dinner, Danny and his father went for a walk. They walked past the village shop and St Bartholomew's church towards the wood. Returning to the place that had been his home for nearly nineteen years felt like the closing of a chapter. Forever. He saw the village with the eyes of an adult rather than the guileless youth who had left a few weeks earlier. Memories piled on memories like dishes in a kitchen, ready to spill over and splinter into a thousand pieces. How could he have not seen how *small* the village was?

Yet everything passes; even when it seems that time goes very slowly, the day comes when you realise how life, at some point, has accelerated in a flash without telling you. Danny felt this and it saddened him more than he could say. He knew when he left to return to the army, he would be leaving more than the village behind. He would be bidding farewell to his childhood, its careless freedoms and rebellions. The thought frightened him. Just for a moment he wanted to run home and hide.

At the edge of the wood, they found a tree stump and both sat down. Stan lit his pipe and smoked it in silence. Danny felt oddly comforted by this. The two of them stared back at the village and watched as orange lights lit up the dark blue of the evening.

'When do you leave?' asked Stan after a while.

'Late next week or early week after when everyone is back.'

Stan nodded. He looked at his son for a few moments. Then, embarrassed, he looked away.

'How do you find it? In the tank?' As ever, his father's words came out in small clumps.

'I don't mind it. We don't spend long, mind you. And we're not facing real fire. I suppose it'll feel different then.'

'It will, son, trust me.'

Danny had never heard his father speak this way. For the first time

Stan spoke of the war. He spoke for an hour, interrupted only by his sobbing. He spoke of the fear he'd felt as they drove towards the killing fire; he spoke of the men he'd killed, their terrified screams; he spoke of the men he'd fought with who died in pain, crying for their mothers, their wives, for God's loving mercy.

Danny put his arm around the former soldier when the recollection became too raw. The pain of remembrance had never left; it never would. A part of Stan did not want the scar to heal. How else would he keep alive the memory of his friends, his brother and those he had killed? Their sacrifice and his actions would have been in vain otherwise.

The price of survival was guilt.

Two days later the forge had a visitor. Lord Henry Cavendish walked in through the open door. Danny was back at work; he wouldn't have it any other way. Nor would Stan, to be fair.

Henry looked at Danny for a moment. Danny seemed to have changed physically. His wide frame had now filled out a little with muscle. There was also something else. It wasn't physical. Danny had never lacked for confidence even with the Cavendish family. Now there was an air about him. If Henry had been forced to put a name to it, he would have called it responsibility. The attractive impudence remained, but this was now allied to, even supported by, a sense of duty. Henry was surprised by how unsurprised he was by this. Already he could see how inevitable it was that he would be promoted again and again. He had an air of leadership. He always had. Henry smiled at Danny and felt a strange emptiness at the thought of what this young man, he had watched grow, would soon be asked to face.

'Lord Cavendish,' said Danny, stumped as to what else to say.

258

'Hello, Danny. They told me you were back. Sorry I wasn't around the last couple of days. Had to go to the factory.'

'I saw Mr Curtis yesterday. He told me you'd gone to Lincoln. I hope everything's all right?'

'It is, thank you. The government has made some special requests of me. Apparently one of my plants can be converted to help the war effort. I can't say much more but I had to oversee the changes with a man from the Ministry. Anyway, I wanted to see if your family could spare you for an evening. We'd love you to dine with us up at the Hall. Could you come in your uniform, Danny?'

Danny smiled and replied, 'Yes, sir.'

Henry left the forge. Danny looked at his father. Stan removed his pipe and without looking up said, 'You're going nowhere until you've finished those damn horseshoes.'

Danny rolled his eyes, picked up the hammer and said sardonically, 'Yes, sir.'

Jane Cavendish met Danny in the entrance hall, her eyes crinkling in a smile when she saw the uniform. A tear, also. 'It's wonderful to see you again. You look so handsome.'

'I always did, sure,' replied Danny, causing Jane to burst out into laughter.

'Lost none of your cheek, I see.'

'The army will never take that,' said Danny, grinning.

'I'm sure your family and friends will be happy to know that. Proud, too, I imagine.'

In fact, Danny's remaining friends in the village had all been delighted by his return and had indicated this in the good-natured abuse hurled in his direction.

Jane led Danny into the drawing room, where he found Henry

Cavendish along with Bob and Beth Owen. This was the first time he'd seen Beth since their departure and the evidence of motherhood was all too clear.

'Beth,' exclaimed Danny and immediately went to hug her. 'What happened to you?'

'You have your friend to blame,' replied Beth, much to everyone's amusement.

Henry then shook Danny's hand warmly and handed him a drink. It looked like it would be the five of them. Danny felt a twinge of disappointment. It would have been nice to see Robert and Sarah.

'I'm afraid Robert's still at school. He'll be pretty miffed at missing you all. He talks of nothing else when he's back. A proper little general.'

'I hope it's all over by the time he leaves,' commented Danny.

'I couldn't agree more,' replied Jane. 'I'm just sorry so many of you will have such a dreadful weight to carry.'

The impact of the war was obvious on the dinner. No longer was it the banquet of times past. However, Elsie still managed to excel herself with a meat pie and honeyed vegetables. The conversation was mainly of the impending arrival of baby Owen. The topic of war was avoided for the most part, a tacit pact among the men. However, the subject could not be avoided for a whole evening. At the end of the meal, Beth was driven back to her cottage just outside the village and the men retired to the drawing room for a night cap.

As Henry poured the drinks, he asked, 'I must admit, chaps, I'm under strict instructions from Robert to find out as much as possible about your training. I hope you don't mind.'

'Of course not,' laughed Danny. For the next twenty minutes, Danny happily took Henry through the events and activities of the previous few months. Bob said little but managed to make a few gentle jokes at Danny's expense, which amused the target as much as Henry.

When Danny had finished, Henry said, 'I won't ask where you're likely to be posted but I think I can guess.'

Danny and Bob exchanged glances. Thankfully Bob seemed to be more in control of his emotions. The fears of the last few months had not been apparent over the evening. The presence of Beth had perhaps acted to reassure and concentrate his mind on the job to be done. At least Danny hoped this was the case. Danny knew there would always be the mask he showed the world. The way he felt would exist, necessarily, one step removed from everyone's view. The doubts, the fears and the insecurities he felt would always be sublimated. His duty would be a shield. Bob would be the same. He would present to the world a version of himself that the world wanted to see. Danny hoped, both for him and for Bob, that when the time came, this version would win out over the true self.

'I imagine it will be hotter than England,' said Bob, with an attempt at a smile.

The evening was drawing to a close. Henry led the two men to the door. They were met there by Jane once more. Offers of a lift back to their houses were respectfully declined.

They stepped out into the night. The chill of winter was creeping into October through the nights. Walking down the path, Danny turned to look back at Cavendish Hall. He saw Sarah at the window of the library. Danny stopped momentarily. Then he nodded. She waved; then, moments later, she was gone.

Danny turned to walk again but saw Bob looking at him strangely.

'You're playing a dangerous game there, my lad,' said Bob softly. For the first time the hunted look was no longer in Bob's eyes. Instead, Danny saw his friend again. Someone who cared about him, who would fight in his corner, who had his interests at heart.

Danny shook his head. 'There's nothing going on. She's too young.'

'Be careful, Danny. They're good people but they're different.'

'Jane Cavendish was one of us,' pointed out Danny, more defensively than he would have liked.

'Jane Cavendish was the most beautiful girl in the county apparently. Still is, looking at her tonight.'

Along with her daughter, thought Danny. Bob, sensing further conversation on the topic of Sarah Cavendish would be unwelcome, wisely began to talk of other matters.

'Do you want to travel down together?' asked Bob.

'No, Bob, I want to have another night in London. I'll leave day after tomorrow.'

They parted at Danny's with a handshake and a warmth that had been missing for a few months.

Chapter Thirty-Seven

London: April, 1941

It was early afternoon. Rather than go to Arthur's house, Danny had decided to stay at the hotel on Piccadilly. He stepped into the foyer and asked if they had any vacancies. A few minutes later he was in a small sparsely furnished room. It felt like luxury to him. The bed was softer than he was used to. Initially this felt decadent, but he soon realised that he preferred a more spartan arrangement. He rose from the bed after a few minutes to freshen up. The water was cold against his skin and acted as a shock to his system. It woke him up after the early start he'd had in the morning that had begun with a lift from the farmer, Gerald McIver, into Lincoln.

Piccadilly Circus was anarchy in Danny's view. So many people, the big red buses, the cars and the horns tooting at pedestrians running across the road. Danny shook his head and laughed. It seemed another world. He looked up at the big signs advertising Bovril, Wrigley's, and Guinness. His heart swelled with pride. The feeling that he had experienced back home with his family in the valley overlooking the village coursed through him now. His thoughts turned to Sarah

Cavendish and, hard as he tried, he could not dismiss her image from his mind. His job had become clear to him when it had previously seemed abstract. He realised it was now more than a job. It was his duty.

With a final brush of his hair, he left the room and bounded down the threadbare stairs to the street. Danny made his way towards the Strand with the intention of returning to Simpson's. As he walked into the restaurant, he saw Abby. She looked for a moment in confusion at the smiling soldier. Then recognition dawned on her. She smiled and walked over to him.

'Hello, stranger.'

Danny followed her to a seat near the window. The restaurant was quieter now as luncheon had finished. Danny ordered the same sandwich dish as previously. Abby made frequent visits to him, and they chatted for as long as was possible. When he had finished his meal and paid, he walked over to Abby, who stood at the exit holding his coat.

'Are you still able to teach me how to dance?'

'Yes,' said Abby, smiling. 'What did you have in mind?'

'I read that Al Bowlly is playing at the Trocadero tonight in Elephant and Castle. Would you like to go there?'

'I'd love to. It's quite near where I live. I can meet you there. What time?'

'Is eight early enough?'

Danny spent the next few hours walking around the city. The barrage balloons overhead blocked out what little sun there was. Thankfully, the rain held off. The afternoon grey became a bayonet-black night. The moon was hidden beneath a dark shroud. Danny wondered if this would encourage enemy aircraft. He hadn't seen any today. Over the last couple of months, the frequency of attacks had decreased. The Battle of Britain long since won. He certainly hoped so.

An hour later, Danny walked out of the tube station at Elephant and Castle. He headed out onto the street and asked directions to the Trocadero. It was still too early to meet Abby. There was a pub near the station. Perfect place to kill time, thought Danny. He popped in and ordered a half pint. He still wasn't a big drinker. Quite a few of the lads in the battalion were. He avoided them. It was evens they would end up in a fight when they went out for a night.

The bar was crowded, noisy and dark. There was a sense of violence about it, too. He regretted his decision to enter but he still had an hour to kill. There were no seats, so he stayed at the bar and nursed his drink. A few people chatted to him. Finally, he drained the rest of his drink and made for the exit.

Back outside in the cold, he saw that there was still another forty minutes to kill. Just then, a siren began to wail. He looked up. The sky was garnished with white puff balls. Somewhere behind the clouds was the drone of something malevolent. Danny sprinted for the tube station as people streamed out of the pub.

A human flood poured down the steps of the tube station, headed for the platforms below. There were a few servicemen around also: Army, Navy and RAF. Danny joined a bunch of them on the platform.

'When is the train due?' he asked with a grin.

The group laughed and opened to let him stand with them. The RAF man answered, 'Blasted things are never on time.' His accent was not local.

'I haven't seen one of theirs in a while now,' said Danny motioning his head upwards. 'You blokes did a great job.'

'Thanks,' said the airman, holding out his hand. 'Dick Manning.'

'Shaw, Danny Shaw.'

The rest of the servicemen introduced themselves. They spoke in low voices to avoid being heard. Manning was shorter than Danny but well made. He had a casual confidence like Danny that the other boys in the group did not seem to have. In fact, they seemed in awe of the airman.

It was clear they were all on embarkation leave. Although none would admit as much, they were probably destined to be heading in the same direction. Airmen were increasingly being sent to patrol the Mediterranean as Britain built up its strength for the North African campaign.

Danny glanced at his watch. It was now after eight. Manning noticed Danny's frustration.

'On a promise, old fellow?'

Danny laughed. 'I wouldn't go that far. I was meant to meet someone at the Trocadero around eight.'

'Don't worry, it'll be over soon. In fact, we should be out any time now. They're probably just checking there aren't any afters.'

Manning's prediction proved to be accurate and soon they were ascending the stairs. Danny walked up with Manning. He turned to the airman and said, 'Where are you from? You don't sound like a Londoner.'

'Nor do you, old chap,' laughed Manning, which made Danny laugh. 'In point of fact, I am from London. Just not this part. How about you?'

'Lincolnshire,' replied Danny. 'We're heading out soon. Thought I might make the most of seeing the big city. I hope she shows up. I was looking forward to seeing Al Bowlly. Where are you going now?'

'Same as you, old boy. I'm going to see Al Bowlly, too. Not sure I'll be able to see him for a while.'

Danny nodded but didn't enquire further. Instead, he said, 'Maybe you can join us, Dick.'

'I'd love to. My girl is meant to be outside.'

'I hope it isn't the same one,' laughed Danny, as they stepped out onto the dark street. The windows were all blacked out and the streetlights had not yet been lit. Danny looked around him and shook his head.

'I don't know how people have put up with it.'

'No choice. It'll be a while, too. This isn't going to be over by Christmas.'

The two men walked along the Old Kent Road towards the theatre, chatting companionably. The Trocadero soon came into view, an enormous red brick building with long windows streaking the façade like tears down a face. The name of the theatre sat just above the windows. There were still no lights. However, lots of people were milling around outside and some even going in. Danny spied Abby and waved. Another young woman nearby also waved in their direction. If Abby was attractive, this young woman was like a Hollywood star.

Danny glanced wryly at his new friend.

'In my next life, I'm going to be an airman.'

Manning laughed good-naturedly.

'There are some advantages, I'll grant you.' He lit a cigarette and offered one to Danny before they separated to meet their respective dates.

'No thanks, never liked them. See you inside.'

Danny walked over to Abby and smiled. 'Thought Adolf was going to put paid to our night.'

Abby laughed. 'Take more than a pipsqueak like him.' She took his arm, and they went inside, down a wide staircase with red felt carpet. On first sight there was a large stage but no dance floor. Instead, it was a theatre with seats. This was a disappointment.

He looked at Abby and said, 'I thought there would be a dance floor, sorry.'

'We've got the aisle, haven't we?' replied Abby with a smile.

They were among the first to arrive and Danny picked out seats near the front and on the aisle. They sat down and Danny asked Abby if she wanted a drink. Just then he saw Manning with his date and waved at them. Moments later they were all together.

'Abby, this is Dick Manning, we just met down at the tube station during the air raid.'

Manning shook hands with Abby and introduced his date, Clare. The two ladies were soon chatting away as they stood by their seats. The sound of the orchestra told them that the show was to begin so they sat down.

It was a variety show. The first few acts were lucky to be bottom of the bill. A comedian with jokes that dated back to Victorian music hall and a juggling unicyclist had Danny's group rolling their eyes. Finally, the orchestra began to play a series of popular melodies. After a few minutes, a diminutive figure carrying a guitar stepped onto the stage to loud applause.

Al Bowlly turned to the orchestra and acknowledged them. Danny felt a shiver of excitement. He'd listened to Al Bowlly on the radio for many years. Now, at last, he would get to hear him in the flesh. He was struck by how small he was. However, there was no denying his charisma. Jet black, slicked back hair, intensely dark eyes, and a swarthy complexion that was unquestionably romantic, certainly if the reactions of the two ladies were anything to go by.

The singer put his fingers onto the guitar. He picked a few chords and then struck three oddly discordant notes. The orchestra joined at this point as Bowlly began to sing Goodnight Sweetheart.

Danny felt a glow as Bowlly's velvet voice caressed each line. This was one of Danny's favourite songs. His hand was now holding Abby's and he felt her grip tighten. The lines of the song were having an effect. The only disappointment for him was he couldn't take Abby to dance. Popular song followed popular song and Danny's enjoyment continued to be bittersweet. He glanced from time to time at Abby. She was enjoying the performance every bit as much as he was.

The second half of the show saw an equally mixed bag of acts but there was no question, everyone was waiting for the return of the South African crooner. His reappearance was greeted rapturously. This time there was no stopping Danny and Abby as well as other like-minded members of the audience. Couples found any available square inch of space they could to dance.

The show ended with a performance of J'Attendrais, the hit song by Charles Trenet. All too soon, they were back out into the chill night air. It was nearing midnight, too late to go anywhere when Danny and Abby said goodbye to Dick Manning and his date. There was no point in trying to keep in touch. The two men's parting was wordless, a nod of the head and a sympathetic grin.

'I'll walk you back,' offered Danny.

Abby glanced at him but saw that he was merely being a gentleman. She took his arm and they walked along the street, just one couple amongst dozens. All clinging onto one another like survivors to the wreckage. The blackness of the night was familiar to Danny, but Abby still hadn't become used to the lack of light. She was glad Danny was walking alongside her. From time to time she looked up at him. He was younger than her, but he had the looks and build of a young Douglas Fairbanks.

They arrived at Abby's flat. It was a building that would have been fortunate to have been labelled nondescript, such was its unsightliness.

'Nice place,' lied Danny with a grin.

'Don't you start,' replied Abby punching him lightly on the arm.

'Well, this is it, then, Abby.' Danny was about to launch into a short speech about how he should get back to his hotel. More flannel. He didn't want the night to be over, but he also wanted Abby to feel safe. The speech was cut short as Abby kissed him. Abby smiled up at him and took his hand.

'It's just as nice inside.'

Chapter Thirty-Eight

Liverpool, England: June, 1941

'So, this is it,' said Arthur, sitting across from Danny, Bob and Phil Lawrence. Over five weeks had elapsed since their return to London. Now they were all sitting in a train carriage destined for Liverpool. They would take a ship from Liverpool to North Africa. Where else? The Germans were besieging Tobruk. The Allies were on the run. Ground won against the Italians was being lost. Yes, it was North Africa. All knew.

The train journey took around five hours. Arthur and Danny played a song pun game to pass the time.

'What's the song where dogs are shouting at birds?'

'A Nightingale Sang in Berkley Square,' replied Arthur triumphantly.

'Swine.'

'What's the song of a naked woman banging on the door of a house?'

'What?' exclaimed Danny, completely at a loss.

'Love Locked Out,' cackled Arthur. This raised a laugh around the carriage, including from Bob.

The hours passed quickly for Danny and Arthur and even more

quickly for Bob. He smiled along with the jokes and even threw in a few comments himself, but his eyes were vacant. Danny knew him well enough to know his friend was petrified. The knuckle-white grip on the seat told its own story.

Every so often Bob would go for a walk into the corridor. It was all Danny could do to stop himself following his friend. His fear was that Bob would try to jump out from the moving train. He knew that to follow him would have been to betray him. But was staying in the carriage not a greater betrayal? If something happened, Danny knew his despair would be great, his sin greater still.

As they neared Liverpool, Bob rose from his seat and walked into the corridor. By now Danny's level of discomfort was overpowering. He had a sense that something was about to happen. This feeling crept into his mind, invaded his conscience and overpowered his guilt.

He had to check.

He rose abruptly from his seat. All at once Arthur got up too. The two men looked at one another.

'Yeah, mate, I don't like this either,' said Arthur.

They walked out into the corridor, past a few soldiers smoking beside the open windows and through to the next carriage. There was no sign of Bob. The two friends glanced at one another. Danny pointed in the opposite direction. Arthur nodded and set off looking. Reaching a door at the end, Danny crossed over into the second last carriage.

There was no sign of Bob.

Only one carriage remained and then he would be at the back of the train. Danny walked rapidly down the corridor, slowed only by soldiers standing by windows, smoking. The train began to slow down as it travelled through Liverpool. Danny could see glimpses of the sea between the buildings. Only a few minutes more and they would be boarding the ship.

The last carriage was less crowded, and Danny made rapid progress. He reached the last compartment. Bob wasn't there. Danny cursed and began to retrace his footsteps. Perhaps he had just gone to the toilet. He made his way quickly back to where he had separated from Arthur. Arriving at the carriage, he saw Arthur standing outside their compartment. He caught Arthur's eyes. It was there. Desolation.

Danny ran forward. 'What happened?'

Arthur held Danny back from going ahead.

'You can't do anything, Danny. The doctor's there.'

'Doctor?' said Danny wildly.

The train came to a halt.

'He's been shot.'

'Shot? What are you talking about?'

'Do you remember Nelson? Young lad from the Midlands. He and Bob always used to hang around one another. They must have had a pact. Nelson shot himself in the leg, but the idiot had it on automatic. It's a mess. Bob caught it bad.'

There was no time to explain any further. An officer came along the corridor calling for the men to disembark. Danny returned to the carriage feeling sick. He desperately wanted to see Bob. He grabbed his belongings from the overhead shelf and followed Arthur quickly onto the platform.

The whole of the platform was a chaos of green uniforms. Danny turned as he heard the shouts of officers, all running around like scared jackrabbits giving orders to soldiers who weren't listening. In the distance, Danny saw two stretchers being loaded onto a waiting ambulance. Danny caught a glimpse of Bob. He was unconscious. He looked around for a way of getting to the ambulance but his pathway to the vehicle was blocked. Then he felt a hand on his arm. It was Arthur. Beside him was Phil Lawrence.

'Leave it, Danny, there's nothing you can do,' said Lawrence. Danny resisted for a moment. 'That's an order, Danny,' continued Lawrence gently.

Danny knew his friends were right. His body slumped. Arthur patted his back. They looked at one another for a few moments. Then a sergeant came along and started to organise the soldiers in Danny's section. A few minutes later, they were marching from Lime Street station towards the docks. As they neared the waterfront, they could see the mutilated buildings. The devastation caused by the heavy bombing over the last few months. Up ahead they saw the troopship. It was painted black. Arthur glanced at Danny.

'Welcome to hell.'

Danny smiled but his heart wasn't in it. The image of Bob, on a stretcher, being loaded into the ambulance, rose before his eyes. He was desperate to know the extent of the injuries. There was no question about what had happened. If he recovered, he would probably be imprisoned. Worse, he would have to live with what he had done for the rest of his life. But hopefully he would live. Hopefully Bob would survive the war. Would he, though? The idea of death rose from time to time in his mind. Normally, it was fleeting. A momentary lapse in his defences. Right now, it no longer felt like an abstract idea. It was real and, with each passing day, its presence was coming closer. He shivered in the cold air.

Fear was something he'd always been aware of. But it felt like something independent of him. It was not tangible, yet it had a presence, like a shadow. You could see it in the eyes of a man, in the changing colour of his skin, the involuntary shake of his hand. Fear was something you felt. But only sometimes and never for long. Never did you think about it or try to trace its source. It was there somewhere. Lurking, smiling at you. Waiting for a moment to make itself known. Then, it would strike, rippling through your body and laying siege to your mind. Poor Bob. He'd known what he was going to do for a long time probably. To have lived with the knowledge of what he was going to do and then to have carried it out. This had taken courage. At that moment Danny realised that courage and fear exist alongside one another. One is a prerequisite for the other. He closed his eyes and offered up a long-forgotten prayer for his friend and for himself.

Night was drawing in. An icy wind beat into Danny's face as he stood in a long queue waiting silently to board the ship. The only sounds were the muffled thud of boots on metal, the lapping of the sea against the side of the ship. No one spoke. Danny paused for a moment before stepping onto the gangplank. He gazed up at the ship and then the reflection of the moon on the water. Then he stepped forward, swept along by the pressure behind him. His body shuddered again; he was impatient, now, to get into the warmth of the ship. Apprehension gripped him. He turned and looked behind him. Phil Lawrence was grim-faced. Arthur, too. They nodded to one another as they reached the top of the gangplank.

The ship's bosun met them.

'What regiment?'

They told him.

'H Deck,' said the bosun not looking up from his clipboard.

The three men followed other soldiers towards a hatch. As they arrived, Lawrence touched Danny's arm and he and Arthur stopped and looked out at Liverpool. The scene below on the quay was chaotic. Hundreds of soldiers were queuing to go up the gangplank. To their right they saw a tank being loaded onto the ship by an enormous crane.

'This is it, boys,' said Lawrence.

'It is,' agreed Arthur, drawing on a cigarette.

They stayed for a few minutes, impelled to watch the scene below, imprinting it on their memories. This would be their last view of England for a long time.

Perhaps ever.

Part 8: Italy 1941

Chapter Thirty-Nine

Naples, Italy: July, 1941

Naples was a kind of heaven decided Manfred. Sure, it was a little too hot. The evident poverty could be overpowering at times and the looks on the faces of the Neapolitans at no point suggested they were welcome, but still …

Naples was a place that the romantic in Manfred could not deny. It was as if God had spread a marine-coloured quilt across the bay, banned clouds from the sky, insisted that music rather than words be spoken, that girls be dark and alluring, that food should be a form of communication not just nutrition. Manfred and Gerhardt tried everything the city had to offer.

'If I live through this, I'm going to live here, Manfred,' said Gerhardt pointing to the Teatro di San Carlo, the opera house located in Piazza del Plebiscito. Manfred looked at him strangely. 'Well, not exactly there. You know what I mean.'

The two boys laughed and ordered another coffee. They were sitting in mute wonder outside a bar watching the world pass them. The most important decisions they had to take that day were what to eat and then where to find female company before they headed out to North Africa the following morning.

'How about we desert?' suggested Manfred as his eyes followed the path of another beautiful young woman passing them on the street. He was only half joking.

'Yes,' agreed Gerhardt, who'd noticed where Manfred's eyes had been fixed. 'Let's desert.'

Manfred looked across the Mediterranean Sea. The coastline of Sardinia had long since disappeared. It was early afternoon. Waves sucked and seethed beneath the stern. A blustery wind grabbed water and hurled it into the air like sugar being thrown at a children's party. The sky was a pale chrome yellow with hints of pink flush. For Manfred, the Mediterranean skies offered infinite varieties of colour and tone. No wonder artists had flocked to the Cote d'Azur, he thought. He sucked in the salty air and let the wind cleanse his face.

This was the second day aboard ship. The texture of the sea and its colour was permanently in flux. The evening before they had left Naples it was a pastel blue sheen, unmarked, chaste almost, reflected against a pale purple sky. This morning, hundreds of miles out from Italy, it was angrier. The turbulence made the water corrugated. This created a rolling rhythm that changed the colour of the sea, sometimes bottle-green, sometimes black, sometimes grey. In the distance there were patches of cerulean blue. Manfred was mesmerised by the colours.

The first morning had brought a welcome reunion with Lothar. He had also been sent for additional training on tank mechanics. Of Matthias, nothing was known. The friends assumed he was probably in North Africa. This was their destination, also. They speculated on the chances of meeting him again.

'He's dead now,' said Lothar. 'He was never meant to fight. Poor guy.'

Then he shrugged a well-you-know-it's-the-truth shrug. They all laughed but inside no one doubted it was true. More of life is determined in the womb than we would like to think. This is not just physical or even intellectual inheritance. Matthias was the son of a university professor. He looked it. He was no Aryan ideal. Too smart, too soft and too weak. Tommy would find him out.

Gerhardt clipped Lothar on the head with his cap. They all laughed. The unkindness of the remark was lost in a greater reality. They were all going to face the same dangers as Matthias. Whatever physical edge the other boys felt they had, it would almost certainly be lost amidst the physical vastness of the desert, the ferocity of the enemy and the appalling anarchy of war.

Beside Lothar was a young man called Sepp. Lothar had befriended him at the last camp they were stationed. He was from a village south of Dresden. In many ways, he was like Lothar. Short, squat and, as Gerhardt had pointed out to Manfred, not the brightest. However, his open smile and manner had instantly appealed to the two boys.

'It could get stormy,' said Sepp.

'What would you know, country boy,' mocked Gerhardt, good-naturedly.

Sepp looked unhappy. He looked up at the sky and said, 'I heard one of the crew say this. Let's see how much you're laughing when the sea whips up.'

Another recruit, Christian, whom they had met at the officer training was already looking green. Christian was quiet-spoken and seemed a mass of contradictions. Bright to the point where anything he said sounded more arrogant than helpful, he was rescued from

281

being ostracised by a cynicism that was as funny as it was reckless. He never referred to Hitler as anything other than 'the corporal'. This recklessness was calculated, however. He never made this reference in the presence of senior officers.

Gerhardt glanced at their friend and then back to Sepp and Manfred. 'I think one of us is ready to go.'

The two boys laughed, albeit nervously. The prospect of being on a ship in the Mediterranean Sea was dangerous enough without the weather adding complications to their journey.

'That's all we need,' said Christian, to no one in particular.

'Cheer up,' replied Manfred. 'We'll be there by tomorrow morning.'

'Oh great, I was worried for a minute there,' responded Christian sardonically. 'I'm going back down below. Wake me when the war is over.'

Manfred stayed on deck and watched as the sky slowly changed from pastel to grey. Clouds lolled into view one after another until they formed an unbroken grey ceiling. By late afternoon this had become a grey-black stucco. Heavy, unyielding – a promise of trouble. The sea changed also.

The gentle pitch had become something steeper. Waves rose menacingly, slapping over the side onto the deck. The rain had been released from the pregnant clouds. Sky and sea became one. Manfred watched all this enthralled. It only occurred to him that he was feeling unwell when he saw a few of his comrades rush onto the deck to throw up. Soon the deck was covered in sea water and vomit.

Manfred went below deck hoping against hope that having something to eat might settle his stomach. The galley was empty save for a few hardy souls intent on showing off their strong stomachs and sea legs. He walked over to one soldier who was in a hammock near to his.

282

'What are they serving?'

'Nothing hot. Apparently, the cook can't keep the pans on the stove,' replied the soldier.

Manfred nodded and went to collect a tray. He returned a few minutes later with sausage and some bread.

'Do you mind if I join you?'

'Go ahead. Johann Kupsch,' said the young man holding out his hand.

'Manfred Brehme. You seem all right,' said Manfred glancing seaward.

'I sail. At least I used to sail. Before all this.'

'Where?' asked Manfred genuinely interested.

'Hamburg. It could be stormy there also,' said Kupsch. He was slightly older than Manfred, very much the Aryan ideal. Like Manfred, he was a Fahnenjunker. Manfred looked down at his food. It was as unappetising a meal as he had ever seen, but he was committed now. He sensed the eyes of Kupsch on him. To turn back now would have been ignominious. He lifted the sausage and began to eat. Bile rose immediately in his stomach, and he fought hard to keep it down.

He glanced up at Kupsch, who had an amused look in his eye.

'Enjoying it?'

'No,' replied Manfred truthfully, putting down the sausage with something approaching relief.

'You did well.'

'Thanks. Doesn't feel like it though.'

However, Manfred was quite pleased at the comment and risked another bite of the sausage. He lifted it up mechanically and did not look at it. This seemed to help, and he was able to swallow it without the desire to gag.

A sudden pitch in the ship had the two young men clutching their trays. Both burst out laughing. The ship was now swooping, soaring then plunging in an endless cycle. Manfred accepted it was only a matter of time before he joined the others atop.

'One good thing from all of this, though,' pointed out Kupsch.

Manfred looked up querulously. What could possibly be good about what he was feeling at that moment, he wondered?

Kupsch smiled at Manfred's reaction before continuing. 'The British will hardly send any planes out in this. Maybe we can get to Tripoli without being attacked.'

This was cold comfort yet it made sense. It was an awful trade off, though: feeling like death on this ship or risking death in more clement weather if it meant running the gauntlet of RAF patrols from Malta.

They parted a few minutes later. Manfred made his way below deck. He moved along the corridor like Charlie Chaplin, rolling and bumping against the walls, against the poor souls who had been unable to make it above and conducted their business in the corridor. The stench was horrible. There was little Manfred could do for them when he was feeling every bit as bad.

He headed into the large area below deck where his hammock hung alongside Gerhardt's. He saw his friend lying there, dead seemingly or, more likely, wishing to be so. Just behind Gerhardt lay Sepp. He was wide awake. He looked at Manfred. He could neither disguise the terror he felt as the waves crashed against the side of the ship nor the nausea. Moments later he turned away and retched on the other side of his hammock. A few other recruits made half-hearted efforts at complaint.

With an enormous effort of will, Manfred levered himself up into the hammock and shut his eyes, praying to a God he barely believed in for some respite.

There was none.

For the next few hours, the ship continued to pitch and roll violently. However, in the hammock there was a rhythm to the movement of the ship. While it may have been disastrous for his stomach, never mind his nerve, Manfred felt confident he could manage.

The noise was another thing. Menacing, strange noises were caused by water smashing against the side of the ship. The scream of the storm. The crashing and clattering of things falling to the ground and then rolling around the floor. The heartrending cries of his comrades ringing throughout the ship, accompanied by the base groan of the metal stretching and rivets rasping in the tempest. Sleep was impossible.

Night came but without a break in the weather. If anything, it seemed worse, although Manfred was past caring. He was now on deck. Sick. He watched the ship plummet into another valley and a large wave rose, crashing over the top of the deck. Manfred was soaking wet. The wind bludgeoned his face and showers of spray blinded his eyes with salty sea water.

The sea was a grey-white lather icing atop grey-black mountain ranges. Manfred felt numb, his eyes were on fire, his stomach empty and sore. He stood on the deck immobile. The cold wetness of his clothes slowly strangled the blood flow to his limbs. He wanted to leave but was unable to move. Instead, he was hypnotised by the sight and sound of the maelstrom.

Finally, he dragged his aching limbs towards the door. It took several minutes but he reached the safety of his hammock. He stripped off his wet clothes and flung them onto the floor. At last, lying in the hammock, sleep came. A fitful sleep, but rest, nonetheless.

He awoke around dawn. Light filtered through the windows. The first thing Manfred noticed was the noise, or lack of it. The ship was no longer rolling violently. The storm had abated.

The second thing he noticed was the ringing in his ears had stopped. It was then that the stench hit him. The smell of stale sweat, damp clothing and vomit assaulted his senses and he nearly retched. He decided to get out into the fresh air.

However, as he jumped down from his hammock, he realised that he ached all over. His eyes and face were smarting from the earlier exposure to the salty wind. He found some dry clothes and dressed slowly. Gerhardt was also awake. His face had a deathly pallor, but he managed a weak smile.

'Am I dead?' he asked.

'Yes, you're in heaven, my son.'

'Nice place.'

'Smells a bit.'

'Bloody hell, does it ever,' said Gerhardt rising slowly. He looked around him and grinned. 'That was the worst day of my life.'

The two boys looked at one another for a moment. An acceptance that worse would follow. Then, Manfred laughed. 'I know what you mean. We must be near by now. I'm going to find out.'

A couple of minutes later, Manfred found a seaman cleaning up the filth on deck. 'How long before we make land,' he asked him.

'If it hadn't been for the storm we would have been there by now. A couple of hours, no more.'

Manfred thanked him and went below deck to relay the news. By now most of the hammocks were stirring. Sepp was up and dressed, although Christian grimly refused to be moved by anything save an undertaker. Manfred and the rest of his friends went to the galley in search of food. With each passing minute on the calmer sea, their appetites returned.

When they arrived, Manfred spotted Kupsch. He motioned for the rest of his comrades to follow him.

'Johann, I want you to meet my friends.'

They sat down alongside Kupsch. Gerhardt asked him what regiment he was in.

'I'm artillery. I shoot the big eighty-eights. Boom, boom.'

The group laughed at this. The eighty-eight-millimetre gun was the deadliest anti-tank weapon in the war. It could knock out a tank from over a kilometre. This was well outside the range of the British tanks, explained Kupsch.

Sepp pointed to him and joked. 'No drinking the night before battle. I want your frigging head to be clear.'

The table, including Kupsch, laughed. He held his hands up and said, 'I promise. Afterwards I get drunk.'

'How come you're not feeling like death, anyway?' asked Sepp.

Kupsch explained about his hobby sailing boats.

'Rich boy, I thought your type was avoiding all this,' said Lothar dismissing him with a wave of his hand.

Kupsch nodded his head. 'Many of my friends are. Sorry, I should say former friends.'

'And you?' asked Gerhardt.

'I don't like Hitler much, but a lot of what he says is right. Germany was a mess until he came along. If this is what we must do to be respected then damn, I want to be part of it. I don't want to spend the rest of my life on my knees.'

The other boys nodded their agreement. He had summed up how they felt. They had grown up in a serf state. No longer should the country accept this status. The youth of Weimar would lead Germany, if not to glory, then at least to prosperity where they would be equals with the other great powers.

The galley produced a big breakfast for the brave souls who were, once again, prepared to eat. Manfred and the boys ate hungrily. By the time they had finished, the galley was full. They agreed to head up onto the deck and spend the rest of the morning waiting to see their destination: North Africa.

Chapter Forty

The weariness and ache in Manfred's bones slowly began to disappear as he stood on the deck with his friends. The sky was a cloudless cerulean blue. Perfect. The sea seemed to be playing a joke on the travellers. Gone was the black and white anger. It had been replaced by a serenity few would have believed possible in such a dangerously spiteful sea.

All around they heard laughter as young men shared their stories of sickness. It was almost as if they had seen the worst of the war. Even Manfred was laughing. No one, aside from Kupsch, had been left unscathed by the tempest. It was easy to laugh at other people and be laughed at too. The catharsis acted to distract the soldiers from what lay ahead. They welcomed anything that took their minds off the future.

Then the laughter stopped as quickly as it had arisen.

Several officers had appeared and began yelling at the young men. There was genuine anger in their voices. They walked along the deck and their presence created a wave of silence that swept the length of the ship.

'What are they shouting about?' asked Lothar.

Kupsch went to find out. He returned a few moments later and reported.

'Some kid was swept overboard last night.'

Or jumped.

They all looked at one another. So, they had not yet reached land and death had visited them. It woke everyone up to why they were on the ship. An awkward silence fell on the group. Eyes avoided eyes.

A voice shouted out from another group.

'Land.'

Manfred and his friends turned around. It was true. Barely there, a hazy grey at the point where sky met sea. The sound of voices returned to the deck as the soldiers started to talk excitedly again. These were young men. They lived in the moment. The past was quickly forgotten, such is the joy of youth. But the memories never leave you. They come back. Later when you are older; when you are better able to understand them; when you feel what you should have felt then: the horror and the sorrow.

'This is it boys,' said Gerhardt.

'Not quite,' pointed out Christian. 'Still a few hours to go. This is hardly a speedboat, or hadn't you noticed?'

Several hats started to beat the laughing 'Professor' Christian over the head. The good humour in the group was now fully restored. They all leant against the railings and allowed a gentle sea breeze to lick their faces. Whatever the future held, they wanted to enjoy these last few moments of peace.

'Nervous?' asked Gerhardt.

'Yes,' replied Manfred. 'You?'

'Yes.'

Silence returned not just to the group but along the deck as the young men watched the ship slowly make its way towards a land where many of them would die in agony.

Manfred took a drag of the cigarette. He had never smoked until he joined officer training. Everyone else was smoking, even Gerhardt. He tried to like it but could not understand the appeal. He was sitting on his hammock, his friends all around.

Everyone was laughing. The mood had relaxed. The prospect of land meant war and possible death, but for Sepp it meant they would be off the water at long last. This was an immense relief.

'You really can't swim?' laughed Christian.

Sepp shrugged. 'No. Never interested. The sea was a long way away and, well, there were better things to do.'

This comment was greeted, predictably, by a few ribald comments on what Sepp had probably never done. In truth, he was hardly alone in this. Virgin men who had been trained to kill.

Manfred remained silent while the others made fun of Sepp. He thought about Anja. He thought about his experience with women, or the lack of it. The others seemed to know so much more. Or maybe they were lying to him and to themselves. Who could tell?

First it was the shout.

Then they all heard it. A light drone at first. Then it grew louder. All at once the deck was a riot of noise and movement. Orders were shouted and lost in the din. Manfred felt himself jostled and pushed as soldiers were ordered to return below deck. Manfred glanced up and saw some of the sailors running to the guns. Then, moments later, driven along by the human wave, he was inside and virtually carried downstairs.

The boys returned to their hammocks. There was no choice as the windows were blocked by the men shouldering one another to get a better view of what was happening. The noise of voices quietened as the hum of the fighter planes grew more distinct.

Manfred looked at his friends. All felt fear and frustration in equal measure. Fear at the prospect of being under attack; frustration they could do nothing to help. The sound of the planes grew louder. The chonk, chonk of the anti-aircraft gun followed a minute later by the regular rat, tat, tat rhythm of machine guns.

Now the planes were a roar overhead. Explosions followed as they dropped their cargo. The sound reverberated around the hold. From each side they heard the deadly sound of gunfire. Manfred glanced down at the hands of his friends. Gerhardt's hands were clasped together, knuckle white.

Manfred's breathing was shallow. He feared taking a deep breath or exhaling too much lest it reveal the fear he was feeling. The siren scream of the planes was the worst: a prelude to death. If you heard the explosion, it meant you were still alive.

No one spoke.

At the windows there was shouting and cheering on the gunners. But no one in Manfred's group spoke. Eye contact was avoided. It would reveal too much. Instead, they fought a battle in their minds. The age-old confrontation between fight and flight.

The sound of the guns acted like a percussion to the main theme played by the aerial combatants. The noise of the plane became familiar very quickly: the hum, the roar, the scream. Finally, there was a cheer amongst some of the men on the starboard side.

The boys turned around. They were hugging one another as there was a sound of an aeroplane splutter, scream and then silence before the explosion. To a man they roared in happiness, in anger and in relief.

'Will they leave now?' asked Lothar following a brief halt to the firing. Manfred shrugged. Gerhardt shook his head. Moments later the assault began again.

Manfred glanced at Christian. His new friend was virtually white with fear. Gerhardt was looking left and right with each explosion. This was less to do with fear than a desire to see if they had been hit. Lothar looked like he was ready to lie down and have a nap. A good actor, nerveless or just plain stupid. Manfred couldn't decide which.

An explosion just outside rocked the ship, and then another. The screams were no longer of aeroplane engines. It was metal tearing. And then they heard a siren.

'We've been hit.'

It was Gerhardt. His voice was toneless. He stood up. The others followed him. Panic flooded the hold. All at once everyone was shouting. Another explosion rocked the ship. This had a different texture. Rather than from above, it seemed to come from within.

'Oh my God,' said Manfred. 'That's the magazine. We must get off. It'll explode.'

Dozens of other soldiers, more alert to the problem, had reached the same conclusion and were soon rushing to the door.

'Grab your life belt,' shouted Manfred over the din.

An officer had pushed his way inside to order men to do what they had already started trying to do. Despite the officer's efforts, panic was rising as the ship lurched on the starboard side. Manfred and his friends made it out onto the deck, which was a scream of noise and confusion. Terrified soldiers were rushing, jostling and fighting to escape the fire that was spreading on the other side of the ship.

The sky was blanketed by puff ball smoke and the air smelled of cordite. Smoke made their eyes water and breathing difficult. Manfred was coughing as he struggled to find something to cover his nose and mouth with.

An officer close by was shouting for them to get to their lifeboat stations. It took Manfred a few moments to get his bearings; then he saw Lothar pointing up to the next level. They followed him up some steps which led to the upper deck. Here it was calmer as the officers had matters under control. Soldiers were engrossed in lowering lifeboats quickly onto the water.

Manfred looked up. It seemed the raid was over. Glancing around at the rest of the convoy it seemed theirs was the only ship to sustain serious damage. The noise level below was, if anything, rising. Another officer appeared and shouted to the sergeant in charge of Manfred and his friends to get a group to help put out the fire near the magazine.

The sergeant turned around and pointed to Manfred, Lothar, Sepp and Gerhardt to follow him. The four men, along with the officer, ran around to the starboard side which was listing now at a slight angle. Below they could see around a dozen men manning hoses trying to put out a fire in the hold below.

The officer shouted over the din, 'The pump below is blocked by a car that has rolled over a line connecting several of the hoses. Get down there and move the car. Be as quick as you can. The ship could blow if the fire gets to the magazine.'

The sergeant took instruction from the officer and then waved at the boys to follow him down below to the hold. They descended two sets of stairs rapidly. A minute later they were now below deck. All around them were tanks, a few armoured cars, and jeeps. The heat was intense but, because the magazine was being hosed up above, the water spray cooled them as they followed the sergeant.

'Grab the rope over there,' shouted the sergeant.

Gerhardt did as he was told and returned with a thick rope. They were now beside the jeep. Simply rolling it forward off the water line was not an option. It was wedged against another jeep, bumper to bumper. They would have to use the rope and pull it a foot to their left to release the line.

Manfred risked a glance at the fire. It had reached the magazine. The fire fighters were losing the battle. Gerhardt helped the sergeant tie the rope around the wheel axle. Then all four men took the strain and tried to pull the car off the line. The effort seemed to tear Manfred's muscles as he pulled with every ounce of his being. At first it seemed a hopeless task. He glanced at Lothar and Sepp. The sergeant had chosen well. Manfred doubted there were two stronger men on board. Slowly it felt like something was giving.

After thirty seconds, they felt the wheel slip off the line. Moments later they heard a roar of approval as more water was released to fight the blaze. However, there was no time to stop and survey their work. The sergeant yelled at them to get back to the ladder. This required no second instruction.

The piercing wail was telling them that it was time to abandon ship.

Chapter Forty-One

'Back to the lifeboat station,' ordered the sergeant. They weaved through the armoured vehicles to the metal ladder connecting the hold to the upper deck. The sergeant stood back and waited as each of the young men clambered up the ladder. Up above, a captain was shouting at them to move quickly. The lifeboats were in the water.

Sepp was at the top first followed by Lothar and then Manfred. Gerhardt virtually had his arms ripped from their sockets as Lothar pulled him up to the deck. The ship lurched a little more followed by an awful silence, probably lasting no more than a heartbeat. Seconds later, there was a tremendous explosion in the magazine.

The ship juddered. Manfred glanced down in horror as the sergeant lost his grip and fell backwards into the hold. He hit the deck with a thump. It knocked him unconscious.

'Quick,' shouted Manfred, 'we have to get him.'

Gerhardt jumped down the steps with Manfred. Lothar joined his two friends a split second later. Manfred was the first to reach the sergeant. He was out cold but still breathing. There was no time to worry about back injuries. The intensity of the heat would kill him in a minute. The fire was almost upon the three men.

Another smaller explosion rocked the vehicles behind them.

Manfred put his hands underneath the arms of the prone man and hoisted him. Lothar grabbed him and threw him over his back like he was a rag doll. Manfred almost laughed at the ease with which his friend handled the sergeant, who was built like a light-heavyweight.

Lothar took him as far as the steps. The heat felt like it was searing the skin of Manfred's face. Worse, the metal ladder was getting hotter by the second. A third explosion rocked the boat. Manfred reached up to stop Lothar falling on top of him. With a final push-pull, the sergeant was hauled up onto the deck by other soldiers waiting for them. The back of his head had a gash and he was still unconscious. Sepp was there and picked up the sergeant as easily as Lothar had. They rushed to the other side of the boat where the lifeboats had been lowered.

They, and a few other soldiers, were the last on board. The decks were empty. The stragglers, including the captain, prepared to jump into the sea to be picked up.

'Where's our boat?' asked Sepp. His face managed the improbable feat of being white with fear and bathed in sweat from his exertion.

Gerhardt pointed down to the sea.

'What about the sergeant? What do we do?'

Gerhardt and Manfred took the sergeant each side. Manfred looked at Sepp. 'Time to jump.'

'I can't swim,' said Sepp, but they were already gone.

Manfred and Gerhardt hit the water with an almighty splash. Immediately they both lost hold of the sergeant. Manfred surfaced first. He looked around. There was no sign of Gerhardt. A moment later his friend appeared. They looked at one another and, in an instant, ducked under water again. The water was as dark as it was cold. The lifebelt prevented Manfred from kicking lower. Panic grabbed him as he tried to untie the lifebelt. The water was cold, his fingers were numb and he could not see what he was doing as the knot was below in the sea. Finally, his fingers latched onto the knot. The water had soaked into the rope making it difficult to untie. He cursed loudly. Finally, he was able to claw one finger into a tiny gap in the knot. He widened it which allowed him to get his thumb in. With a yell he ripped it apart and ducked under the sea. Despite the poor visibility, Manfred could see Gerhardt a few metres deeper. He had grabbed the sergeant by the scruff of his uniform.

Lungs beginning to burn, Manfred surged towards the two men and came underneath the sergeant and began to kick upwards. Moments later two other men entered the water a few feet away from them. They kicked over to Manfred and Gerhardt to help them drag the sergeant towards the boat.

Manfred swam alongside the boat also. The men on the boat had hauled the sergeant on board. All around there was bedlam. Shouting, more explosions from the ship.

'Where's Lothar and Sepp?' asked Gerhardt.

Then he and Manfred realised why there was so much shouting. Clinging to the boat they both turned around and looked up. Silhouetted against the smoky sky were Lothar and Sepp. They seemed to be arguing.

'Jump,' shouted Lothar.

'I can't,' replied Sepp.

'What do you mean you can't? The damn ship is about to go.'

'I can't,' persisted Sepp. Lothar looked at him like he was insane.

Down below they could hear the shouts of the other soldiers. The lifeboats were beginning to move away from the ship. Behind them the sound of popping was becoming more persistent. The ship listed another couple of degrees; the dying screams of the ships structure grew louder.

'I can't swim,' shouted Sepp. His voice was almost shrill with panic.

'You have a life vest, you moron,' screamed Lothar. 'Jump.'

Sepp looked down and then back at Lothar. 'I'll die.'

'You'll die here too.'

Another explosion and the boat listed more. Both boys fell backwards against the cabin wall. The ship was now at a forty-degree angle. Gravity pulled both boys backwards. Lothar felt the panic rising in him also. There was no way they could get back up to the railings now because the angle was too steep. They had nothing to hold on to.

Sepp looked at Lothar and realised he was about to condemn his friend to death. His eyes filled with tears. They looked at one another; then Lothar turned away. There had to be another way. The idea came to them at the same time.

'The other side. It's nearly in the water,' shouted Lothar.

The two boys moved around the ship clinging to the walls. The intensity of the heat grew with every step. Another small explosion rocked the boat and this time it listed even further, so much so they were able to run more freely. They reached the other side of the boat a minute later. They were now only a few feet off the water, but the ship was in danger of sinking. If it did, they would go down with it.

'You'll have to jump in.'

Sepp's terror had returned. He shook his head. Lothar looked from Sepp to the fire. The ship was in its death throes. The noise of screaming metal was reaching deafening levels. Breathing was almost impossible now. The smoke didn't so much obscure his view as blind him. He felt the panic rise in him also.

Suddenly, a red-hot iron bar fell, hitting Sepp on the side of the head.

'Sepp,' screamed Lothar at his friend.

Manfred and Gerhardt sat on the boat yelling in vain to their friends. Two men with oars began to row away from the boat.

'What are you doing?' screamed Manfred. 'Our friends are still on board.'

'They're dead men,' came the reply.

A lieutenant looked at Manfred and said in a tone that brooked no debate, 'We must go. The ship will either explode or sink. Either way we are at risk.'

Manfred knew he was right. He looked at Gerhardt. There was nothing else to say. Their friends were going to die while they both sat on the boat and watched. Manfred felt sick. He had to fight hard against the nausea he was feeling. He began to cough as the impact of so much inhaled smoke began to tell. All at once his vision blurred; his movements slowed as if his body was now unwilling to continue with this exercise in futility: the act of survival. He wanted to surrender himself to the darkness assailing him. His hearing dulled as it usually did when he was on the point of sleep. Just then, as his body was shutting down he heard the muffled sound of an explosion from behind. Sea water flew fifty feet in the air and splashed over him. The water jolted him awake.

He glanced up sharply and saw that the ship was listing at an extraordinary angle. It was moments away from sinking. He could no longer see his friends. The lifeboat was moving further and further away from the ship towards one of the other boats in the convoy. Tears blinded his eyes. He knew it wasn't from the smoke either. He wiped them away with the palm of his hand. The saltwater brought its own stinging rebuke and he cursed himself.

Slowly the boat drew further away. Up ahead they heard yet another muffled explosion and the ship listed onto its side. Then, with shocking rapidity, it disappeared under the bubbling water. The surface was littered with debris.

The lifeboat continued drawing away from the catastrophe as if it were trying to distance itself from a mistake. Theirs was the only ship that had sunk. A couple of others were smoking but any damage appeared to be limited. Each ship's horn blew, almost as an act of defiance. Soon the air was filled with the noise of the ships' shrill sirens and horns.

Manfred looked at Gerhardt. His head hung with sadness but in his eyes was anger. Manfred felt the anger, too. It began to swell inside him. The hatred felt trapped inside. He wanted to explode.

'Why are those idiots making this noise?' he snarled to no one in particular.

No one answered. They were all young men. All in a state of shock. This was their first exposure to war. Further up the boat, he caught the eye of Christian. He was crying. Whether this was through fear or the loss of his friends, Manfred knew not.

The lifeboat pulled up alongside another ship, just as the noise began to abate. They were now at least a kilometre away from the remains of the Aachen.

Sepp collapsed to the ground. His head was bloodied. Lothar fell to his knees. He could feel movement in his friend's chest. He was alive. He pulled Sepp towards the railings. Climbing over them himself, he pulled Sepp underneath. They both fell into the water. It was a short drop, no more than a few feet. The cold water seemed to revive Sepp.

'What the ...'

'We're in the water,' said Lothar, pointing out the obvious.

Even in Sepp's groggy state this much was plain.

'I can bloody well see that,' replied Sepp irritably. His head was pounding and his panic at being in the water he detested so much was compounded by another realisation.

'Where is the lifeboat?'

Lothar was wondering the same thing at this point. But a bigger problem was quite literally in front of them.

'Move,' ordered Lothar.

'What?'

'Move, the damn ship is going to sink. We need to move.'

Sepp was now fully awake to the problem. His head was hurting damnably, and the death throes of the ship were doing little to help an already hellish situation.

'How?' asked Sepp.

'Use your legs to kick. It's called swimming, you moron.'

Lothar was already beginning to move. Sepp, seeing no other choice, began to kick instinctively away from the ship. An explosion prompted a renewed energy to his efforts, but he was tiring fast. The cold of the water, the fear and the soaking clothes acted to slow him down.

Lothar was cutting through the water easily. He was an experienced swimmer. Within a matter of seconds, he was thirty metres away from Sepp. He continued swimming; then he paused to take stock. He turned around.

Sepp seemed hardly to have moved.

'Move,' screamed Lothar. His voice was shrill with the dread that was now engulfing him. Sepp's arms began to flail in the water. What progress he was making seemed paralysingly slow. Lothar looked on with desperation. The sound of metal ripping and rending drowned out his shouts. He had a decision to make. It was life and death, possibly both Sepp's as well as his.

Seventeen years old.

He began to swim towards Sepp.

A few strong strokes and he was within fifteen metres of his friend. Sepp was still near the ship, holding onto a piece of debris. Lothar could see that Sepp was unaware of the imminent danger. The ship was listing at a grotesque angle and seconds away from falling on his friend. There was nothing he could do.

He shouted at his friend, 'Sepp!'

Sepp glanced up. There was a look of relief on his face as if he was glad to see Lothar was safe or perhaps it was something else, the moment of acceptance. Lothar watched in horror as the ship collapsed over Sepp. The impact of tonnes of metal sinking created a vortex that began to force the water downwards, dragging everything with it. Panic gripped Lothar as he felt himself being dragged under the waves.

Deeper and deeper he went. His lungs were bursting, breathing impossible. With a strength borne of the terror consuming him he kicked and raked his arms at the same time. Somehow this managed to counteract the force of the downward pressure and he began to move up. He reached the surface moments before passing out.

A cough awoke him. He didn't know how long he had been out for. His body began to expel the water he had swallowed on the way up. He vomited the fear and the sea water from his body. Around him lay signs of wreckage. But Sepp was gone. He took off his life vest and dived beneath the water.

Visibility was non-existent. He surfaced again and swam towards the fizzing white foam where the ship had last been before the sea had claimed it. Diving once more he could see little beyond a few metres. Once again, he resurfaced. As he did so, something broke the surface further ahead. It was a man.

'Sepp,' screamed Lothar.

He swam over to the floating body. It was Sepp. His lifeless body was slumped head down in the water. Lothar pulled his head back. He slapped Sepp's face lightly. Then harder, no response. Tears stung his eyes. He shouted in his ear.

Nothing.

Lothar now understood three things with utter clarity. Sepp was dead. He could not be revived. The chill of the sea and the weight of his clothes were beginning to tell. He was at the end of his physical resources. Finally, with an increasing feeling of desperation, he realised he was alone. The ships were far in the distance. He began to yell to attract their attention.

Just at that moment the sound of his cries for help were drowned out by the sound of the ships' horns.

For one minute or more they blew. Lothar looked on in incredulity. Why were they doing this? Why weren't they looking for him? Tears of rage streamed down his face, and he began to yell at the ships when the blaring noise had ceased. But even as he yelled, he could almost see the sound of his voice disappearing into the vast emptiness around him.

He needed a life vest. Keeping one arm on a piece of the wreckage, he looked around at the charred brown debris scattered like autumn leaves on the dark blue sea. Around fifty yards away he could see something that resembled a life vest; it was bobbing up by a piece of the wreckage. For a moment he thought about swimming over to it. But his muscles were stiffening in the cold like an old man. Then he looked at Sepp. His friend was floating face down thanks to the life vest. The horror of what had to be done was all too clear. He slapped the water angrily and shook his head. There was no choice. This was about survival.

With the last remaining reserves of his strength, he pulled Sepp towards him. He released his hold of the debris and began to kick frantically under the water to keep himself from submerging. With increasing desperation, he searched for the knot on Sepp's life vest. It took seconds to find. Precious seconds that further exhausted his spirit. The knot was loose. Sepp couldn't even do that right.

Lothar took a deep breath and ducked under the water. The salt stung his eyes, but he couldn't shut them now. He tore open the knot of the life vest. His lungs screamed in pain as he wrestled it off his friend.

His head popped up above the water and he gulped in air. Then he held his breath and scrambled to put on the vest. Its buoyancy gave him both the physical and spiritual lift he needed. Just as he tied the knot, he caught sight of his friend. Without the vest, Sepp's head slowly sank beneath the water. His funeral lasted seconds.

There was no prayer for the dead.

After a few moments staring at the sea where his friend had been, Lothar looked towards the convoy. He began to shout. After a minute of yelling himself hoarse he stopped.

The silence screamed in derision. All was a void. Just him and the clicking sound of the water lapping around his body waiting for its opportunity to claim him like it had done Sepp. His situation was impossible. There was nothing he could do. Swimming to the ships was out of the question. Attracting their attention impossible.

All was lost. It was hopeless.

He began to cry. The sobs wracked his body in a way they had not done since he was a small child. He slapped the water again in frustration as the tears of desolation gave way to anger.

And then all was silent again. Lothar bobbed on the water, watching the ships receding slowly into the horizon. Angrily he threw away a piece of debris that had floated alongside him. For the first time he became aware of the wreckage that was around him. Twenty metres away, sitting on top of one of the large pieces of floating debris, was a leather bag.

Curiosity overcame Lothar. He swam towards the debris. When he arrived, he reached over to the bag and opened it. The interior of the bag was dry. He felt a hard metallic object. As he put his weight on the floating debris, it tipped over, submerging Lothar for a moment. He kept his hand above the surface, though, ensuring the bag did not fall in the water. He resurfaced and coughed angrily.

He stared dumbly at the ships sailing away from him into the distance. Then he looked at the object in his hand.

It was a gun.

He looked inside the magazine.

Empty.

Lothar jerked his head up towards the heavens and screamed an oath to the divine practical joker. He kicked towards the metal debris again, where the bag remained. Placing the gun carefully on the metal remains of the ship, he reached inside the bag and felt around the interior once more. His hand fell onto a slim metallic object. He lifted it out. A bullet. Another search of the bag proved fruitless. With an oath, he hurled the bag angrily across the water.

Taking great care, he loaded the bullet into the magazine. In the distance he could see the convoy silhouetted against the sky. He felt sick with fear. Once again, the cold water began to numb his senses, slow his thinking and strip away his willpower. He looked again at the convoy; then he looked at the gun.

In the silent expanse of the sea, he knew he had a decision to make.

Chapter Forty-Two

Manfred and Gerhardt were the last two to be pulled onto the ship. On the deck, near them, they could see the sergeant being given first aid. He was alive but it was difficult to gauge the extent of his injuries. Manfred felt a pair of arms help him as he was in danger of collapse. He was shivering from the cold, or shock, he wasn't sure.

'Come along,' said a voice, helping him to his feet. 'We need to get you changed.'

At first Manfred went along with him and then an image of his two friends rose in his mind. He stopped and looked around wildly.

'No,' he shouted.

The hubbub around him quietened. At that moment Manfred realised he was responsible for this. He felt his face redden in embarrassment. All around he could see faces looking at him.

'Our friends are out there.'

It was Gerhardt.

There was a sigh and then a lieutenant came over to the two boys and said, 'No one could have survived the sinking.'

There was no malice in his voice. No attempt to dismiss their view. It was just a gentle nudge towards reality. They knew he was right.

Once again, Manfred resisted, with all his might, the desire to cry. The hard, cold truth was out there in the vastness of the sea. Death would visit them all many times over the next few months, perhaps years. They would have to grow a shell that would help protect their mind from the fear and the fragility that would shadow them every waking moment.

'Hurry,' ordered the lieutenant. 'We're not stopping to look for anyone. The British may return. We still have a few hours before we make port.'

Manfred and Gerhardt turned around and said, 'Yes, sir.'

Gerhardt looked at Manfred and then the lieutenant. He nodded in acceptance. Manfred's shoulders fell. He knew the officer was right. The lieutenant put his hand on Manfred's arm. It was over. He had to move now. To stand still would have been to object to the implied order. He felt empty, cold and scared. They had not even reached Africa and a taste of what was to come had proven terrifying and unexpected. Afterwards he would discuss this fear with Gerhardt. No one else.

He pushed forward in a line with the others. Gerhardt fell in step with Manfred. They walked along the deck in silence; then Gerhardt said what was on both their minds. 'There was nothing we could do. He should've left Sepp.'

'Would you?'

'I'd have thrown him in.'

'Me too,' said Manfred. There was no humour in his voice. Instead, there was anger. This, oddly, was not directed towards the British but instead towards Sepp. In Manfred's mind, Sepp was responsible for Lothar's death, if he was dead. He thought about the life vest. He turned and gazed out towards the debris. The sun glinting off the water made it difficult to see anything clearly.

Just behind Manfred walked the lieutenant. He saw Manfred

looking out to sea. The two boys had fallen behind the others. The lieutenant walked alongside Manfred to make them move faster. Manfred glanced down and looked at the object in the officer's hand. The officer looked at Manfred sympathetically. He was probably only a few years older than Manfred. He understood how it felt to lose a comrade. He had seen his fair share over the last eight months convoying in the Mediterranean.

'You don't give up, do you?'

Manfred smiled grimly. He nodded at the object and said, 'May I?'

'Make it quick,' said the lieutenant handing Manfred his binoculars. 'And keep moving.'

The binoculars weighed heavily on aching muscles. They were probably powerful enough to see home, he thought. Manfred walked to the side; he put the binoculars to his eyes. It took a moment to adjust to the glare from the water. His hands and body shook from the cold or, perhaps, the shock. It made the wretched task of searching for his friends even more difficult. Teeth chattering, he carefully scanned the debris which was spread out across a hundred metres of water. They were at least a mile away or more now. Suddenly some movement caught his eye. He stopped. Gerhardt and the lieutenant stopped also.

'What's wrong?' asked the lieutenant irritably. 'I told you to keep moving.'

'It's Lothar. I can see him. What's that he's holding?' replied Manfred. His eyes watered at the bright sunlight reflecting from the sea. He tried to keep his gaze fixed on his friend to see what was in his hand.

The three of them stopped. Manfred could hear his heart thumping against his chest and the chill of the wet clothing against his skin. He sensed the lieutenant and Gerhardt standing either side of him.

'What's happening, Manny?' asked Gerhardt. There was an edge to his voice. Manfred guessed this was a warning about the growing irritation of the lieutenant.

Manfred didn't care. Their friend was alive, yet the ship was sailing away from him. They had to turn around. He was about to say as much when he saw what Lothar was holding. He stopped breathing. A seagull cried overhead. Manfred felt his head swimming. He exhaled.

'I think he's holding a …'

As Manfred said this a shot cracked the silence of the sea.

Acknowledgements

It is not possible to write a book on your own. There are contributions from so many people either directly or indirectly over many years. Listing them all would be an impossible task.

Special mention, therefore, should be made to my wife and family who have been patient and put up with my occasional grumpiness when working on this project.

My brother Edward, and John Convery helped in proofing and made supportive comments that helped me tremendously. I have been very lucky to receive badly needed editing from Kathy Lance who has helped tighten up some of the grammatical issues that, frankly, plagued my earlier books. She has been a Godsend!

My late father and mother both loved books. They encouraged a love of reading, particularly about history. My father's taste in music is also reflected in the references to the late, great Al Bowlly.

I would also like to thank Charles Gray whose advice in the legal field and on the football field is always valued.

My sincere thanks to Marina McCarron who read the manuscript and provided many suggestions that have made it a much better book.

Following writing, comes the business of marketing. My thanks to

Mark Hodgson and Sophia Kyriacou for their advice on this important area. Additionally, a shout out to the wonderful folk on 20Booksto50k.

Finally, my thanks to the teachers who taught and nurtured a love of writing.

About the Authors

Jack Murray lives just outside London with his family. Born in Ireland he has spent most of his adult life in England. His first novel, *The Affair of the Christmas Card Killer* has been a global success. Five further Kit Aston novels have been published: *The Chess Board Murders*, *The French Diplomat Affair*, *The Phantom*, *The Frisco Falcon*, *The Medium Murders* and, most recently, *The Bluebeard Club*. Several characters from this series also appear in this book. Jack has also written two other detective series: the Agatha Aston Mysteries set during the mid-Victorian era and the DI Nick Jellicoe police series set in the late 50s and early 60s.

J Murray

Jack Murray is the nephew of the author. Jack is currently at Portsmouth University studying Computer Games Technology. He is also an avid student of World War II and tanks. Jack has provided research and contributed ideas to the development of this story.